RESCU

MW00940096

RESCUE HER HEART
By
KC Luck

20180419

Thank you for your interest in *Rescue Her Heart*. I sincerely hope you enjoy the story. It was a pleasure to write. If you find time, a review, or even better, a referral to another reader, is always appreciated.

Please enjoy!

KC

CHAPTER 1
NAT

Captain Natalie (Nat) Reynolds was in orbit around the small planet of Prospo. The craft was a P-527 patrol starship and a mainstay of the Space Rangers who kept tabs on the planets in the 8th Galaxy. Nat was assigned to a four-planet cluster and so far, things were quiet as a mouse. *Down-right boring*, she thought, which was fine by her. Although not afraid of action, in fact her body had scars to prove it, she had accepted this route in order to get her head on straight. The last assignment had been a hard one and among other things, she lost a fellow Ranger pilot as well as a dear friend. *But let's not think about that, shall we?* Nat thought and reached for the console in front of her. Punching a button, the sound of Def Leppard music suddenly filled the cabin. It was a seriously old school Earth sound, but Nat loved the hair bands from a century ago and since it was just her on the ship, she cranked the volume up to the max. The P-527 patrol ships were the biggest in the class which could still be piloted solo and Nat had insisted on it. She did not want to be saddled with a new partner. After ten years with the Space Rangers, she had earned her right to pick and choose assignments. There would come a time for a new partner, but the scars were still too fresh, both on her body and in her mind. *Just let it go,* she told herself. There would be time to think about it not to mention discuss it with counselors in the future. Right now, all she wanted to do was enjoy zipping through space at near light speeds and take in the sight of Prospo below her. It was one of her favorites with its tropical climate, turquoise blue oceans, and white sand beaches. *Maybe it is time for a nice long vacation down there.* Being fiercely devoted to the Space Rangers and always willing to sign up for every mission, it had been years since she took time for herself.

As she pondered it, the red light over the radio receiver started to flash. Clicking off the music, Nat acknowledge the transmission. "Base to Catwoman," said a voice over the speaker. When they used her callsign, she knew it was head-quarters and wondered what was up.

"Go ahead, Base," Nat acknowledged.

"Nat, we just received a report of fuel theft at the Prospo petrobay," Base said. "Sounds like somebody filled up the tank of a small starship and then ran out without paying." Nat raised her eyebrows. Stealing fuel was hardly a major crime and for a second Nat felt a bit irritated to be asked to respond to it, but then she reminded herself the assignment was her choice. If it meant handling the minor stuff, so be it.

"I'm on it, Base," Nat said. "I'll let you know what I find out."

"Roger, Catwoman. Base out," the voice said and Nat switched over to the commercial aviation frequency.

"Captain Natalie Reynolds to Prospo Control," she said. "Request for landing."

"Acknowledged, Captain," Prospo Control answered. "Come on in." Nat shook her head a little at the casualness of the answer, but then reminded herself it was not a military planet, only a recreation one. *I should think of it as a nice change of pace*, she thought as she piloted the ship through Prospo's atmosphere and made her approach. Within fifteen minutes she was on the ground of the landing bay, surrounded by beautiful civilian ships. As she disembarked, she could not help but appreciate the smooth lines and modern styles of the different spacecraft. One of the smaller crafts caught her attention more than the others. It was an Avalon Mercury Model 3370 and about the size of her military P-527 craft, but much flashier. Walking closer, Nat wondered what something like it cost. She had accumulated a few million credits over the ten years. It was easy to save when a person worked nonstop and never spent any money. Adding in the hazard pay and survival bonuses, and her bankroll was impressive by anyone's standards. *What if I just gave up the Space Rangers and bought one of these to cruise the galaxies with?* she wondered. It did not sound half bad, at least until she considered what life might be like without the Space Rangers. With her parents and brother light years away in another galaxy, Nat had no one else in her life. The Space Rangers were her family. A lonely life flying around in a pretty starship would not fill the void she sometimes felt and she knew it. With a sigh, Nat turned away and headed toward the aviation tower. She had only taken a step when a man spoke behind her.

"Hey there," he said. Nat turned to see an older gentleman in designer pilot's overalls walking toward her from around the Avalon Mercury. "I saw you looking her over. What do you think?" He was smiling, clearly proud of the craft. Nat could understand why.

"It's gorgeous," she admitted. "I wouldn't mind having one someday." The gentleman nodded.

"A good choice," he said. "And you're in luck. This beauty of mine is for sale. Interested?" Nat hesitated. She had only been half serious when she thought about someday having one. Now it almost seemed like fate. Before she could come up with an answer, the gentleman held out a business card.

"No rush," he said. "I've not even listed her yet. Take my card and give it some consideration. I wrote the price I'm looking for on the back. Let me know." Nat took the card and smiled. *Why not think it over?* she thought.

"Thank you, I will," she told him as she read the card. Dr. Manny Lopez. "It's been nice to meet you, Dr. Lopez."

Dr. Lopez leaned in to read the nametag on her chest. "Same to you, Captain Reynolds. Safe flying."

"You too. I'll be in touch," Nat said and gave him a nod as she started walking toward the aviation tower again. Flipping the card over, she read the amount the Avalon Mercury would cost and was pleased to see it was not unrealistic. Putting the card in her pocket, she promised to think about it more seriously later. *You just never know,* she thought and walked through the door into Prospo Control. She went straight to the main desk and was greeted by the SN-0406 android running things there.

"Welcome. Captain Reynolds I presume?" the android asked. Nat nodded.

"Yes. I'm here to take a statement about a fuel theft," Nat said. The android's lights blinked happily.

"Perfect," the machine said. "Sergeant Baxter is waiting for you in his office. He can give you all the details. Right this way." The android turned on a set of four wheels and headed for a door across the room. Nat followed and after a moment was standing across the desk from a handsome black man. "Sir, Captain Reynolds to see you." Sergeant Baxter stood up and held out his hand. Nat shook it and, when he motioned for her to have a seat, took a chair.

"Sorry to bring you down here for something so minor," Sergeant Baxter apologized. "But stealing fuel must be reported to the petroleum cartel. No way around it." Nat nodded.

"No problem," she said and took her comm device out of her pocket. She opened the notepad feature and prepared to listen. "What exactly happened?"

Sergeant Baxter leaned back in his chair and gathered his thoughts. "About 1300 hours a small ED-90 ship got into line," he started and Nat was surprised. ED-90s were relics. She had not seen one since she was a kid and they were old then. Seeing her look, Baxter nodded. "I know. A classic. But this one was a wreck. The fuel attendants said they were amazed it could actually fly."

"Interesting," Nat said typing in the information. "Then what?"

Baxter shrugged. "After about thirty minutes, it fueled up. After the fill-up, it moved away from the hoses but rather than stop and pay, it accelerated," he explained. "Blasted through our airspace and out into orbit without a word. Didn't clear with the tower or anything. Damn dangerous."

"No kidding," Nat agreed. "And no one got a tail number?" Baxter shook his head and leaned forward again.

"Apparently something which could have been numbers was on the side, but too faded to read," he said. "There was one thing left behind though." He picked up a piece of paper and held it out for Nat. She took it from him. It was a handwritten note.

SORRY I CAN'T PAY. I HOPE YOU UNDERSTAND BUT I NEED THE FUEL TO GET HOME.

"Wow," Nat said. She had never seen anything like it. *What criminal writes a note apologizing for stealing?* she wondered. "How did you get this?"

"Released from the side port in a communication canister," he answered. "As the ship lifted off."

"Crazy," Nat said. She took a picture of the note with the camera on her comm device and then handed it back to Baxter. "What about video? I imagine you have the hoses under surveillance." Baxter took the paper and stacked it on the desk.

"We do. Not sure it will show much, but I can have the techs pull it. Give me a half hour," he said. Nat nodded.

"Works for me," Nat said as she stood up. "I'll grab a bite. What's nearby?" Baxter stood up as well and walked her to the door of his office.

"Flight Deck Diner is right across the tarmac. Can't miss it," he said.

NAT SAT ON A STOOL at the counter of the diner with her veggie burger and fries. She could not figure out what kind of crook left a note behind. *Why bother?* she wondered and was lost in thought when a man sat down on the stool next to her. He leaned toward her.

"Hey there, Ranger," he said. "What brings you to a dive like this?" Nat started at the interruption of her thinking and frowned. Noticing, the stranger smiled. "Aw now, don't look like that. It messes up that pretty little face of yours." Nat sighed. *Great*, she thought. *A come on.* It was the last thing she wanted or needed. Trying to ignore the guy, she dipped the last of her fries in ketchup, ate them and started to stand up. She tossed a few credits on the counter and turned to go. Before she could, the man put a hand on her arm. "Whoa," he said. "What's the hurry?" Nat turned to look at him with an icy glare. The man pulled back his hand. She watched his face slowly turn red and she knew what was coming next. "Oh, right, let me guess," he said with a sneer. "You like girls."

"Exactly," Nat snarled. "So buzz off." The man answered with a mean laugh.

"Sure thing, dyke. But you don't know what you're missing," he said. Nat strongly considered head-butting him between his eyes, but then decided he wasn't worth it. With a disappointed shake of her head, she left the asshole at the counter and walked out. He did not know how lucky he was actually. Nat knew she could have kicked his sorry civilian ass without breaking a sweat. She had more experience fighting hand-to-hand than she ever wanted. *But what purpose would it serve?* she thought. Mean people stayed mean, even when they got their stupid heads cracked. Nat kept walking and went back into the Prospo control center hoping the security video was ready to roll. She did not want to stay on the planet any longer than necessary.

CHAPTER 2
CATHERINE

The piece of junk ED-90 rattled its way through space. Catherine Porter did her best to keep it flying in a straight line, but it was not easy. Her experience flying was limited as her father had done almost all of it for all of the eighteen years of her life, or at least up until he disappeared the month before. It was only out of dire necessity she was driving now, but she knew she had to get to the planet Untas where her aunt lived and figure out what to do with her life. Besides, her aunt needed to understand her brother was missing and Catherine only hoped the woman would have some insight as to what Catherine should do next. Normally, when a person disappeared from Prospo, it was a kidnapping, but Catherine was sure that was not what happened. Not only had there not been a ransom note so far, but her family was broke. It was why the only spaceship Catherine could afford was the ED-90. It was even cheaper than a between planet transport ticket, except Catherine had not calculated in the cost of fuel. The dealer at the starcraft lot had promised her the tanks were full, but it was bullshit and by the time she realized it, the traveling shyster had picked up stakes and moved on. All of which was why she resorted to stealing the fuel she needed. Catherine hated having to do it, but no matter what she thought of, there were no more credits in the bank. *At least I left a note*, she thought, which Catherine realized was lame under the circumstances, yet she needed the people at the fuel station to know she was sorry and not a real criminal. *Someday, when I am rich, I'll go back and pay them for it*. Catherine held onto that thought as she fought the steering controls and prayed she was going the right direction. The orbital position system was up and the holograph showed the planets in relation to her location, but Catherine only half trusted it considering the rest of the ship was falling apart.

Gritting her teeth, Catherine willed the junker to keep flying. It was at least two days flight to get to Untas and she was not one hundred percent sure she stole enough fuel. Already the gauge was jumping around and she was only a couple hours in. Glancing at the holograph, Catherine noted the only planet between where she was and where she needed to be was Taswa. It would do her no help. The thing was basically a rotating block of ice with an environment of a continual blizzard. Nothing inhabited it, not even a military outpost. There definitely was not any fuel to buy, or in her case, steal. *I'll just have to make it*, she thought and tried to relax. She could not fly for forty-eight hours all twisted up like a spring about to go off, but it was hard to let go. The last thirty days had been hell.

First, her father did not come home one night after stumbling off from their shop to find a new bar which would let him open a tab Catherine knew he could not pay. She had long ago learned not to worry until a couple of days went by as her dad would often find a woman to take him in and shack up with her until he sobered up. *Or when they threw him out as they realized he was a penniless drunk*, Catherine thought. Only this time her father did not come wandering home after all. After the third day, Catherine went looking for him. She started with his favorite watering holes only to hear over and over that her dad was a worthless deadbeat. Each time she would walk back out trying to keep her head held high and let the mean words roll off her, but at night she cried herself to sleep, her fury mixed with despair. Finally, when a week had passed, she went to the cops. The response there was not much friendlier. They knew Catherine's dad all too well. A drunk they picked up at least once a week and had to put in the tank to dry out. They had to admit he had not been seen in a while but told her to just go home. Like a bad penny, the cops were sure he would show up again in due time.

But he did not. With no other ideas, Catherine went to the medical center actually hoping he was there, but they had no record of a forty-five-year-old unidentified drunk man being checked in for anything. She had stumbled home after that, tired and without hope of ever finding him. When she got to the corner market her father owned, which she had not opened since he went missing, she found the doors locked. This was an especially big problem because she and her dad lived above it in a dismal flat. The notice on the door clearly outlined the problem. No rent had been paid in six months. Catherine was suddenly homeless at eighteen. Only by climbing the fire escape was she able to jimmy the apartment window and get inside long enough to pack one bag and grab her stash of credits under the loose floorboard in her corner of the room. There was not much, but she had saved it slowly over the last five years. It was her dream money of someday getting out of her pathetic life.

Taking it and running back down the ladder as the sound of police sirens started to come closer, Catherine did not know what to do other than try and call her aunt. Catherine knew her father and his sister were not close, but she was the only person Catherine could think to turn to at the moment. With no money to even afford a comm link, Catherine used some of her precious credits to go to a cafe and make the call from a station there. She nearly cried when her aunt answered and was clearly concerned when she saw Catherine's face.

"Oh my God," she said. "Catherine, is that you?" All Catherine could do was nod as the sobs started to come. "Honey, what is wrong?"

"It's Dad," she choked out. "I can't find him." Catherine's aunt was quiet for a long moment.

"I see," she finally said. "How long?" Catherine gulped in a breath.

"Almost a month," she answered. "And they locked me out of the shop and our apartment. I don't know what to do." Again, her aunt did not answer immediately. It was so long in fact, Catherine looked up to make sure they still had a connection. What she saw made her stomach clench with panic. Her aunt's face was no longer friendly.

"He inherited that from our parents. They trusted him with it before they died," she said, her voice hard. "And he let it slip away." Catherine suddenly felt the need to defend her dad.

"He did the best he could," she argued. "After mother died, it was hard for him." Catherine watched her aunt frown.

"How do you know anything about when your mother died? You were four," she said. Now

Catherine was getting angry. *Why is she being so mean?* she thought. *What did we ever do to her?*

"Dad told me about mom all the time. About how wonderful and kind she was to anyone who came into the store. How beautiful she was," Catherine said. "How much I looked like her." Her aunt's face did not react and stayed cold.

"Well, she was a good woman and could have married far better than my brother," she said. "It was a horrible thing which happened to her. A horrible accident." Catherine had heard enough. She did not call her aunt to listen to insults about her father. It was clear there would be no help from her aunt and Catherine lifted her chin in defiance.

"Well," Catherine said. "I simply wanted to let you know about your brother. I need to go." At last her aunt's face softened.

"Catherine, wait," she started. "Don't go." Catherine waved her hand dismissively at her aunt's image and slung her ratty backpack onto her shoulder.

"Never mind. Goodbye," she said. As she reached for the disconnect button, her aunt leaned in closer to the monitor so her face filled almost all of the screen.

"Please take a transport here," her aunt said. "Just do that. We can work out the rest." Catherine shrugged.

"I'll think about it," she said and hung up the call. The timestamp let her know she had used up more credits on the call than she wanted. She was about out of money and knew if she did not get more soon, she would be sleeping on the street. With no other options, she went back to the bar her father most liked to frequent. It was early and the place was empty. When the owner saw her, he rushed around the bar and helped her up on a stool.

"Catherine, baby," he said. "What is going on? Where's your dad?" For the second time, Catherine started to sob. The man she had met on occasion when her dad took her along was being so nice. She remembered his name was Marcus and he was old and fat, but right now he was a lifeline. *Maybe he can lend me the money to get to Untas where my aunt lives*, she thought and started to blab out her whole situation. Marcus listened and nodded, a look of sympathy on his face. When she finished with her plan to borrow enough credits to take a transport to Untas, he patted her hand gently. Catherine tried not to flinch when she felt his short, fat, sweaty fingers touch her. *He's a friend of my dad's. It's okay.*

"I will help you," Marcus said and Catherine could not believe her ears. "I don't have enough to spare for you to take a transport. They are ridiculously expensive, but I have enough credits for you to buy a cheap ship and fly yourself there. Can you do that?" Catherine nodded, smiling for the first time in almost a month. Marcus smiled back and turned to open a cupboard which hid a safe. Glancing back at her for a moment, he paused. Catherine gave him the most hopeful look she could muster and Marcus licked his lips before he looked back at the dial and entered the numbers. As he prepared to open the safe, he paused. "Can you go lock the front door? I don't want anyone to come in and rob me while I have this open," he said. Catherine understood and jumped off of the stool to go to the front and turn the deadbolt. When she returned to the bar, Marcus was counting out credits. Catherine's eyes widened when she saw the small pile he was making for her. Like he said, it was not enough to get a ride to Untas, but it would be her ticket to safety.

Once he was done, he looked up and their eyes met. He nodded and pushed the credits over to her. She picked them up with a shaking hand, afraid at any second he would change his mind. When he smiled again, Catherine took that as a good sign and slipped the money into the front pocket of her backpack. "Are we okay now?" Marcus asked, making Catherine jump. He had come around the bar and was standing right next to her. Catherine took a step back, suddenly uncomfortable, but smiled to cover it.

"Sure, Marcus," she said. "But I should get going. I want to look for a ship right away." Marcus licked his lips again and Catherine felt a hint of fear bloom in her stomach.

"This won't take long," he said and unhooked his belt. "Just kneel down right here." Catherine froze. She could not believe what she just heard and yet a part of her could.

"There are no free rides," her father told her almost every day of her life. She heard it so often, she almost believed it. But not quite. Catherine smiled as sweetly as she could and stepped closer to Marcus. She saw the lust in his eyes and it gave her power.

"Thanks for everything, Marcus," she said and when he looked surprised at her tone, Catherine did not hesitate. She brought her right knee up as hard as she could into his groin. Marcus let out a squeal and crumpled in front of her.

"You bitch," he whispered through teeth clenched with pain.

"Don't you forget it," Catherine said and walked fast to the front door, unlocked it, and bolted from the bar.

CHAPTER 3
NAT

Leaning forward, Nat watched the video monitor. It was a bit hazy as the Prospo fuel bay was not well lit, but she could make out enough of the details. While the images of various spacecraft rolled by, Sergeant Baxter returned to the room carrying two cups of coffee. "Here we go," he said as he handed one to Nat and then sat down in the other chair beside her. "I can't promise it tastes any good, but it is hot and strong." Nat gave him a nod.

"No problem. Thanks," she said. She was well used to military coffee, so figured this could not be any worse. Taking a faint sip of the hot liquid, Nat realized she was wrong. The coffee was abominable. Seeing her reaction to the taste, Baxter chuckled.

"Sorry, but I warned you. For some reason that damn SN-0406 android they assigned us can't make a decent pot of java to save its life," he explained. Nat smiled and set the nasty brew aside. She would make herself a nice espresso once she was back on her ship. "Okay," Baxter continued. "Thanks for waiting. Let me rewind this video along to the timestamp we are looking for." He pressed a few buttons and the screen flickered. Everything in the picture started zipping around backward. "It will just be a minute to get to the spot." He leaned back in his chair, sipped his coffee, made a face at the flavor, and then set it down near Nat's. "Incredible. It's like the damn 'droid tries to make it bad."

"It is pretty horrible," Nat admitted. Baxter laughed.

"Yes, it is," he leaned back again. "So, tell me, Captain. How long have you been with the Space Rangers?"

"I just started my eleventh year," Nat answered.

"Wow," Baxter said. "You don't look old enough to have a decade under your belt already."

Nat shrugged. "I joined the day after I turned eighteen. Growing up, it was all I ever wanted to do," she said.

"And you like it?" Baxter asked. Nat thought about the question for a second but then nodded.

"It has its highs and lows. I would lay down my life for my Ranger brothers and sisters, but the red tape gets a little thick sometimes," she answered.

"Ever think of retiring? Isn't ten years the cut off for the elite forces?" he asked, picking up his coffee, apparently willing to risk tasting it again. Nat gave him another shrug.

"I've considered it," she said. *Just this morning while I checked out that luxury starship in fact*, she thought. "But for now, I'm content. It really just depends on what the future holds for me."

Baxter nodded. "Gotcha. Well, if you ever do and want a job, I'm always looking for good cops down here. It's about as laid back as you can get," he said. From what Nat had seen so far, what he said was an understatement.

"Thank you, sir," she said. "I'll keep that in mind." Just then the image of an ED-90 came on the screen. "Hold on, I think we found it."

Baxter pushed the pause button and the video stopped. He leaned in and checked the timestamp. "Yep, that's the one," he said. "Like I said, the crew reported the ship was a piece of junk. Looks like they weren't kidding." Nat had to agree. The small, one passenger craft showed a lot of neglect. Scanning it from tail to nose, she did not see any clear identifying markings or numbers. The paint was so faded though, she was not especially surprised.

"Can you back it up all the way and then let it run? I can't quite make out the driver," Nat asked. Baxter obliged and after a moment, the footage ran forward again. Nat watched as the ED-90 made it to the front of the line and stopped. The attendants hooked up the hoses and then moved on to the next ship in line. Once the meter clicked off on the ED-90, one guy came back, unhooked it and waved the ship forward to the pay station. Everything seemed normal until the tiny spaceship accelerated past the cashier and raced out of the landing area. People started yelling for the pilot to stop, but it was wasted breath. The ED-90 clearly had no intention of paying and was flying away. Nat remembered the note of apology Baxter showed her earlier. "And where did they find the canister?" Baxter pointed to a spot on the screen and Nat saw the small dot resting on the platform. While she watched, an attendant picked it up. After he inspected it for a second, he called over to what Nat guess was a supervisor and handed the object off.

"That's Dave Lewis," Baxter said. "He runs the place during the day shift and is the one who called us."

"I see," Nat said. The whole situation was puzzling. She still could not get all the pieces to fit together. *Why steal the fuel?* she wondered. Filling up the small tanks of an ED-90 would cost almost nothing. *And then why apologize for it?* She shook her head. "Okay," she continued. "I did see a face in about the last five seconds of the clip. Let's back it up and enlarge the frame."

"You got it," Baxter said and, in a minute, the monitor was filled with the picture of a young woman. *Can't be more than eighteen*, Nat thought. *And she looks scared as hell.* Nat studied the graphic. The girl was incredibly pretty. Dark hair down to her shoulders framing large brown eyes. *I think I could look at that face all day.* "Good looking, kid," Baxter said, interrupting Nat's thoughts. "Wonder what her story is." Nat wondered it too.

"Can I get a printout of this image?" she asked.

Baxter nodded. "No problem," he said and reached around to turn on the printer behind him. "Just gotta let this relic warm up and then I can have it for you." Nat continued to examine the picture while she waited. She found the woman's image captivating. It was as if Nat somehow knew she was supposed to know her.

"Did your tower track her on radar when she left the fuel bay?" Nat asked. Baxter sighed.

"I wish," he said. "But since she didn't send out any comm she was about to exit the airspace and leave the planet, no one was looking for her. I called the guys up there and they told me she came and went too fast to get a lock." Nat frowned feeling frustrated by the lack of efficiency she was finding with the civilians on the laid-back planet of Prospo. Then she had an idea.

"Print me a shot of the ship too," she said. "There can't be too many places the girl is headed if she left orbit. I'll go run her down."

"Really?" Baxter asked. "Is it worth it? It's just a little fuel and I only called you because petrol crimes are a mandatory call." Nat paused. He was right. *Was this really worth pursuing?* she thought. For reasons even she could not explain, it felt like it was and so she nodded.

"I want to do this," she said. "Besides, things were getting a little too quiet for me anyway." Baxter grinned and punched the buttons to print out a picture of the runaway ED-90.

"I bet," he said and waited for the printer to finish. He handed the images to Nat. She glanced at them, pausing at the photo of the girl again. *So young to be on the run from something*, Nat thought and then stood up. Baxter did the same and they went to the front desk. As soon as they were within earshot, the SN-0406 android spoke up.

"Perfect timing, Sergeant," it said. "A Level Orange bulletin just came in. Seems a meteor shower is set to pass through." Nat watched Baxter frown and study the monitor the android was pointing too. Meteor showers were not necessarily a problem unless they came too close to a planet's atmosphere. Then it depended on the size of them. Nat knew a Level Orange bulletin was only semi-serious, so she waited patiently until Baxter finished reading the brief. He turned to Nat.

"Well that means your manhunt for the ED-90 is out," he said. "A pretty substantial number of small meteors is set to blast past Prospo over the next few hours. All craft are grounded until the all-clear." Nat felt an unexpected surge of disappointment. *Where is all that emotion coming from?* she wondered. It was completely out of character for her to feel much investment in anything, particularly for some thief running away in a piece of shit spaceship. *It's probably for the best.*

Nat shrugged. "So it goes. Good break for the girl, assuming she's clear of the shower's lane. Now she gets away scot-free," she said.

"Good point," Baxter agreed. "Some people are just born lucky. And don't worry about the girl being caught off-guard by the shower. We will be sending out an all-points bulletin to any spacecraft in the area warning them of the danger and the mandatory requirement to either land or clear the airspace. Our thief will have plenty of notice."

"Fair enough," Nat said. She put out her hand and Baxter gave it a shake. "Thanks for taking the time to show me the video."

Baxter smiled. "And thank you for being so quick to come answer our call," he said. "Sorry it didn't work out to be an arrest for you." He motioned to the video screen capture printouts she still held in her hand. "You want me to shred those for you?"

Nat looked at the pages again. There was absolutely zero reason to keep them. *And yet*, she thought. *I really want to.* "You know, I am going to hold on to these," Nat said. "And keep an eye out for this girl or this ship. It could still turn up."

"Well, if it does and I can help you in any way, speak up," Baxter said. "So what will you do while you're stuck for a while on Prospo? Lots of great beaches to check out. Surfing. Swimming. Sunbathing. Or there's restaurants galore, with—" Nat held up her hand to interrupt him with a polite smile.

"I plan to head out the minute the all-clear is sounded," she said. "So, I'll go back to my ship and relax in my quarters. Catch up on some reading." She stepped away from the counter and started slowly toward the exit. Baxter followed suit and walked her to the door.

"I hear that," he said. "And if and when you do retire, keep in mind what I said. A job here for you, anytime you want it."

"I appreciate that," Nat said and walked outside. Evening was coming on and, with a glance at her comm device to check the time, she was surprised at how late it was already. For a brief moment, Nat reconsidered Baxter's advice about finding a restaurant and having dinner. Something cooked in a kitchen larger than the three by three foot galley she had back on her ship. Then she remembered the diner and how much she disliked having to interact with people in general. Even when she wanted to be left to herself in public, her muscular body wrapped in her tailored Space Ranger uniform always drew attention. It did not help that she was naturally good-looking with olive skin, sandy blonde hair, and intense blue-gray eyes. On nights she went out, it was not uncommon for her to receive propositions from both men and women. Nat always said no. It was an easy choice for her. People simply were not interesting and she was far happier being alone.

CHAPTER 4
CATHERINE

She was making good time and starting to feel confident in her progress when the first pinging noise sounded off of the hull. *What in the hell was that?* she thought. It was not like she was back on the ground of Prospo where she could run over something. She was in open space. There should be absolutely nothing to hit. Shaking her head, Catherine tried to convince herself it was a fluke. The ship was settling from old age or something. Then she heard it again, only this time it was more of a banging noise and she felt the craft waiver from the impact. *Something definitely just hit the side of my spaceship. But what? There's nothing out there.* Just then she noticed a small flashing red light on the instrument panel in her cockpit. It was faint, as if the bulb was nearly done for, but once she saw it, Catherine knew it was not a good sign. Pressing it with a shaking finger, her holographic map was immediately replaced with a bulletin.

WARNING: LEVEL ORANGE METEOR SHOWER EXPECTED IN THE PROSPO AIRSPACE STARTING AT 1900 HOURS. ALL CRAFT IN THE AREA ARE ADVISED TO LAND IMMEDIATELY.

Catherine looked at the clock on the dashboard. It read 1915 hours. *Oh, you have got to be kidding me*, she thought realizing her bad luck was continuing all the way up into space. *But it is only Level Orange, so that can't be too bad, right?* Just then another rock, bigger than the other two, ricocheted off of the windshield. Although it did not crack the thick, space tempered glass, it startled the hell out of Catherine. It was followed by the sound of pinging and clanking from smaller pieces all over the ship. *I need to turn around*, she thought. *Or I'm going to get shot to bits.* But Catherine also knew she could not go back. There were no more credits in her account to live on and, even if there were, she was a criminal now after stealing the fuel. The only choice was to keep going on toward Untas and pray her ship held together. Clamping her hands tighter onto the steering wheel, she gritted her teeth and willed the little craft to fly faster. A minute passed and there were no more pings of meteors hitting the ED-90. When it was quiet for a full five minutes, Catherine relaxed and let out the breath she had not realized she was holding. It was going to be okay.

The next meteor was the size of a gallon of milk and it hit Catherine's spaceship so hard it nearly knocked her out of her chair. "Shit!" she yelled as she fought to keep the craft from going into a spin while a rainbow of different lights started flashing on the console. An alarm sounded and it was followed by a screeching voice so loud it made Catherine wince.

"Hull damage warning," the voice blared. "Structure integrity at 63%." Pressing a button to silence the alarm, Catherine did not like the sound of that news and realized her plan to keep flying on to her aunt's planet was not going to work. Now she would be lucky to make it back to Prospo and she knew it. Pressing a button on the dash, she brought back up the orbital positioning device. The little green dot she knew was the ED-90 was just starting to cross through the farthest edge of the planet Taswa's orbit. Unfortunately, landing there was not an option. Everyone in the solar system knew Taswa was uninhabited because it was not much more than a frozen hunk of revolving ice. Even landing there to wait out the meteor shower was out of the question. The environment was basically a perpetual blizzard. Even the best pilots dismissed Taswa as a place to layover.

With no other options, Catherine sadly started a slow turn to reverse direction back to Prospo. With a little luck, she would get back on planet undetected and then be able to consider her options. Although the idea of getting arrested was not appealing, dying in a meteor shower was even less so. Just as she was thinking about her options, a series of six more small meteors pounded off the side of her spaceship in rapid succession. They shook the ED-90 to its core and the alarms sounded all over again. "Hull damage warning. Structural integrity at 44%" the voice screeched. Slapping the button to silence the alarms, Catherine bit her lip and did her best to ignore the reality of her situation. *There is no way I'm going to get blasted to bits by some pieces of rock up here after all I have been through*, she thought. *No way!*

The biggest meteor yet slammed into her windshield and this time it did leave a hairline crack. Before the warning voice began to blare again, Catherine knew the "structural integrity" number just went down. A lot. "I have to land," she whispered as the reality of what was happening finally settled in. She let her eyes drift back to the holographic map. Right in the center was a glowing blue planet. Taswa. If she made a dash for it, there was a chance she could get there and out of the path of the meteor shower before she was pummeled to bits. What happened when she got there, she had no guess except that it was probably not going to be a good time. Turning her ship again, she locked in the coordinates for Taswa and pushed the rocket boosters all the way to high. The sound of tiny rocks made a tinkling symphony across the ship's hull as the meteor shower gained momentum. Catherine knew it really would come down to her making it to Taswa before a rock big enough to breach the ship hit her. She was in the race of her life.

Catherine watched the blue planet rapidly grow bigger in her windshield. A quick glance at her map told her she was within minutes of the planet's atmosphere. As if pushing the small spaceship along through sheer willpower, the ED-90 closed the distance in a hurry while the ship's alarms blared out warning after warning. Catherine had stopped bothering to silence them. She was committed to her course and she knew it. It was Taswa or bust. Now she knew she would just have to hope someone would bother to come looking for her, which seemed unlikely. There was no one who gave a damn about her. Catherine felt tears threaten and she shook her head angrily. *Feeling sorry for yourself won't get you through this, Catherine Porter,* she thought. *Now hit the damn mayday button and let's ride this out.* Reaching out, she punched the large red button with the white letters SOS on it. It immediately started to flash, but Catherine hardly noticed with all of the other blinking warning indicators in front of her. Instead, she put all her focus on the quickly advancing blue planet in front of her.

"60 seconds to entry," a different, much more calm voice said over the speaker. Catherine appreciated the change. It was nice to have something sound confident. Flexing her hands, she took a series of long deep breaths to calm herself. She knew her piloting experience was crap and the idea of blasting into a blizzard made her heart nearly stop with fear, but Catherine also knew she had zero other options. "45 seconds to entry," the voice declared again. Catherine licked her lips and tried to swallow but her mouth was beyond dry. "30 seconds." Taswa filled her windshield now. It was actually quite pretty, with its swirls of blue in a dozen different hues all laced with white. *This won't be so bad*, she thought and then the ED-90 punched through the cloud cover and into the storm.

Fierce winds grabbed at Catherine's spaceship and tried to slam it to the ground, but she fought with all her strength to stay airborne. *Not that I have any idea what way is up and what way is down anymore*, she thought. All she could see out the window was white. Only by watching the instrument panel could she keep on a semi-level course as she whipped along, occasionally seeing a black outcropping of rock whizz by her. The question now was where and how to land. Her holographic map was proving to be about useless as it only showed fields of white glaciers on all sides. Then she had an idea. *What if I just fly around here in circles for a few hours? And let the meteor shower pass?* It would use up more of her precious fuel than she wanted, but under the circumstances, it seemed like a minor problem. If she had to arrive at Untas on fumes, so be it. She could wait for the all-clear message and then return to space to finish her journey. Catherine almost kicked herself for not thinking of it sooner.

As she continued to cruise along being buffeted by the wind and feeling pellets of ice spray over her windshield, Catherine began to think Taswa was not really so bad. Certainly not a place to live, but not the horror it was made out to be by pilot friends of her father's. Mostly, it was just cold. Catherine likened it to being stuck in a subzero freezer and turned up the dial for the heater to take the chill off the inside of the cabin. Feeling the heating elements kick in, she let herself relax a little. The last hour had taken a lot out of her and she could feel the adrenaline from it all just now starting to drain from her body. Hopefully, the worst part of the trip was behind her. As she twisted her head from side-to-side to work out the kink which had developed there during the stress of flying through the meteors, Catherine saw the flashing SOS. Feeling almost embarrassed at having turned it on in her near panic, she leaned forward to shut it off. Just as her fingers grazed the white letters, the ship suddenly swung hard left and Catherine had to grab the wheel again with both hands. *What was that?* she thought just as the ship was pounded with more wind. The storm appeared to be picking up steam and Catherine did not like it. *Is the meteor shower still going on?* It felt like it might be time to leave Taswa after all.

As if hearing her thoughts, the blizzard roared even louder and rocked the small spacecraft hard from right to left, as if trying to shake it to pieces. Catherine fought the wheel as best she could, but she quickly realized she was no longer controlling what was happening. *This is not good*, she thought and peered as hard as she could through the windshield to try and see what was ahead. There was nothing but white. *But wait. What is that?* Something was starting to materialize out of the blowing snow. It was massive and edged in gray and in a flash, she realized it was a mountain of granite. Panicked, Catherine wrenched on the wheel to try and pull up, but it was too late.

The ED-90 flew headlong into it, and only by luck and her last attempt to steer did the craft avoid being smashed to pieces immediately. Instead, it glanced to the side and, plowing up plumes of snow, slid along the mountain face. Catherine could hear the wrenching of metal as the small ship, her one last hope of getting anywhere safe, was torn apart around her. For a moment, she wondered what she could try next, but then it did not matter. The craft came to a final collision and slammed to a stop. Catherine was thrown forward and her head hit the console. She had time for one fleeting thought. *I'm going to die... but does that really matter?* She suddenly did not think so and then everything went black.

CHAPTER 5
NAT

Nat was settling in to enjoy a good glass of red wine and the next book in the classic storyteller Sue Grafton's private eye series when the SOS alarm came over the ship's speaker system. Anytime a distress call was set off in a fifty-million-mile radius of a Space Ranger ship, all available pilots were notified. When Nat went to check the monitor to see the location of the mayday, she froze. It was at the center of the reported meteor shower and near the cusp of the ice planet Taswa. Although it was possible she was wrong, Nat somehow knew in her heart the ship in trouble belonged to the beautiful young woman in the runaway ED-90. In a split second, she made the decision to go after her.

Slipping into the pilot's chair, she fired up her P-527 spacecraft and radioed Prospo's aviation tower while buckling into her harness. "Control, this is Space Ranger Captain Natalie Reynolds requesting clearance for takeoff to answer a distress call," she said. There was a pause and Nat knew her request was causing some discussion up in the tower, but she did not wait. Slowly she accelerated the thrusters and lifted off of the tarmac.

"Captain, please be advised a Level Orange meteor shower warning is in effect," Control finally responded. "Leaving Prospo airspace is not recommended."

"Affirmative, Control," Nat said. "I am aware and I acknowledge your recommendation. Am I clear for exit?" There was another pause and while Nat felt her frustration starting to rise, she used the time to move her ship into position to blast out of the Prospo atmosphere. *If they don't answer with a yes in the next ten seconds, I'm going anyway*, she thought. It would get her in hot water with command later, but in the moment, she did not care. She knew she had to get to the girl before it was too late. Nothing else mattered.

"Captain, you are clear," Control said. "Godspeed." Nat nodded with satisfaction and, throwing caution to the wind, pulled back on the thrusters to blast out into space. The P-527 shuddered a little with the sudden intense acceleration, but Nat handled it easily. As the blackness of open space enveloped her, she brought up her navigation system and checked the last location of the distress beacon. It blinked faintly from within the Taswa atmosphere and Nat swore under her breath. She was well aware Taswa was a hostile place with nonstop artic-like conditions. Chances of survival if stranded there long term were next to zero. It left Nat no other option than to use her hyperdrive booster to close the distance fast enough. Only there was one big problem. Flying at that speed through a meteor shower was a good way to kill yourself. Even hitting a small meteor could rip through any ship's hull. It would take impossibly good pilot skill and a whole lot of luck to make it through and get to Taswa in one piece. Fortunately, Nat was an impossibly good pilot. *Now I just need to count on the luck part*, she thought. *And I am long overdue for some of that.*

Typing in the coordinates for the planet Taswa, Nat saw the edge of the meteor shower quickly approaching. It was a wide swath of tannish-brown dust and debris slinging through open space and so far, nothing looked big enough to be a real problem. Her goal was to blast through the area fast enough to miss being hammered to bits by too many rocks and make her approach to the quickly growing blue orb off to her left. Once launching to hyperdrive speed, she calculated being at the beacon site within eight minutes. As she put her hand on the throttle and prepared herself for the physical shock of such rapid acceleration, she heard a transmission come through from Space Ranger Command. "Catwoman, this is Base, do you copy?" Base said. Nat considered for a moment of not answering. She knew what they were going to tell her and the result would put her in a horrible position. Still, her training and loyalty left her no option but to respond.

"Base, this is Catwoman, go ahead," Nat said.

"Catwoman, we show you on radar and please be advised you are in danger of entering a Level Orange meteor shower," Base said. Nat rolled her eyes. *No shit*, she thought.

"I see it, Base. I am responding to the SOS alarm," she said.

"Another unit has been deployed from the far side of Taswa, Catwoman," Base explained.

"They won't get there in time," Nat said. There was a pause and Nat knew she did not have time for a conversation right now.

"Neither will you," Base finally responded. "You are ordered to reverse your position and return to Prospo."

"Base, I am engaging hyperdrive. I will be at the beacon in under seven minutes," she said. "I will report in when I have reached the crash site."

"Catwoman, you will not engage hyperdrive and you will return to Prospo. Be advised, that is an order," Base said. Then the voice on the comm link softened. "Nat, this is suicide. Just turn around." Nat considered it. She had no reason to risk her life for the woman on the video. They had never met and there was nothing connecting them to each other. *So what am I doing?* she wondered. *Why do I feel such a need to rescue her?* Nat shook her head in frustration. No matter what she thought, the intense feeling inside her insisted she find the woman. Somehow, she knew it was her destiny.

"Sorry, Base, but I have to do this. Catwoman, over and out," she said and shut off the comm link so she could focus. Taking a deep breath, she grasped the throttle once again and before she could chicken out, yanked it backward. Instantly, Nat was pushed back into her seat as the P-527 surged forward. She gritted her teeth as the force of acceleration shook the entire ship. Rocks began to strike the hull and sounded like hail on a tin roof. There was no way to avoid it and Nat could only hope nothing too big caught up with her. She looked at the digital clock on the dash and knew she would be hitting Taswa's orbit in less than two minutes. *Come on, baby*, Nat thought as she rode the ship forward. *90 seconds and I'm out of this*. Then she saw it. A meteor the size of a cow spinning end-over-end and directly in the way of her trajectory. Nat had two choices. Try to steer around it or shoot it with her blasters, hoping to break it up small enough that the remnants did not puncture her windshield. With only nanoseconds to decide, Nat activated the P-527's space cannon and pulled the trigger. Twin energy blasts shot out from under her ship and struck the meteor dead center. Nat watched the rock explode seconds before she raced through what was left of it.

Coming out the other side, Nat blinked with surprise when she realized she was alive. Letting out a whoop of excitement, Nat grinned and rode her spaceship as it looped around into the relative safety of Taswa's atmosphere. The key word was relative. As soon as Nat punched through the cloud cover, icy gusts of almost hurricane-speed winds ripped at her craft. The entire vessel shook and Nat could see nothing through the windshield glass. Snow and ice clouded the air and left her no option but to rely on her advanced navigation systems to get her safely to the distress beacon. Following the blinking dot, Nat wrestled to keep the P-527 airborne and within a minute she was over the downed ship. *I did it*, she thought with extreme satisfaction. *Now if only I am in time.* Using infrared imagery, Nat scanned the ED-90 wreckage. A single faint red blob appeared and Nat's heart surged with relief to know the woman was at least still alive.

Moving her ship as close as possible to the ED-90 and then setting it to autohover in place, Nat unbuckled and quickly put on her spacesuit. She grabbed some medical supplies and an emergency blanket and, with not a moment to spare, she opened the hatch. Dropping the ramp, she jogged out into the open. The wind was incredible and at first impact, nearly sent her sprawling in the snow. Leaning into it,

Nat used all her strength to shuffle along to the downed wreck. What she saw filled her with fear. A gash had ripped through the center of the craft and snow mixed with ice was blowing into the cabin. The inside would be at subzero temperatures by now and Nat knew the girl had to be half frozen if not dead. Still, she pushed on and climbed in through the torn opening. It cut the wind some, which helped, and Nat turned on her headlamp to see the interior of the ship better. The ED-90 was as much an old piece of shit on the inside as the out. For the life of her, Nat could not understand how the thing could still fly and vowed to find the person who let the young woman try to travel off-planet in it and kick his ass.

Within a minute, Nat was in the cockpit and saw the girl slumped over the controls of the craft. Her face was pale with a hint of blue around her lips. The wind had blown a thin layer of snow and ice over her body like a blanket. Nat did not hesitate. She immediately wrapped the girl in the emergency blanket and picked her up, not even stopping to check if the woman was still alive and made her way back to the exit. As soon as she stepped out, the Taswa blizzard threatened to rip the girl from her arms and Nat had to battle every step back to the P-527, which was rocking precariously in the gale. Thankful to make it, Nat climbed back inside her ship and used her elbow to hit the button to close the ramp. Even though her starship was unsteady, it was a huge relief to be back onboard and safe. *Now I just need to save this woman*, she thought.

Nat carried her through the craft to the small sleeping quarters and set her gently on the bed. Pulling off her own spacesuit, Nat assessed the situation. She was not sure how severely the girl was injured aside from the small cut on her forehead, but it was clear the woman was nearing, if not already, slipping into a hypothermic state. The key now was to raise the girl's body temperature as soon as she could, and this would require removing her freezing wet clothes. *Don't think about it*, Nat thought as she went to the cabinet and took out scissors. *This is just a rescue and I'm an experienced captain in the Space Ranger Corps.* Nat turned back to the woman and forced herself to be all business. Using the scissors, she cut away the emergency blanket and peeled it back. Next, she slipped the blade under the woman's shirt and sliced it down the middle. The fabric fell away and Nat realized the woman was braless. Nat forced her eyes away and, with shaking hands, pulled off the girl's boots and socks before focusing on removing her pants. It was difficult to cut through the thick fabric and knowing precious time was slipping away, Nat tossed the scissors aside and gripping the cloth, yanked with all her strength to tear the pants apart and off the girl's body.

Suddenly the woman's eyes flew open and stared at Nat. "What are you doing?" she asked through chattering teeth. Nat froze as she looked into the stranger's brown eyes and tried to remind herself she was doing nothing wrong.

"I need to get you warm," Nat answered. "And first that means removing your wet clothes." The woman nodded and closed her eyes.

"Okay, but I'm still so cold," she murmured and rolled over to curl up on her side. Nat looked down at the woman who was now free of her freezing clothes but left with only a pair of bikini underwear. She grabbed a blanket and put it over the woman but quickly realized it would not be enough. She had to have a direct heat source. Racking her brain, Nat could think of no options but for one. Body heat. Again, reminding herself she was a professional and what she was about to do meant the difference between life or death, Nat stripped off her own clothing down to her underwear and slipped under the blanket. The girl's skin was like ice, but Nat did not hesitate and pressed her own body against the woman's back while wrapping her arms around her in an enveloping hug. As they spooned together, Nat could not believe how slender and petite the girl felt in her arms. It had been a long time since she held a woman. Feeling a shiver coming on, Nat hugged the woman a little tighter and heard her sigh. Responding to the warmth and comfort of Nat's body, she snuggled back against her. The sensation was so tender and sensual, Nat had to work to stay relaxed and not react. The feeling was sweet torture.

CHAPTER 6
CATHERINE

C atherine was feeling warm and content as she slowly started waking up from the best sleep she had in a month. *Or even longer*, she thought with a sigh. Rolling over, she felt the softness of skin and the firmness of muscle and snuggled against it, even throwing her leg over. *So nice.* Then her eyes popped open. *What in the hell?* She had no idea where she was or what had happened. The last thing she remembered was flying through a wicked storm on Taswa. Catherine had no idea how she ended up here. Realizing she was in the embrace of a stranger, she pushed back and scrambled to a sitting position. The stranger, a woman Catherine realized, opened her eyes slowly and looked at her. "Who are you?" Catherine asked, surprisingly not alarmed considering she just realized she was nearly naked. For some reason, the stranger did not frighten her. Pulling the blanket up to cover her breasts, she waited for an answer. The woman, who Catherine realized had the fittest body she had ever seen, raised up on an elbow.

"Captain Nat Reynolds, Space Rangers," she answered. "This is not what it looks like." Catherine could only nod, still completely confused. "The real question here is how do you feel?" Nat continued. In her surprise at the strange situation, Catherine had not thought about how she felt. Now she realized there was a light throbbing coming from her forehead and she reached up. Her fingers found a goose egg.

"Well this doesn't feel so great," she said. "Did I hit my head?" Nat nodded and swung her long legs over the side of the narrow twin-size bed they were sharing. She stood up, slipped a classic Space Invaders video game t-shirt over her head, and then handed a second navy blue Space Ranger t-shirt to Catherine. Happy to have it, Catherine put it on. It was two sizes too big but at least she felt less vulnerable.

"You did," Nat said finally answering the question. "When your ED-90 ship hit a glacier. Frankly, you're lucky to be alive." Catherine could hardly believe it as she remembered almost nothing after flying into the Taswa atmosphere. Then she had a thought and looked up at Nat.

"Did you save me?" she asked. She watched Nat blush a little, and Catherine found herself thinking it was incredibly sweet. Nat shrugged.

"It's my job," she replied. "Are you thirsty? Hungry?" It was clear the woman was changing the subject, and Catherine let it go, although a part of her got the sense Nat came to rescue her out of more than duty. *Which makes absolutely no sense*, Catherine thought. *We've never even met before.* Suddenly a realization came to her, and she felt a lump of panic growing in her stomach. *Unless she knows I stole the fuel and came here to arrest me!* Before she could figure out what to do, Nat turned back to her. Catherine saw her frown as she took in Catherine's anxious face. "What's wrong?" Nat asked looking worried.

"I, um," Catherine started, not sure what to say without giving away anything in case Nat did not know about the stealing. "So, are you like a cop?" She saw Nat raise her eyebrows at the question.

"Not exactly," she said. "Why? Are you worried about what happened on Prospo?" Catherine gulped. Having no idea what to say next, she just nodded, no doubt looking as guilty as she felt. Nat laughed.

"Well, I have to say, the note was a cute touch," she said and then, still smiling, went back to the original topic. "Now, how about telling me if you are thirsty or want something to eat?" Catherine relaxed. Still not sure what exactly was going on, but because it felt like everything was good between them, Catherine smiled back.

"I'm both," she said and tried to think of the last time she really ate or drank anything substantial. *A week?* she wondered. It was hard to find food when a person was broke.

"Well alright then," Nat said and went from the sleeping quarters into the small galley. From where Catherine sat, she could see into the room through the wide door. "How about some hot tea?" she called back. "Probably a good idea to keep warming you up." Although she rarely drank anything but soft drinks, warming up with hot tea sounded good.

"I would like that," she said and then had a memory of how warm she felt when she was curled up in Nat's powerful arms. Catherine blinked. *Where did that come from?* she thought. Before she had a chance to analyze it further, the entire ship gave a lurch to the right. It was quickly corrected, but Catherine was still unsettled. "Where are we?" she asked. Nat poked her head out from the galley.

"Still on Taswa," she answered. "I'm waiting for the all-clear on the meteor shower before taking us back up. Don't worry. This P-527 is reinforced to sustain winds much higher than these. Just a little bumpy at times."

"Oh," Catherine said, wondering where Nat would take her once they could fly again. *Maybe my little ship is still okay?* she wondered. It would give her a chance to keep going to Untas. "Is my ED-90 around?" she asked. "I have somewhere I need to go."

Nat snorted. "That contraption should never have been in space to begin with," she said. "But it is out of its misery now."

"Oh," Catherine said again and felt a sense of hopelessness start to creep up on her. Her last few credits went into buying that spacecraft. Now she had absolutely nothing. Nat walked back into the sleeping quarters with the tea and handed one to Catherine before sitting on the edge of the bed.

"What were you thinking trying to go anywhere in that thing anyway? It was a deathtrap," she said. Catherine hung her head a little, and Nat noticed. "Hey," Nat continued a little softer. "I didn't mean to hurt your feelings, but your ship was not space worthy, it's as simple as that." Catherine nodded without looking at Nat and sipped her tea. The last thing she wanted to do was think about her situation. Everything felt so safe and stable here on Nat's ship. Worrying about her dad and money and being homeless would just spoil it. "You want to talk about it?" Nat asked, clearly sensing Catherine's dismay. Catherine shook her head.

"Not really," she answered.

Nat nodded. "Okay," she said. "Well then let's take a closer look at that cut on your forehead. I have a first-aid kit, but I need to wash away some of the blood first." Alarmed, Catherine put her fingers to the bump again. *Blood?* she thought.

"Is it bad?" she asked. Nat set her tea down and slid closer. She gently pushed a lock of Catherine's hair to the side. It was so tender, and Catherine was starting to feel so down about her situation, she actually felt the sting of tears. Nat froze.

"Am I hurting you?" she asked sounding confused. Catherine shook her head and without thinking, just leaned in and rested her head on Nat's shoulder. A sob slipped out.

"No," she whispered. "You are being so nice." Now a few tears did come. "It's just everything else in my horrible life."

She felt Nat take the tea from her hand and turn a little to set it down before putting strong arms around her and pulling Catherine in close. It was too much, and Catherine could not hold back all her feelings of fear and anguish any longer. She let it out and sobbed into Nat's chest until the sadness ran its course. As the crying started to subside, Catherine slipped her arms around Nat's waist and hugged her back, nuzzling her face up under the other woman's chin with a sigh. It felt so good to be held, and Catherine could not think of the last time someone let her just cry. "Thank you," she whispered into Nat's neck and felt her new friend stiffen in response. Suddenly Nat was pulling away and abruptly stood up.

"I'll get the first-aid kit," she mumbled and turned to go back into the galley. Catherine shook her head confused. *What just happened?* she thought and wrapped the blanket around her, suddenly feeling uneasy. Nat came in with a box marked red and white and set it on the bed but did not sit down again. Catherine could tell Nat was unhappy, but she did not know why.

"Did I do something?" Catherine asked. Nat frowned and opened the box to fetch out some alcohol wipes.

"Not at all. Everything's fine. I just need to do my job, that's all," she said. *Do her job?* Catherine wondered. *Like arrest me?* Catherine swallowed. "Am I going to jail?" she asked, ready to face whatever Nat said but scared to death as well. She did not think she could survive in prison.

"What?" Nat asked sounding confused for a second. "Good grief, no. I won't let that happen." Catherine let out a big breath of relief. She thoroughly believed Nat would protect her even though she hardly knew the woman at all.

"I don't know what to say," Catherine said. "First you rescue me from the storm, and now you will help me with the cops." She paused to think of the right words and then looked into Nat's eyes. "You're my hero," she said. Their gaze held and Nat's face was completely unreadable. The stranger's gray-blue eyes, so intense yet inviting, locked on Catherine's and the passion behind the look was so strong, Catherine felt it to her core. A warm feeling started blooming inside her, and she bit her lip, not sure what to do next. Before she had to decide, an alarm started beeping in another part of the ship. She watched Nat drag her eyes away and start toward the front of the spaceship. "What's wrong?" Catherine asked.

"Nothing," Nat said. "It's just the all clear. The meteor shower has passed." The woman disappeared for a moment, and the alarm stopped. As she came back in, Catherine could not read her face, but Nat did not look happy.

"What does it mean?" Catherine asked. Nat stopped, and not looking at Catherine, pulled a fresh pilot's uniform from her locker. She started to get dressed.

"It means it is time to go," she answered. "We can't stay down here forever." Catherine frowned at the announcement. She liked it here with Nat on the ship, even if it was in the center of a perpetual blizzard. Going back to reality was the last thing she wanted. In another minute, Nat was back into uniform, and she finally looked at Catherine. "You know I don't even know your name," Nat said softly. At this, Catherine smiled.

"I'm Catherine Porter," she said. Nat nodded, taking it in.

"Pleasure to meet you, Catherine," she said softly. Again, their eyes held for a breath and then Nat turned sharply away. "I don't have another seat in the cockpit, so you have to stay back here. Try and rest. We will be back at Prospo soon enough," she said. Without waiting for a response, Nat disappeared toward the front of the ship. Catherine lowered her chin and tried to make sense of everything. *The feelings, the looks...* It was all so confusing. *Maybe a nap will be the best thing.* Catherine snuggled back down into the bed and wrapped the blanket around her. She sighed at the softness of the pillow and realized it held the scent of Nat. It made her feel warm and safe all over again. So much so, a part of Catherine missed having the woman with her in the bed. *But that's crazy, right?* Catherine was not sure. Her feelings were so mixed up, but there was one thing she did know. More than anything, she wanted to keep Captain Nat Reynolds in her life.

CHAPTER 7
NAT

Leaving the Taswa planet behind, Nat took a deep breath to try and calm the emotions raging inside her. *Catherine*, she thought. She was trouble. Catherine brought out something in Nat she had not felt before. An intense need to protect her and find a means to take away the deep sadness she could see the girl felt. When she held Catherine in her arms only a short while ago, with her such obvious grief, it nearly broke Nat's heart. *How can someone so young and so sweet carry such a burden already?* Right then and there, Nat had made a promise to herself to find a way to help Catherine. She did not know the root of the problem yet, but there would be time to dig deeper into that later. *And there will be a later if I have any choice in the matter.*

Even though they just met, Nat felt a deep commitment to the young woman in the sleeping quarters behind her. The look they shared spoke straight to Nat's soul and moved things there which would be changed forever. *It moved other things too, and you know it, Nat Reynolds*, she thought and frowned. The physical chemistry was undeniable although Nat was confident Catherine had no idea it was happening.

If she had to guess, the thought of being with a woman had never crossed Catherine's mind. *Which means I need to take that part of things out of this equation.* The intense passion she felt for the woman needed to be put in a box and locked away. Catherine could never know how much Nat wanted to touch her, to kiss her. *To take her.* Nat shook her head with frustration. Those thoughts had to stop and the help Nat was offering had to be unconditional. "Okay," she whispered. "Back to work. Time to be the professional I know I am." Regaining control and setting her resolve, Nat keyed the comm link. "Catwoman to Base," she said.

"This is Base. We're happy to hear from you, Catwoman," Base responded almost instantly. Nat smiled. Even though she was sure there would be a bit of hell to pay for her disobeying orders, the relief she heard in the voice of the Base Dispatcher made her feel good.

"All is well here," Nat said. "Reporting the recovering of one female survivor from a single ship crash on Taswa. I am in route to Prospo to have her checked at a medical facility." There was a pause on the radio. *Here it comes*, Nat thought as she waited for the reprimand and hoped it was not too severe. *But it will be worth it, no matter what they say.*

"Excellent work, Catwoman," Base said. "However, Command is requesting you return to Base. They would like to speak to you about your decision to complete the rescue against a direct order to abort." There was a pause, and then Base continued in almost a whisper. "You kind of pissed them off, Nat." Nat nodded. It was to be expected, and at some point, she would have to face the music, and she knew it. *But I don't want to do it right now*, she thought, worried it would interfere with getting to the bottom of whatever was wrong with Catherine. Trying to think of a good excuse to not return to Base directly, she heard a noise behind her and glanced back. Catherine was standing at the entrance to the cockpit. She still wore Nat's blue t-shirt, which hung suggestively above her knees.

"I got you in trouble, didn't I," Catherine said looking crestfallen after having heard the comments from Base. Nat saw the look and felt the now ever so familiar need to get up and pull the woman into her arms to comfort her. Instead, she shrugged, trying to make light of the situation.

"It was my choice. I wouldn't change it," she said. Catherine clearly was not buying it and stepped forward into the small space until she was beside Nat's chair. She put her hand on Nat's shoulder, and Nat could almost feel the heat of her touch through the cloth.

"I know, but you didn't have to do it," Catherine said. "I hate that now it is a problem. Go wherever they want you to go. I'll just—" Catherine paused as she seemed to be trying to think of a good lie. "I'll just take a public transport back to Prospo." Somehow, Nat knew the girl had no means to take a transport anywhere. If she brought her back to Base, Catherine would basically be stranded.

"Catwoman?" Base called. "Do you copy the last transmission?" Nat tilted her head, looking at Catherine, and thought about everything. She did not want her time to be over with her yet. It was as simple as that and with a nod, Nat turned back to the comm link.

"I copy, Base," Nat said. "I am requesting seventy-two hours emergency leave. I will return to Base at that time." She glanced back at Catherine and saw the woman's mouth was open with surprise. Nat chuckled knowing she was making the right choice even if there was hell to pay later. Surprisingly, Base came right back with an acknowledgment.

"Your leave is granted, Catwoman. Conditions are to ground your P-527 immediately. What is your destination?" Base asked. "Prospo?"

"Affirmative," Nat said with a big smile. "I will check in at aviation control as soon as I arrive."

"Very good," Base said. "Enjoy your break, Nat." Nat clicked off the comm link and turned back around to Catherine. Surprisingly, the woman had tears in her eyes and Nat worried she had assumed too much.

"Should I not have done that?" Nat asked trying to figure out the problem. Catherine shook her head.

"No," she said. "Does this mean we can be together a little longer?" Nat felt her heart surge with excitement as she realized Catherine wanted to spend more time with her too. She would analyze what that all meant later, but for now, Nat just grinned and nodded.

"Three days on a tropical planet," she answered. "Just you and me."

SMOOTHING THINGS OVER with Sergeant Baxter had gone easier than Nat had even hoped. After landing back on Prospo and requesting a quick meeting with the sergeant to explain her emergency leave situation, he had been more than understanding. "Sometimes a person just needs a break,"

he said. "Now, about the girl in baggy clothes out in my waiting room?" Nat had nodded and tried to make light of it.

"Crashed on Taswa of all places," she said. "I barely found her in time." Baxter whistled.

"No kidding. And the ED-90?" he asked.

"Toast," Nat answered. "I don't yet know all the details, but I get a sense the woman has limited resources. I'd like to pay for the missing fuel on her behalf and be done with the matter."

Leaning his elbows on the desk, Baxter clasped his hands together and pressed them to his chin thoughtfully. "I guess I could lose the paperwork on this one," he murmured. "But you owe me one, Captain." Nat grinned, and the sergeant returned it.

"Deal," she said. Baxter laughed and stood up to come around the desk. Nat got up, and they shook hands. "So, three days here. Any plans?"

"None," Nat answered. "Which is frankly just how I want it."

Baxter nodded. "Those are usually the best vacations of all," he had said.

Now, she and Catherine were in an Ubercab heading away from the spaceport. Catherine was shaking her head in disbelief. "So, just like that, I'm okay? No charges?" she asked. Nat smiled.

"No charges," she replied. Suddenly, Catherine frowned.

"But wait," she said. "Did you pay for the fuel?" Nat paused, already sensing her answer would not be popular.

"I did," she said softly. Catherine closed her eyes and leaned her head back on the cab's seat.

"I never wanted that," she said sounding almost embarrassed. Then she sat up and fixed Nat with a serious stare. "But I'll pay you back. Every last credit. I promise."

"If that's what you want, then okay," Nat said. This seemed to satisfy Catherine, and she went back to smiling. Nat wanted to smile too, but her next question was one she did not want to ask, even though she knew she had to. Nat took a deep breath and just got it over with. "So, where do you need to go? I assume you'd like to return home and change," Nat said and swallowed hard before the next sentence. "And check in with whomever." Catherine looked surprised and glanced down at her clothes as if forgetting she was still in Nat's t-shirt and sweatpants, which were rolled up at the ankles because they were inches too long. Then Nat saw her shoulders droop and she instinctively knew Catherine had no place to go and possibly no possessions other than what might have been on the ED-90 back on Taswa. Slowly, she took Catherine's hand, and the girl squeezed it almost desperately. She looked up into Nat's eyes, and Nat saw hints of fear and desperation there.

"I don't have any place," she whispered, color rising to her cheeks. "I was going to Untas to start over."

Nat did not hesitate. Right or wrong, taking care of Catherine was all she wanted. "Then you'll come to the hotel with me," she said. Catherine opened her mouth to protest, but Nat held up her free hand to stop her. "No arguing. Just like with the fuel, you can pay me back later." Catherine was quiet, and again Nat wondered if she had gone too far. *Does she think I mean one bed?* she wondered feeling awkward as hell. *Oh God, how do I handle this?* Since her every spare second was basically taken up by the Space Rangers, Nat did not have a lot of experience with dating and zero experience with straight girls. "I'll get us two rooms," she blurted at last. "I didn't mean to make you uncomfortable." Catherine turned to her and blinked with surprise.

"You're not making me feel uncomfortable at all," she said. "It's just I can't believe all of this is happening. My life's been a little, well, it's been shit lately and now all of a sudden it's wonderful." Her face softened. "Because of you." Nat felt herself starting to blush and tried to shrug it off.

"Just helping a friend in need," she muttered and then to change the subject, leaned forward to the divider window of the Ubercab and knocked. The driver slid open the portal. The sound of loud music blasted through.

"What's up?" the driver yelled over the music.

"Change of plans," Nat yelled back. "I want to go to the Royal Venus instead." The cabbie whistled.

"Nice choice," he said and made a U-turn in the street. Other shuttles, cars, and mopeds honked and swerved all around him. Nat leaned back, and the driver closed the portal, shutting out the music again. She looked at Catherine whose eyes were wide.

"Are you kidding?" she asked with a voice full of wonder. "The Royal Venus? That place is so beautiful, but my God, it will cost—"

Nat cut her off with a smile. "Don't say it. This is my vacation, and I haven't taken one, well, to be honest, I've never really taken one," she said. "If I want to splurge, I will." Catherine laughed and clapped her hands.

"I can't believe this!" she said, so excited it made Nat's heart happy. No matter how many credits it set her back, she could care less. *You only live once*, she thought and remembered how close she had come to dying not too long ago. *It is time to do some real living.*

Nat kept that same thought once they arrived at the Royal Venus. Rather than take just any room, she asked for a deluxe luxury suite with a premium view of the ocean, no matter the price. The desk clerk smiled warmly at the request and took Nat's credit card with pleasure.

CHAPTER 8
CATHERINE

"Oh, shut up! You have got to be kidding me," Catherine said as she walked into the luxury hotel room. It was so beautiful and spacious she found it almost overwhelming. "This is impossible." Nat laughed from behind her as she followed Catherine.

"Not sure about impossible, but yes, this is gorgeous," she agreed. Catherine thought gorgeous was an understatement. The suite was multiple rooms, all with high ceilings, plush carpet, and spectacular furnishings. Catherine skipped happily to the center of the large room and spun in a circle with her arms out. The place was magical. It made her realize just how dismal the flat she had shared with her dad above the corner grocery store was in comparison. *Don't worry about that right now*, Catherine thought. *Just appreciate all of this.*

"I take it you like the place?" Nat asked. Catherine stopped and looked at the woman, the one who saved her life and took care of her and now brought her here. *My hero*, she thought and laughed as she stepped over and threw her arms around Nat's neck.

"I love it," she said. "I have never felt so special." Catherine saw Nat's smile fade, and her eyes became serious in an instant. They ran over Catherine's face and then stopped to meet hers to hold there.

"You deserve to feel special, Catherine," she said. The moment held, and Catherine felt so many emotions churn through her she did not know what to do next. Before she could act on any of them, Nat gently took Catherine's arms from around her neck and stepped back. Catherine watched the woman put on an awkward smile. "So," she said clearing her throat. "Which bedroom do you want?" Catherine blinked with surprise.

"You mean there is more than one? How many rooms does this place have?" she asked. Nat genuinely laughed at Catherine expression and took her hand.

"Come on, let's explore," she said and pulled her toward a doorway. Catherine giggled and followed along as they stepped into a giant bedroom with a king-size canopy bed and floor to ceiling windows with a view of the ocean.

"Ohhh," Catherine said. "Can I have this one?" Nat nodded at her with the sweetest look on her face.

"Yes, you absolutely can," she answered. Catherine let go of her hand and ran to flop onto the bed. The mattress was so soft Catherine sighed with delight. *It will be like sleeping on a giant cloud*, she thought. Nat came to the side of the bed and looked at her and Catherine almost reached out to pull her down but then hesitated when she saw the hardness in Nat's eyes. It was clear the woman did not want to be on the bed with her and feeling a little embarrassed, Catherine sat up.

"Sorry," she apologized. "I'm a little overwhelmed."

"Maybe we should order some room service," Nat said steering the conversation onto a safe topic. "I know you must be hungry."

"Famished," Catherine said and could not believe they were going to actually order room service. It was all so extravagant and fun. "What can we have?"

"Whatever you want," Nat answered. "What do you like?" Catherine wondered if she should order something fancy to look sophisticated in front of Nat but then thought better of it. Catherine was authentic if she was anything else so she smiled and nodded.

"Pizza! Loaded, please." Now it was Nat's turn to look surprised, but then she laughed, and Catherine watched her walk over to the comm link for the room. In a moment, she had room service on the phone and was ordering a pizza with all the works.

"And do you stock Mars Select Reserve?" Nat asked over the link. She listened and then nodded. "Perfect. Two wine glasses please." Nat hung up and turned back to Catherine. "I guess I should have asked, but do you like red wine?" Catherine shrugged, but in reality, had never tried it or any alcohol to be exact. Watching her dad drink himself to death was a bit of a deterrent. Still, if Nat liked it, she would happily try.

"I won't know until I have some I guess," she answered.

"Fair enough," Nat said. "Well, we have about a half hour, what do you want to do while we wait? Check out the view? Watch television?" Catherine tilted her head and considered the question. Then she had a thought.

"Does this place have a bathtub?" she asked. "I would love to clean up and relax. I'm a little sore."

"After the crash you had, I'm not surprised, and yes, I am certain this place has a bathtub. Let's look," Nat said and led the way to a different doorway. It was, in fact, the bathroom, and like the rest of the suite, it was huge and luxurious with a soaking tub sitting in the middle of the marble floor. Catherine sighed. *More heaven*, she thought. "Well, I'll leave you to it," Nat said with an awkward tone as she backed quickly out of the room. Catherine turned to see the door close and worried she was somehow upsetting Nat but was not sure how or what to do about it. With a sigh, she resolved to talk about it with her after the bath but for now, was going to enjoy a good soak.

As the water ran hot and filled the tub, Catherine stripped down and climbed in. It felt exquisite. The room where she grew up did have a bathtub but it was shallow, and there was never enough hot water. This was worlds apart. As the level rose, she let her mind drift while her hands roamed over her body. She could tell she was growing skinny from not eating enough, but as she cupped her breasts, she was glad to feel they were still full and firm. Her thumb rubbed over a nipple, and it tickled her so that she squirmed a little. She realized they were surprisingly sensitive and hardened immediately in the hot water. Catherine touched herself again, and this time the tickle was more of a throb. Gasping with surprise, an image of Nat suddenly came to her. The tall, strong woman with the great body wrapped around her in the bed back on the spaceship. Catherine frowned a little, feeling confused but also excited. *What if it was Nat's thumb brushing my nipple right now instead of mine?* she thought, and another more intense throb rolled over her only this one did not stop at her nipple but ran all the way down her belly.

Instinctively, Catherine followed it with her fingertips until she was poised just above her lips. She hesitated. It was not like she hadn't touched herself before. On a few nights, when her dad was out on a bender, she would be reading a book with a love scene. It would turn her on, and she would rub her body to try and release the ache. Now she had a similar ache, only this time the wanting was much more intense. *But Nat is just in the other room*, she thought. *It wouldn't be right and yet ...* The thought of Nat so close by sent a tingle up Catherine's spine and she gave in to the wanting. Slipping her finger down, she rubbed a circle around her clit, finding it hard and swollen. Suddenly she was so turned on she squirmed. With a fingertip, she flicked the mound gently, and it felt so good she nearly cried out. Suddenly Nat was all she could think about, and she froze. *Would Nat touch me like this if I asked her?* Catherine was not sure. There were so many mixed signals. *And do I want her to?* Catherine was never attracted to women. *So why am I aching for her?* It was not right. *I need to stop*, Catherine thought with almost a sob. *It is not fair to either of us.* She pulled her hand away and was trying to control her breathing when there was a light tap at the door. Catherine jumped feeling guilty.

"Yes?" she squeaked out.

"The food is here," Nat said through the door.

"Oh, okay," Catherine said with a sigh of relief. *What if she somehow heard me in here?* Catherine thought. She would die of embarrassment. "I'll be right out." There was no answer, so Catherine figured the coast was clear, and she hopped out of the tub. A fluffy, white rob hung on a hook near the shower, and Catherine donned it with glee. It was too big, but that did not matter. She snuggled it all around her as she tied the belt and relished the soft cloth against her naked skin. *More heaven. This place is too much.*

Catherine went into the living room and saw Nat standing just outside the open doors leading onto the balcony. She held a glass of wine and had changed out of her pilot's uniform into jeans and a t-shirt. Hearing Catherine, Nat turned and smiled. Catherine smiled back and flounced over to the closest couch to plop down in a cloud of terrycloth robe. "Good bath?" Nat asked. Catherine could not contain a sigh.

"Wonderful bath," she said, and it was all she could do not to finish the sentence with "but I missed you."

"That is what I wanted to hear," Nat said, and she set her wine on the coffee table near Catherine before walking to the room service cart near the door. Catherine noticed a second empty glass and the opened bottle of wine. Deciding to take the bull by the horns, she helped herself to a long pour. Picking it up, she smelled the liquid and grimaced. Looking up, she saw Nat coming back with the pizza box. The woman laughed at Catherine's expression. "An acquired taste," she said. Catherine was not to be deterred. If Nat liked it, she would like it. Taking a tentative taste, the wine slid smoothly over her tongue. It was a little fruity, but not sweet. Not horrible, but not her favorite either. *Better than scotch though*, she thought, remembering her dad's drink of choice. She tried some of it once when she was fourteen to see what it was like. It tasted so bad, she could not even get it down. This was far better.

"I think I could learn to like this," she said and drank again. A warm glow was already starting in her stomach, and she loved it. She saw Nat pick up her own glass and sip as well. Their eyes met for a moment, and Catherine decided it was time to get things out in the open. Lifting her chin, she took one more drink for courage and then set the glass down. "So, Nat," she started. Nat raised an eyebrow.

"So, Catherine," she said. Catherine giggled. The wine was really making her feel even happier than before.

"So, Nat," she started again. "You like girls, don't you?" For a second, Nat did nothing, and Catherine started to feel a little awkward, but then the woman slowly nodded.

"Yes," she said. "I very much do." Catherine nodded feeling bolder than usual. *It has to be the wine*, she thought.

"I thought so," she said. "Well, I want you to know you are special to me. I owe you everything." "But?" Nat said quietly.

"But I am not attracted to women," Catherine finished and picked up her wine to drain the glass. Once it was empty, she reached for the bottle to pour more and peeked a look at Nat to see if she was mad. Catherine was relieved to see the woman looked thoughtful, but not upset.

"Duly noted," Nat said. "And we should probably eat something before you have much more of that." She motioned with her chin toward the wine. Catherine giggled again, unable to help herself. Nat was so nice all the time. Truly a great friend. Leaning back with the wine, Catherine drank a little more before snuggling deeper into the couch cushions.

"Whenever you want," she said and watched as Nat plated two slices and handed one to her as she sat down on the couch a few feet away. Catherine drank more and rolled her eyes.

"Don't be like that," she said and scooted over to sit right beside Nat. "I didn't mean you had to sit across the room, silly." Nat took a bite of pizza and Catherine could tell her friend was frustrated. Not sure what to do about it, she had more wine. Nat pointed at Catherine's pizza.

"Eat please," she said, and Catherine could hear in the tone it was not a suggestion, but an order.

"Okay," she said. "Sorry." Catherine ate the pizza, and it was the best she ever tasted. It seemed like everything at the Royal Venus was magic.

CHAPTER 9
NAT

Nat was furious at herself. She knew better than to get caught up in some fantasy about being with the young woman she first saw on some surveillance video. *I was making something out of nothing from the very beginning*, she thought and started to feel like a fool. Slowly, she stood up from the couch and walked to the windows at the balcony. Pulling the sliding door open, she stepped out and let the sea breeze roll over her. Closing her eyes, she listened to the waves crashing and took a deep breath. *I am a decorated captain in the Space Ranger Corps. I am a warrior. This is nothing.* Nat opened her eyes and exhaled. There was a sound behind her and Nat turned to see Catherine standing in her robe at the door. She looked confused and a little upset. "Nat, I'm sorry," she said. "I didn't think you would get angry. I just, well, I'm not—" Her voice trailed off, and Nat gave her a small smile.

"It's okay, Catherine," she said. "I'm not angry. Just a misunderstanding. Now come on and check out this view." Catherine obliged and came to stand near her. They stood there in silence for a minute, and the only sound was the ocean.

"I can't believe how beautiful everything is," Catherine said in almost a whisper. "This view. And the rooms. God, even this robe." She plucked at the cloth. "All of it." Nat looked over to see the girl gazing up at her. "Thank you," Catherine said. "Thank you for everything." Nat sighed and put an arm out for Catherine to step into. Together they walked back into the hotel suite, and Nat led them to the couch. Catherine sat down, but Nat was not interested in sitting. She was too restless now. Picking up her wine, she finished the glass and checked the bottle. They would need to get another one soon if the plan was to just stay in and drink too much. *That is a dangerous idea*, Nat thought and set the bottle down. She looked at where Catherine was sitting and noticed the woman was watching her with uncertainty. It was the last thing Nat wanted to see on the woman's beautiful face. After thinking a moment, she had an idea.

"You need new clothes of your own," Nat said. "Go get dressed. There's a big mall across the boulevard out front." She smiled to soften her tone. "What do you say we go shopping? My treat." Catherine started to smile too.

"Really?" she asked.

Nat laughed, letting all of the frustration over the situation she found herself in slip away. In her heart, she knew Catherine making things clear sooner rather than later was probably for the best. Now there would be no confusion.

"Really," Nat answered. Catherine leaped off of the couch and threw herself against Nat in a hug. Instinctively, Nat wrapped her arms around the woman and hugged her back. She could feel Catherine's naked body through the fabric of the robe and closed her eyes to stop from reacting. *Nobody said this was going to be easy*, she thought. As much as she reasoned with herself, the chemistry was still there. It would just take time for her to snap out of it, or at least that was what she hoped. After patting Catherine platonically on the back, she stepped away. "Go on," she said. Catherine nodded and rushed off to her room to get dressed.

THE MALL WAS GIGANTIC and packed with tourists. Every imaginable kind of shop was there. Electronics, jewelry, shoes, and clothes. Lots and lots of clothes. Catherine was like a kid in a candy store, pointing at items in every window and laughing with delight. Nat could not have been happier. "Haven't you been here before?" Nat asked at one point. "You grew up on Prospo, didn't you?" Catherine had sobered at the question, and Nat regretted asking it, but then the woman shook her head and smiled again.

"It was a bit out of reach to come here," she said, and Nat thought it was a perfect answer.

"Well then, I am happy to be the one to bring you here," she said and meant it with all her heart. She might not have a future with Catherine, but these moments were perfect. Catherine gave her a quick hug and then raced off to look in another window. Nat caught up with her and then she saw it. A drop-dead dress. It was a sheath of silver and would look fantastic on Catherine. "Come on," Nat said and took Catherine's hand. "We are going in here."

"But Nat," Catherine said. "We can't shop here. It's the most expen—"

"Don't say it," Nat said. "My credits work here as much as anyone's." They stepped into the lobby of the department store and were surrounded by racks of classy, expensive, and beautiful clothes. Everywhere Nat looked she saw things Catherine would look spectacular in. A clerk came forward. She was an elegant female alien with a bob of silver-gray hair framing smooth skin tinged with a flattering hint of green. She was dressed impeccably, and Nat could see her light-yellow cat eyes took them in with a look.

"Hello, may I help you?" she asked warmly with only a touch of an Heulian accent. Nat liked her immediately, especially when she considered how she and Catherine looked. *Probably not a lot of girls in baggy sweatpants and a Space Ranger hoodie wander in here*, she thought and was grateful there was zero judgment in the alien's entire demeanor.

"Actually, I believe you can," Nat said. "My friend lost her luggage and now needs some new clothes." The clerk nodded and held out her hand.

"You are indeed in the right place then," she said. "I'm Ms. Violet. And who do I have the pleasure of helping today?" Nat took her delicate hand and shook it.

"I'm Nat," she answered and turned to Catherine. "And my friend is Catherine." Ms. Violet nodded and held her hand out for the woman.

"Please come with me," she said as she started to take her along. "Is there something specific you want to start with?" Catherine looked back at Nat, her eyes wide with excitement. Nat gave her a wink.

"She needs everything, Ms. Violet," Nat said to the re-treating figures, one the picture of elegance and the other a rumpled mess. She saw Ms. Violet lean into Catherine.

"Well, that makes it the most fun," she heard her say. "We will start with the basics."

While Nat waited, she set up a tab with a substantial deposit of credits. Once that was settled, a helper was dispatched, and the shopping began in earnest. Sitting on a lounger with a glass of champagne in hand, Nat watched as Catherine came out to show off outfit after outfit. Everything looked perfect, and Nat could see why Ms. Violet was successful at her job. She was dressing Catherine in young, fashionable clothing with a flattering mixture of classy and sexy. As far as Nat was concerned, she could sit there all day and watch Catherine twirl in front of the mirrors, but when the helper, a flamboyant cat mutant named Jared, came with a fresh glass of champagne, he had a note for her. "What's this?" Nat asked taking the piece of folded paper from him.

"It's from your lady friend," he purred with a sly smile. Nat set the champagne aside to read it.

PICK SOMETHING FOR YOU TOO! I FEEL TOO SPOILED! PLEASE?

Nat laughed. *Fair enough*, she thought and waved Jared over. "Seems I need to find an outfit. What do you suggest?" she said. The cat mutant's eyes widened with excitement.

"With that body? Oh, honey, I have just the thing," he said and raced off. In a minute, he was back and waved for her to follow. When she saw what he picked, Nat had to admit, it was a hell of an outfit and was about the last thing she would have ever have picked out. Slipping into the cream-colored pants of leather so soft it made Nat think of butter, she had to admit they hugged her ass like a glove. The sleeve-less chocolate brown rayon shirt was a perfect contrast and left her well-defined arms exposed. Taking it all in, Nat shook her head. There was no place in her life for an outfit as sexy as this one, but it was still fun to try it on. Getting ready to take it off again, there was a tap at the door. "Ms. Nat?" the helper asked. "Ms. Catherine wants you to show her what you've picked out." Nat snorted a laugh. It was not exactly like she picked it out, but it only seemed fair to go parade it for her. Stepping out of the fitting room, she saw Jared's feline features light up when he saw her. "Even better than I imag-ined," he said.

"Thanks," Nat said with a grin and decided to have some fun. "Don't suppose you have a jacket that goes with this that I can throw on really quick?" Jared clapped his paws.

"I do!" he said and sprinted from the room. He was back in thirty seconds with a supple leather jacket which brought it all together perfectly. Nat slipped it on and had to admit it felt terrific. *I might be buying this piece for myself at least*, she thought and with a smile started to make her way to the wait-ing area. As she hit the door, she mustered all her confidence and put a little swagger in her step. Catherine and Ms. Vio-let were waiting for her, and both stopped to stare. Ms. Vio-let smiled first, and with a nod of appreciation, Nat watched her wave the staff out of the room as she made a subtle exit. Now she and Catherine were alone, and when Nat saw what Catherine was wearing, she froze in mid-stride. It was the sil-ver dress from the window and was so spectacular on her Nat was speechless. The two women stood and stared at each other for a moment and then Catherine came closer until they were only a few inches apart.

"Nat, you look..." Catherine started and then she shook her head, clearly not sure what to say. Electricity filled the air around them, and Nat swallowed hard to try and keep herself in check.

"Catherine, that dress..." she was able to growl out. Catherine nodded.

"I knew you liked it," she whispered. Nat raised an eyebrow.

"I more than like it," she said. A bit of color rose to Catherine's cheeks, and it was just enough for Nat to get under control again. She stepped back and cleared her throat. "Well, I want you to get it," Nat said and started to turn away.

"But where will I ever wear it?" Catherine said. Nat paused and thought about it. Then she looked back with a grin.

"I know a place. We're going out tonight, and that dress will be perfect," she said and then walked back to the dressing room knowing she would be buying her clothes too. As the door closed behind her, Nat let out a long breath and rested her head against the mirror. *God, I want that woman*, she thought with a moan. She was playing with fire, and she knew it. Straightening up, she took off the jacket and started on the shirt when there was a tap at the door. "One sec," Nat said thinking it was the helper, but then the door opened, and she saw it was Catherine, only she was not in the dress anymore. Instead, she was in a lacy white bra and panties. Nat felt her jaw drop. "What are you doing?" she whispered to

Catherine. With a playful smile, Catherine turned in a slow circle.

"I just thought you should see these too, since you're buying them and all," she said. It was too much, and Nat let instinct take over. She grabbed Catherine around the waist and pulled her into the dressing room with her. Catherine let out a happy squeak of surprise.

"Nat, what are you doing?" she asked as Nat pressed her up against the wall. She leaned in with her body and held Catherine in place with her hip while planting one hand on the wall on each side of her face.

"What do you think you are doing, Catherine Porter?" Nat growled. Her heart was racing a million beats a second, and she was not sure what she was going to do next. Catherine tilted her head back and looked into her eyes.

"I can ask you the same thing," she said trying to sound confident, but Nat noticed the tremor behind the words.

"I'm going to kiss you, that is what I'm doing," Nat said and moved in closer until she could feel the heat from Catherine's breath on her lips. Catherine gave a slight shake of her head.

"No, you're not," she said. "We talked about this."

"You're standing in my dressing room in the sexiest damn bra I have ever seen. We didn't talk anything about that," Nat replied. Catherine licked her lips, and Nat knew the woman wanted to be kissed. She could feel it in her soul. *But does she want all of me?* Nat thought suddenly. *Or is this just a big tease?* Slowly, Nat backed away and a flicker of disappointment shown in Catherine's eyes for an instant, but then it was gone. "You're right. We talked about it," Nat said. She rubbed a hand over her face and realized it was shaking. She laughed. "I love the underwear, Catherine. Please get it too. Thank you for showing it to me." Catherine did not move for a second, but then laughed too.

"You're something, Captain Nat Reynolds," she said as she opened the door. "But I'll figure you out yet." Then she was gone. Nat shook her head. *Well, if she does figure me out, that will make one of us*, she thought and started to get undressed.

CHAPTER 10
CATHERINE

T he shuttle lifted off smoothly, and Catherine looked out the window at the city below, awash with hundreds of thousands of lights against the dark night backdrop. It was mesmerizing. She had never really paid attention to it when she flew with her father in the past. *But my eyes are opening to a lot of things lately*, she thought. Turning to Nat, who looked stunning in her new outfit, Catherine smiled and took the woman's hand to squeeze it. Nat turned from looking out her window and raised an eyebrow. "What's that for?" she asked. Catherine giggled, simply overwhelmed with all of the excitement of everything she was experiencing.

"Just a thank you squeeze," she said. "Don't worry." Nat grinned and shook her head.

"I'm not worried, Catherine," she replied. "I just hope you like the place I'm taking you."

"Why won't you tell me where we are going?" Catherine said. So far, Nat would not reveal details other than it was a satellite club with dancing. The idea they were going off-planet to a place was thrilling. Everyone knew the most exciting and upscale bars in the galaxy were those which revolved around Prospo. *Plus, I am dressed to kill*, she thought. The sheath dress of shimmering silver was a perfect fit and hugged her every curve. Nat's eyes had turned hungry when Catherine came strolling out of her room at the last minute before the shuttle arrived and it made Catherine feel powerful and sexy. Wherever they were going, she knew her look would attract some attention, and for once, she welcomed it. *Why not have some fun?* For too long her wardrobe was recycled designer jeans and sweaters from the second chance thrift store. People in high school were not fooled, and sometimes kids could be awful mean. *If they could see me now.*

The shuttle arrived, and Nat jumped out to come around the landing platform to open Catherine's door. Flattered, Catherine held out her hand for Nat to take and exited with all the grace she could muster. As she looked up, she noticed a couple of women at the edge of the platform vaping and they were both staring at her. It was the same hungry look she noted with Nat back at the room. Blinking with surprise, Catherine did not know what to make of it. *Where are we?* she wondered and then saw the club's sign. *Sappho In The Sky Girl Bar.* Her mouth dropped open with surprise. Nat had taken her to a lesbian club. Holding back from where Nat was trying to lead her by the hand, Catherine felt a hint of panic. *I won't fit in here.* "Nat, I don't know if I can go in there," she said. Nat paused and turned back. Her look was warm and understanding.

"I need you to trust me," she said. "Everyone here is open-minded about straight people, or at least as long as you are with me. I promise you will have fun tonight." Catherine knew she trusted Nat completely. With her life, in fact. Slowly, she nodded and squaring her shoulders, let Nat lead her forward and into the club. When they walked inside, Catherine's eyes widened. The place was wall-to-wall with females of every shape and size. Humans, aliens, mutants. They were all in attendance and intermixed in small groups and couples, yelling over the sounds of dance music spinning from a six-armed DJ in the corner. The best part though was no one gave her a second glance as she let Nat guide her through the throng to the bar, which was three layers deep with people ordering drinks.

"This is crazy," she yelled over the noise of it all. Nat leaned in close.

"But you're okay?" she whispered into her ear. Catherine thought about the question and realized she was fine. The place felt fun.

"Yes," she answered. "But I can't believe you brought me here without telling me first. Very brave, Nat." Nat shrugged.

"If you'd said no, I would have turned us right around and taken you somewhere else in a second," she said, and her face turned serious. "I never want you to do something you don't want to do." Catherine gave Nat's arm a hug.

"I know. That's what I find so special about you," she said. "You make me feel safe." Their eyes held for a second and Catherine could tell Nat wanted to tell her something important, but then they were both enveloped in a friendly hug.

"Hey!" said a stranger. "My God, is that you Nat? And who's this hot mamma? Yowza!" Catherine saw Nat grin as she turned to the stranger and laughed.

"Vic Patterson. Well, I'll be damned. Fancy meeting you here," Nat said. Vic threw her head back and belted out a laugh.

"You know I pretty much live here," she said. "But not you! What's it been? Three years?" Nat kept grinning.

"Something like that," she answered and turned her attention to Catherine. "Let me introduce my friend, Catherine Porter. It's her first time." Vic's eyes narrowed playfully.

"Ohhhh, a fish!" she said with another big laugh. "Well, welcome Catherine. That is an incredible dress." Catherine could not help but laugh along with Vic. The woman was hefty, probably well over three hundred pounds, and her relish for life was evident in every ounce of her.

"Thank you," Catherine said. "But I'm not sure I like being compared to a fish." Vic patted her on the shoulder good-naturedly.

"I'm sure you'll be fine," she said and turned back to Nat. "Come sit with us. I think you know everybody and we can make room." Nat nodded.

"That sounds perfect," she said. "Lead on." They all walked together to a corner of the club. Catherine tried to keep her nerves under control. She was not sure she was ready to meet a bunch of Nat's friends, but if it made Nat happy, she would do it. *I just hope I live up to expectations,* she thought but then frowned. *Although I'm not sure what those would be. We're just friends, and this is hardly a real date.* Everything was always so confusing. Luckily, when they approached the large horseshoe shaped booth, everyone was happy to see them. A long-haired blonde at the center of it all, with a very masculine woman beside her draping an arm possessively over her shoulders, looked the most overjoyed.

"Captain Nat," she said. "If I live and breathe, you are the last person I expected to see in here. I thought you were on emergency leave?" Nat nodded.

"A little R&R is all," she said. "Long overdue."

"I hear that," the blonde said. "Well pull up a chair. And who's with you?" Nat put her hand on Catherine's back and smiled.

"This is Catherine Porter. A new friend of mine," she said and looked at Catherine. "And this ringleader is my longtime friend Dee. She's a Space Ranger dispatcher."

"New *friend?*" Dee asked, and Catherine did not miss the emphasis. Nat nodded.

"Yes, *friend*, Dee," Nat replied.

"Well then come sit by me, Catherine," a girl with slicked back black hair said happily as she slid over to make room.

"My *straight friend,* Alex," Nat corrected.

"Oh," Alex said. Then she shrugged and patted the seat beside her. "I'm sure it's not catching." Catherine giggled. Alex was fun and after a look to check with Nat, who nodded with a smile, she took her offer.

"Nice to meet you, Catherine," Alex said and held out her hand. Catherine shook it.

"You too," she said.

"Yes, nice to meet you," Catherine heard Dee say, and she looked up to say hello. The protective glare she found on Dee's face gave her pause. Clearly, Dee was not thrilled Nat was there with a new "straight just friend." Trying to look as innocent and reassuring as possible, Catherine smiled at Dee.

"You as well," she said.

Undoubtedly sensing the chill in the air, Nat jumped in and made the rest of the introductions before offering to fetch everyone some drinks. "Nitro-gold tequila shots for everyone!" Alex exclaimed. Nat laughed.

"Fine," she said. "Anything else? Catherine?" Catherine shook her head. It felt like a situation where she wanted to stay as in control of herself as possible.

"Maybe just a coke?" she asked. Nat raised her eyebrows, but thankfully let it go as she turned to the rest. A few more orders were tossed out, and Nat left. Catherine felt her nerves tighten in her stomach at being left alone. Taking a deep breath to steady herself, she looked to Alex, the friendliest of the group. "So how long have you known, Nat?" Catherine asked.

"The real question is, how long have you known Nat?" Dee interrupted. Catherine felt a blush coming on but tilted her head with a touch of defiance.

"Not long. She rescued me, you know," Catherine said. She saw Dee's eyes widen for a moment and then narrow.

"Wait a minute. You're not the woman Nat risked her life to go fetch off of Taswa are you?" Dee asked. Now Catherine did blush. Seeing the reaction, Dee shook her head. "Oh, fuck me," she said frustrated. "Just what Nat needs. She always did have a hero complex." This time the heat rising to Catherine's face was a touch of anger.

"Hey," she said. "You can criticize me if you want. But not Nat. I've never met someone more humble and kind."

"True that," Vic jumped in. "And you'll have to excuse Dee. She's a bit defensive when it comes to her friends. Right, Dee?" Dee nodded.

"You know it," Dee said. "But especially Nat. Her last mission against the Space Pirates really messed her up, and the last thing she needs is..." She looked at Catherine and then paused as if finally realizing how mean she was coming across. "Well, she just needs some support and not head games." *Space Pirates? Messed her up?* Catherine thought.

"What do you mean? What happened?" Catherine asked. Before Dee or any of the others could comment, Nat was back with a tray full of colorful liquids.

"Here we go," Nat said cheerfully as she sat the different drinks around the table. When she put down the tequila shots, Alex slid one over to Catherine.

"Nitro gold. Loosen everybody up a bit," Alex said as she gave everyone at the table a warning look, especially Dee. Dee saw it and shrugged.

"Fair enough," she said and picked up the shot glass. Catherine shook her head.

"I'm seriously going to pass," she said.

"Oh, come on—" Alex started when Vic raised her hand.

"Here comes trouble," she whispered to the group, and everyone including Nat turned to look. A gorgeous woman in a black dress as tight as Catherine's and a head of long deep purple hair was swaying toward them. Sexiness radiated off of her, and it only took Catherine a second to realize the woman was making a beeline for Nat.

"Nat Reynolds," the woman cooed. "Where in the world have you been?" Catherine turned to look at Nat who seemed almost mesmerized by the appearance of the sexy stranger.

"Hi Olivia," Vic offered up. "Good to see you." Olivia smiled, and it was all heat. She shifted her gaze from Nat and looked over the group until her eyes stopped at Catherine. Narrowing them a bit, Olivia looked Catherine up and down appraisingly. After a pause, she held out a perfectly mani-cured hand tipped with long burgundy nails.

"I don't believe we've met," Olivia said. "I'm Olivia." Catherine instinctively stood up and took the woman's hand. When Olivia saw the silver dress, her eyes narrowed even more, and it made Catherine feel powerful.

"Nice to meet you, Olivia. I'm Catherine Porter," she said and then tilted her head. "Nat's friend." Now Olivia raised her eyebrows and turned to Nat.

"Nat, you devil. She's a little young," Olivia said with a sensual playfulness. Catherine saw Nat blush.

"She's just a friend," Nat said. Olivia looked pleasantly surprised at the news.

"Oh really," she said and then took Nat by the arm. "Well, then she won't mind if we dance." Olivia pulled Nat out onto the dance floor and slid her arms around Nat's neck. She started to sway to the music, her body moving dangerously close. In response, Nat took Olivia by the hips and began to follow her moves. Catherine slowly sat down, unable to take her eyes off the couple. A knot started to tighten in her stom-ach.

"That's Nat's ex," she heard Dee say, and Catherine turned to look at her. "Cheated on Nat about three years ago when Nat was out on a six-month deployment. Tore her up a bit."

"Yeah," Vic said. "She's trouble." Catherine saw Alex and the others at the table nod in agreement. Catherine turned back to watch Nat and Olivia. The music changed to something slower and sultrier. Olivia took full advantage and slipped even closer, pressing her hips suggestively into Nat's. With a glance over at Catherine, Olivia smiled and making sure Catherine was watching, started running her hands over Nat's shoulders. The two of them started to move together in rhythm to the music. It was the most sensual dance Catherine had ever seen.

"You're just going to sit there and watch this?" Catherine heard Dee say to her and without looking, Catherine picked up the tequila shot from the table. In a swift motion, she downed it, picked up a second one and stood up. *Oh, hell no*, she thought and headed for the dance floor.

CHAPTER 11
NAT

Nat was conflicted as hell. Olivia. Curvy, sexy, Olivia, who was her ex, but who Nat knew was a tiger in bed. *But she's a cheater, and you know it*, Nat thought as the woman ran her hands over Nat's shoulders and pressed her hips forward to make friction between them. *God, that feels good.* She had not realized just precisely how pent up with sexual frustration she was until this minute. There was never a time when Nat was more aroused than since she met Catherine. That woman really had her number, and Nat knew it. As Olivia leaned in, Nat could smell her perfume, and she closed her eyes, wanting the woman in her arms to be Catherine. Not Olivia. *Catherine.* The one who Nat wanted to touch and taste. *And take.* As she relished the fantasy, she heard Olivia whisper in her ear. It took a second for Nat to comprehend Olivia's question. "Have you fucked her yet?" Olivia murmured. "Does she scream like me?" Suddenly snapping back to reality, Nat opened her eyes and saw the woman dancing with her as the person she was and not who she was pretending to be tonight. Olivia was a bitch, and everything was a game with her. Nat was about to walk away from the dance floor when suddenly Catherine was beside them. She held a small glass of tequila in her hand.

"Nat, you forgot to take your shot," she said and then tossed her head with a little laugh Nat had never heard from her before. It did not travel to her eyes, which were shooting daggers at Olivia. "I think Alex will steal it if you don't drink it now." Even though Nat did not know quite what was going on, she was thankful for the interruption and took the glass.

"Well, where's mine?" Olivia snapped. Catherine shrugged.

"You weren't here when we ordered, but I'm pretty sure Vic has extra. You should go ask her," she said and smoothly cut between her and Nat. It was such a surprise to have Catherine suddenly so close, Nat almost dropped her drink. Out of the corner of her eye, she saw a very pissed off Olivia stride away. The whole situation was crazy, but Nat knew one thing, and it was she was not going to waste the drink or the opportunity. She belted back the tequila and then tossed the glass to Alex who she saw was watching the entire interaction with a big grin on her face. Only Dee was not smiling, yet she did not look angry either. Nat could not read her face, and before she could make it out, she felt Catherine's hands on her face. "Look at me, Nat," she said. Nat obliged and saw a look of possessiveness in Catherine's eyes that sent a ball of heat straight through her. *What has gotten into this woman?* Nat thought but was not about to interrupt it. She gazed at Catherine and lowered her head until they were nose-to-nose.

"Is this better?" Nat asked, and Catherine nodded a little. "Now hold me close. Like you were with Olivia." Nat raised an eyebrow but did as she was told and a little more. She slipped her hands onto Catherine's hips and then pulled her in with force. Once they were in full contact, Nat started to grind her hips with the music and took great pride in hearing Catherine gasp with surprise and pleasure. It was all Nat could do not to groan she was so turned on. Never had she wanted anyone as much as she wanted Catherine. Never. As if feeling the heat too, Catherine leaned forward until her breasts were brushing Nat's and they were riding the beat as one. Tilting her head back, Catherine looked up at Nat with half closed eyes.

"Kiss me," she demanded, and Nat did not hesitate, trying to go slow but her heart was pounding. As soon as their lips brushed, Nat felt her entire body stiffen with desire. The heat coming off of Catherine was incredible. Not holding back now, Nat pulled Catherine even closer and kissed her with all the pent-up passion inside her. Slipping her tongue along Catherine's bottom lip before tickling it just inside her mouth, she heard a moan come from Catherine's throat. Encouraged, Nat plunged deeper and was rewarded by the tip of Catherine's tongue touching hers. Nat shuddered. It was too much. She pulled back and pressed her forehead to Catherine's while they danced.

"Let's get out of here," Nat breathed. "Please." Catherine nodded, and without missing a beat, Nat gave a wave to her friends and then took Catherine by the hand to lead her out of the bar. The wait for the shuttle back to the planet was excruciatingly long as all Nat could think about was how Catherine's mouth tasted on hers. *So luscious*, she thought shifting from foot to foot as she held Catherine in front of her and tried to be patient. Finally, the shuttle made it, and Nat held the door as Catherine slid past her. Running to the other side, Nat got in, typed their destination into the GPS and for once was thankful the planet to satellite shuttles were unmanned craft. Nat wanted no distractions. As soon as she hit GO, Nat turned to look at Catherine. The woman's face was flushed, and her eyes were sparkling with passion. Without letting Catherine change her mind, Nat moved closer and pressed her face into Catherine's neck to nuzzle the soft, smooth skin there. As Nat let her lips slowly linger over the skin, she could feel Catherine's pulse beating. It was racing and knowing the girl was as turned on as she was, Nat pulled Catherine onto her lap. Catherine giggled at the unexpected move but did not complain. Nat decided to press things further.

Reaching up, she turned Catherine to face her and looked into the woman's eyes. They were half closed with need and Nat did not hesitate. She pulled her in close and kissed her, slipping her tongue into Catherine's mouth just enough to make the woman moan. Bold now, Nat put her hand on Catherine's leg, only at the hem of where her dress had ridden up. The skin was on fire, and it took every ounce of Nat's willpower to go slow. Gently she moved her hand up until her fingertips were under Catherine's hem. Catherine broke off of the kiss and gasped. "Nat, what are you doing?" she asked.

"Do you want me to stop?" Nat asked with a growl. Catherine paused.

"I don't know," she whispered. Nat hesitated. Her whole body was aching to move forward, but she remembered what

Catherine said in the hotel earlier. She was not attracted to women.

"Do you trust me?" Nat asked. Catherine gave a little nod. "I promise I will stop whenever you say." Nat did not wait for an answer and inched her hand higher onto Catherine's thigh. Catherine slapped her hand down and stopped Nat's progress. She held onto Nat's wrist and moaned.

"Nat," she said. "I just—" Catherine did not finish and instead loosened her grasp on Nat's arm. Slowly, Nat slid her hand higher. Her fingertips felt the lace of the white panties she knew Catherine was wearing and Nat closed her eyes to relish the moment.

"Oh God," Catherine said in a breath. "Oh God." Nat moved slow, knowing at any second Catherine would say stop. She let her fingers brush lightly over Catherine's mound. It was swollen and moist. Catherine flinched, and Nat had to freeze to stifle a moan of her own. "Wait, Nat," Catherine whimpered into Nat's neck. Nat did, hoping the shuttle would hurry up with its descent. She wanted to get Catherine back to the hotel and undressed as quickly as possible. The thought of the woman naked under her made Nat shutter with lust. *How can I want her so much?* she thought. Nat was never shy about sex and knew passion, but Catherine had her head spinning and her knees weak. At last the shuttle arrived back at the hotel's rooftop landing pad and stopped.

"Are you ready?" Nat said before she moved. Catherine did not say anything, and Nat looked into her face. She saw tears.

"I can't do this," Catherine said. "It's not that I'm not turned on, but I am just not like that." Nat felt a dagger of ice rip through her heart. *How can she say it when she is sitting on my lap shaking with desire?* Nat wondered feeling frustration rising.

"But," Nat started and then paused. Arguing would do no good. If Catherine said she was not ready, Nat would not press her. She just knew the night ahead would be long. "Okay," she said. "Let's just go back to the room and get some sleep." Catherine shook her head.

"I don't think that's a good idea," she said. "I need to find another place to stay I think." Now Nat's heart really did ache. This was the last thing she wanted.

"Where will you go?" Nat asked, and Catherine shrugged.

"I have a few friends I can stay with. It will be fine," she said and slid off of Nat's lap. "You should go. I'll just wait here and give you a minute." Nat blinked. The girl did not even trust her alone in the elevator. Now she felt angry but checked it and pulled out her wallet. Taking out a few credits, she handed them to Catherine.

"For the Ubercab," she said and started to climb out, but then hesitated. Turning back, she noticed the anguish on Catherine's face but forced herself not to react. Enough was enough. "Do you have your room key? You know, just in case." Catherine nodded without looking at her and with that, Nat closed the shuttle door and stalked across the roof.

Once back in the lavish hotel room, Nat was beside herself with frustration, arousal, and disappointment. She knew Catherine wanted her as much as Nat wanted Catherine, but the girl could not see past the labels. *Who be it for me to fight that battle?* Nat thought and wished there was more wine left.

Slugging back what was there, Nat tried to figure out what to do next. A run sounded good. A pulse-pounding, grueling race down the street would do wonders for all her pent-up emotion. Unfortunately, it was after midnight, and even the streets of Prospo were not that safe. She would just have to work out in her room. Striding to her half of the suite, she yanked off her clothes and put on shorts and a sports bra. Then she dropped to the floor and knocked out twenty-push-ups. Transitioning immediately to a high knee sprint in place, she ran until she could hardly catch her breath and then dove back the floor for more push-ups. Almost frantically she pushed herself from one exercise to the next until her heart was racing and sweat was pouring off her body. It was not enough, and she kept going, wanting to pound out everything within her. The pain over the last year. The lust for Catherine. All of it.

Finally dropping to the floor in a spent pile, she heard the front door to the hotel room open. *What the hell?* she thought and dragged herself to her feet to walk out into the front room. Catherine was standing there. She would not meet Nat's eye. "I have nowhere else to go," she said. Nat's heart nearly broke at the defeated sound of the woman's tone. It was all she could do not to take her in her arms, but she resisted.

"It's okay, Catherine," she said instead. "You're welcome here. Always. Go ahead and get some sleep. I'm going to take a quick shower." Catherine looked up, clearly noticing for the first time Nat was half naked and glistening with sweat from working out. Nat saw the girl's eyes widen a little and she knew she looked good. Her muscles were swollen from the workout, and her body was ripped, all of it accented by the glisten of perspiration. Nat smirked and took pleasure in seeing she was not the only one who was frustrated. "See you in the morning," Nat said and with that, headed for the bathroom.

CHAPTER 12
CATHERINE

C atherine threw herself down on the bed and covered her face with her hands. She had ruined everything. *How could I have let things go so far?* she thought and moaned with frustration. Now all she had accomplished was hurting the one person who made Catherine feel special. Nat was the most incredible woman she had ever met. *Don't forget sexy,* said a little voice in her head. "Stop it," Catherine said back to it and slapped her hands down angrily on the lavish bedspread. It was precisely that kind of subliminal thinking which was making her crazy and letting her do things she should not do. Taking a deep breath and trying to steady herself, she sat up and looked around the room. Her deliciously soft robe was thrown over the chair where it landed when she raced in to dress hours ago. She thought of the fun she had getting ready to go out and how excited she was to put on the silver dress. Catherine ran her hands over it now and felt the sleek fabric, so shimmery and sexy. *I wore this for Nat. I wanted her to be attracted to me, but then I tell her no when things get too hot.* Catherine stood up and shook her head angrily, realizing she was being nothing more than a little cocktease and hated herself for it. None of it was fair to either of them.

Unzipping the dress, Catherine slipped out of it. She went to unclasp her bra and caught her image in the mirror. Delicate white lace. Innocent, but then not in the least. *Just like me*, Catherine thought and puffed out an annoyed breath. She pulled off the underwear and slipped naked into the robe. Knowing sleep would be impossible right now, she wandered into the front room, hoping there might be wine left. As she crossed the space, she could hear the sound of Nat's shower and the memory of the woman standing in her workout clothes all hot and ripped popped into Catherine's head. A bloom of heat flared low in her belly, and she growled with frustration. Her body kept betraying her mind, and it had to stop. Distracting herself, she went back to searching for the last of the wine but could not find it. She wondered if Nat had taken it into her suite and Catherine contemplated going in to look for it. *Now, why would I do something as disrespectful as that?* She bit her bottom lip and knew exactly why. As crazy as it was, she wanted to see Nat come out of the shower. *Or I could even see her in the shower.* The hot bloom she felt from before now turned into a throb which ran lower and she wavered. *I could just help wash Nat's back as a way to apologize.*

Throwing caution to the wind, Catherine strode across the room and, hesitating for the briefest moment at Nat's bedroom door, opened it and went in. Steam billowed from the attached ensuite, and Catherine followed its trail until she was standing in front of the shower door. Licking her lips, she mustered her courage and let the robe slip to the floor. It was now or never, and she knew it. Taking the last step, Catherine opened the glass, and more steam billowed out, but through it, she could see Nat standing beautifully under the hot spray. With her head tilted back and her eyes closed, she looked a million miles away. Trying not to startle her, Catherine stepped into the shower and pulled the door closed. "Nat," she murmured. She saw Nat frown and then open her eyes. They widened with surprise.

"Catherine, are you crazy?" she asked. "I'm only human."

"Shhhh," Catherine said and took the liquid soap from the shelf to pour it into her hands. "I just want to help wash your back. To say thank you for everything." She watched Nat's face to see if she should continue. A myriad of emotions rolled over it until finally the woman gave a nod and turned around. Catherine paused when she noticed the scars. There were four, all about two inches long, and looked like they were made by something hot. She could tell they were relatively new from the pink around the edges. "Oh Nat," Catherine said, feeling her heart hurt knowing what she was seeing was part of the story of space pirates Dee was trying to tell her at the club. Somehow, somewhere, a person had wounded this special woman, and it made Catherine furious to think about it. "Do they hurt?" she asked. Nat shook her head no.

"It's okay, Catherine," she said. "You can touch them. Unless they freak you out."

"They don't," Catherine said and reached out to run her soapy hand across the muscles of Nat's back. She felt the woman stiffen in response.

"Just relax," Catherine said and moved closer to use both hands now. Sliding them all along Nat's shoulders, she felt the woman slowly loosen. Encouraged, Catherine trailed her hand down Nat's spine and worked the lower muscles. "Does that feel good?" she asked.

"You have no idea," Nat murmured, and Catherine smiled with satisfaction until she was finished. "Now my turn," Nat said as she twisted around to stand face-to-face with Catherine. Their naked bodies were so close to touching Catherine could feel the heat between them. She licked her lips and knew letting Nat touch her anywhere would be trouble. *But I want it. I so want it*, she realized and handed the soap over before turning to face the wall. There was a pause, and she thought for a second Nat had changed her mind, and then she touched her. The heat of the water, the woman's strong hands, the slippery soap. All of it felt exquisite, and a moan slipped out before she could stop it. Clearly encouraged, Catherine felt Nat move closer until now their bodies were touching.

Catherine's physical reaction was so intense it shocked her. Immediately her nipples tightened, and an ache ran between her legs. She felt Nat's hands still moving, only now they were sliding away from her back and coming around to cup her breasts. Nat teased the nipples gently, and Catherine felt her knees start to buckle. *Too much*, her mind screamed, but then Nat's strong arm wrapped around her waist and held her tight so she would not fall. The woman's other hand lingered at Catherine's belly, and there was no doubt what could happen next. Conflicted as hell, Catherine knew she had to stop this now, or there would be no turning back from it.

"Are you okay?" she heard Nat breathe in her ear. *Am I okay?* Taking a deep breath, Catherine nodded and gathering all her courage, put her hand on top of Nat's. Before she could back out, Catherine slid Nat's hand down until it was on top of her sex. Even if she wanted to wait now, Nat did not let her.

The woman pressed with a gentle finger until Catherine felt it slide her lips apart and left her clit exposed. Unable to help it, Catherine shivered with want. She felt Nat's lips kiss the side of her neck and her arm was still wrapped tight around her waist to hold her, but Catherine's real focus was on the woman's hand. The magical touch which was now tracing a circle around Catherine's clit, softly at first, but then started to add more pressure. Catherine shuddered. Never had she felt so on fire. Whenever she touched herself, it was good, but this sensation made her dizzy. Amazingly, Catherine realized the pleasure was only just beginning as now Nat used her fingertips to rub directly onto the pleasure spot in long slow strokes. The rhythm started to build a tightness in Catherine she never felt before. A longing for release filled her mind as Nat moved faster. Involuntarily, Catherine felt her hips buck against Nat's hand, pressing the touch even harder.

"Oh my God, Nat," she said as the finger kept probing and prolonging the waves. "How are you doing that?" Nat growled behind her and kept going, faster and faster over the top of the clit. Her whole body quivering now, Catherine threw out her hands to brace herself against the wall and for a fleeting moment thought she should stop this before she lost control altogether. "Nat," she started. "I don't know -" It was too late. Everything inside her exploded, and the orgasm ripped through her with such force she let out a little scream of pleasure.

CHAPTER 13
NAT

"Why does everything feel so good with you?" Nat heard Catherine murmur and she opened her eyes to see it was morning. The woman was wrapped in her arms, spooning like they had back on the P-527 in what seemed like forever ago, but in reality, was almost no time at all. She felt Catherine rub her hand tenderly along her arm and the girl sighed. It was a sound Nat could wake up to every morning for eternity. *But it won't be*, she thought and pulled Catherine into her a little tighter knowing time was short for them. *I will face it all later. Just not now.*

"Good morning," Nat said in answer. "Sleep okay?"

"Mmmmm," Catherine breathed. "Never better than this, which is crazy considering everything." Nat felt some unease at the comment, not sure how much the words reflected their ever more complicated relationship. As if sensing the change in her, Catherine rolled over and looked into Nat's face.

"I don't mean you," she corrected. "Well, okay, maybe a little is you, but you're the good crazy. It's my father who is my real worry." Nat relaxed at the tenderness in Catherine's words but also wanted to know Catherine's story. Whatever made the woman worry was something Nat needed to hear.

"Can you share?" she asked. Catherine let out a deep sigh and Nat could see the hesitation on the woman's face. "It may help," Nat continued. Nodding, Catherine sat up, realized she was naked and blushed as she pulled up the blanket. The look was so sweet, Nat chuckled. "Let me get our robes," she said. "And then I'll order us breakfast. We can talk on the balcony and watch the waves." Catherine nodded, and Nat hopped out of bed, unconcerned about her nakedness as she walked across the room to go fetch their things from the bathroom. When she returned, Catherine was looking thoughtful. "What is it?" Nat asked as she slipped on the white terrycloth.

"I'll share if you will. I want to know who hurt you. About the scars," she said. Nat froze. It was about the last thing she wanted to talk about, but she also knew sharing should go both ways. *Within reason*, she thought.

"I'll order room service," Nat said. "Then we can see." It was all she was willing to commit to for now.

AS THE SOUND OF THE ocean rippled through the air and they sat on the room's balcony, Nat sipped her coffee and watched Catherine eating her breakfast with relish. A double-stack of waffles with a mound of strawberries all bathed in whip cream. Taking another bite, Catherine closed her eyes and gave a little sigh. "How can this taste so good? What is it about this place?" she asked. Nat chuckled.

"It is pretty impressive, I'll agree," Nat answered and meant it. Never in her life had she felt happier. *Or more alive*, she thought. Catherine's presence had a profound impact on her. Nat knew it, and frankly, it scared her. In less than forty-eight hours, the fantasy would be over, and Nat would be back in uniform ready for duty. *But where will Catherine be? Who says we can't make it work out?* Nat sighed. *Just about everybody in the galaxy, that's who*. Nat had worked hard to avoid getting entangled in relationships with the one mistake being Olivia. Just like everyone predicted, the long stretches of time apart killed any closeness.

Even though she knew Dee and the others wanted to tar and feather Olivia for cheating on Nat, she did not blame her. Nat just had not been there enough to satisfy the woman. Something she refused to put Catherine through. *Assuming the girl even wants me that way*, she thought. After last night, Nat had no idea where they stood, but the last thing she was going to do was ruin this moment together. The sweet normalcy of it touched her heart. Looking up from her coffee, Nat saw Catherine watching her. "Where did you go?" she asked. "You suddenly looked sad." Nat put on a grin and shook her head.

"It was nothing," she said and noticed the breakfast plate was empty. "Wow, you killed those waffles." Catherine leaned back in her chair still giving Nat an appraising look.

"You're changing the subject," she said.

"Maybe I was thinking about how I could talk you out of that robe?" Nat challenged hoping the aggressive pass would throw Catherine off the scent. As she watched Catherine blush and tug the robe closed, she knew it worked.

"I'm pretty sure that wouldn't make you look sad," she murmured as she glanced away. Nat laughed. *She has a good point*, Nat thought and for a moment had a warm tingle run through her as she remembered the shower and feeling Catherine quivering against her. *Maybe that is the best answer to any of this. Pick her up, carry her to bed and take her over and over until she is out of my system.* Nat licked her lips at the thought, and this time Catherine laughed, still blushing but now with more heat than embarrassment. "Now I'm certain that was not what you were thinking," she said. "So spill it." Nat sobered, feeling the ache in her change from longing to sadness.

"I was thinking I'm going to miss you," she said softly, but when Catherine's face fell, and she actually saw the first glisten of tears, Nat leaned forward to change the subject. "But I don't want to talk about it. What I want is to find out why in the hell you were trying to fly to Untas in a thirty-year-old ED-90?"

"Okay," Catherine said as she wiped at her eyes. "So. My ED-90." She sighed. "I didn't have any other option. I need to go see my aunt about something." Nat frowned.

"You couldn't take a public transport instead? They run at least four times a day. Albeit a long and uncomfortable ride, but far safer than the ED-90," Nat said. Catherine picked up her orange juice and did not meet Nat's eye.

"I couldn't afford it," Catherine admitted as she took a sip. "Actually, I used the last of my credits to buy the ship I did have." She looked at Nat almost defiantly. "Nat, I won't hide it from you, I don't have a credit to my name." Nat paused to consider her words. What she said explained a lot, but also just added more questions.

"But what about family? You mentioned an aunt," Nat asked. Now a sad look crossed Catherine's beautiful features, and Nat hated to see it but needed to know the answers.

"My mother died when I was a child and my dad's a drunk," she whispered. "And now he's missing. I've looked everywhere for him. Bars, cops, hospital. He's vanished, and I am not sure if I think he's dead or just deserted me." Nat heard the hurt in Catherine's voice, and it made her angry. *What kind of bastard does this to his daughter? Especially one as wonderful as Catherine?* she wondered.

"So how does your aunt fit in?" Nat asked. Catherine shook her head.

"I thought she might know something so I called her. She was mad when I told her, but she also asked me to come to Untas and see her," Catherine answered. "So, I was, by the only means I could figure out." She looked up and smiled a little. "And then I met you." Nat smiled back, but she was also calculating what to do to help Catherine. She would use her contacts to make sure Catherine's dad truly had not been found dead in a ditch. Then she would get her to Untas. *But how? Get her a seat on a transport?* Nat thought. *And just say good-bye?* The idea of it made her stomach hurt. "Sorry to just dump all of this on you," Catherine said, breaking into Nat's thoughts. She was clearly embarrassed and lowered her head to hide behind her hair. In that instance, Nat realized how young and afraid Catherine was, and it made her wonder the girl's age.

"Catherine, how old are you?" Nat said. Catherine looked up surprised.

"Why?" she asked. "How old are you?" Nat shrugged.

"Twenty-eight," she answered. "But I was asking you." Catherine hesitated and then with a blush admitted she was only eighteen. "I just graduated from school last month." Nat's mouth dropped open. *Well at least she's out of high school*, she thought and remembered Olivia's crack at the bar about how young Catherine was, which Nat had disregarded as bitchy and not thought about it. Nat tried not to look as surprised as she felt but was too late.

"What?" Catherine said with a hint of defensiveness. Nat raised her hands in mock surrender.

"Nothing," she said. "I was just curious." It was a bit of a lie as the information was unsettling. Not so much the number of years difference, as it did not matter to Nat, but instead she was worried about the gap in life experience. Nat had been through space battles and the rigors of military life. She had survived rocky relationships and made lifelong friendships. Now Nat realized Catherine had none of it. "I was only making sure no laws were being broken," Nat said trying to make things a little more playful. Catherine blushed and looked away again.

"Cute," she said. "Well, for the record, you're the first person to ever touch me like that." Nat froze. *What is she saying?* Nat thought as a mix of emotions raced through her. Nat cleared her throat. "So, uh, you're saying—" Catherine cut her off.

"Yes, I'm saying I'm a virgin, and I've never..." she paused clearly searching for the right word. "Never felt like that." Nat swallowed hard.

"You mean have an orgasm?" Nat asked. Catherine looked at her, and there was an intensity in her gaze.

"Yes, Nat, you're the only one," she said.

Nat had no idea what to say. Clearing her throat, she picked up her coffee cup and tried to take a sip. Her hand was suddenly shaking so bad, she had to set it down before she spilled it. She stared at the table. Never in her wildest imagination had she thought Catherine was so innocent. The passion Nat felt for her had nothing to do with being her first. *But you are, so now what are you going to do?* she wondered feeling an entirely new closeness to Catherine. *And responsibility.* "I don't know what to say," Nat said. "I hadn't realized." Suddenly she heard Catherine's chair pushing back and looked up to see the woman getting up to leave the table. Her eyes were snapping with fury.

"Well, sorry to surprise you," she said as she headed for the balcony door. Nat jumped up and was beside her in a moment. She put her hands on Catherine's hips and turned her around so she could look into the woman's face. Nat hesitated unsure of what the right thing to say was, but then decided to just be honest.

"It's a good surprise," she said and realized at that moment how true her words were as she remembered the feel of Catherine against her. Knowing no one had ever been with the woman filled Nat with a renewed passion. "I like being your first." Catherine slipped her hands around Nat's waist and leaned into her as she rested her head on Nat's shoulder. She sighed.

"What we did," she started and then paused. "How it felt. Nothing was how I imagined it would be, but I wouldn't change it." Her words made Nat's heart ache. There was nothing she wanted to hear more than that confession, but it also filled her with fear. *How can we make this work?* she thought. Catherine was eighteen and had a world of experiences ahead of her. Being tied down to a Ranger who was gone six months at a time was no way to live. Nat thought for a second of saying exactly that, but then stopped. They still had a couple days. Anything could happen. Pulling Catherine in close and wrapping her arms around her, she kissed the top of her head.

"I wouldn't change it either," she said. "You're a special woman, Catherine." Nat knew then she would do anything to help her.

CHAPTER 14
CATHERINE

Catherine was restless. Nat was gone. Off on some errands she had to do alone. It was all slightly mysterious, but Catherine guessed there was something to do with tracking down her father. When Catherine tried to come along, Nat asked her not too. It was clear she did not want Catherine on hand if the news was bad.

And at this point, it has to be bad, right? she wondered. It had been well over a month, with no word and no sign of him. The thought she was possibly alone in the world clenched at Catherine's heart. With her mother dead from an accident when Catherine was four and now her father gone too, there was no one she could turn to when it mattered. *Other than Captain Nat Reynolds.* Catherine sighed as she pictured the woman's face. Nat was quickly becoming her world and Catherine had to admit she could not remember a time when she felt safer or happier. The woman was so strong and smart. *And sexy.* The thought caught Catherine off guard. She was still wrapping her head around the fact Nat was female. It never crossed her mind growing up she would fall for a woman. Not that Catherine had a problem with lesbians or any alternatives. The galaxy was filled with every variation of human and alien imaginable. Her high school was mixed, and one of her few friends was gay. Still, now that she thought of it, she rarely found herself particularly attracted to the boys either. It was more about the person and appreciating a good body, and Nat definitely fell into that category. The woman's physique was incredible. Remembering Nat walk boldly across the bedroom that morning to get their robes gave Catherine a bit of a tingle even. Yet therein was the real problem. Catherine had no idea how to make Nat feel as good and appreciated as Nat made her. *Let's not forget satisfied too.*

Plopping down on the couch, Catherine groaned with frustration. Satisfying Nat was the biggest problem of all. The thought of trying to navigate how to touch her and pleasure her scared Catherine almost to death. She did not want to do it wrong and wished she had access to a private comm link so she could at least watch a few videos on the topic. Catherine laughed. It would be just her luck that Nat would walk in and catch her in the middle of watching porn. Then she had a sudden thought. *I wonder if Nat likes porn?* Catherine blushed just thinking about it. There was so much more she needed to learn about Nat. Catherine wanted to be everything for her. More than just her lover though. She did not miss Nat's reaction when she learned Catherine was only eighteen. As much as the woman tried to cover it, Catherine could tell it caught her off guard and concerned her for reasons Catherine did not understand. It was true she did not know as much about the world as Nat, but life for Catherine with an alcoholic father who was gone half the time was not easy street. There were a lot of days she stayed home from school to run the store. She handled the money for the most part and took care of things in general. Unlike a lot of her classmates who were only worried about sports, grades, and getting laid, Catherine was worried about having enough money for food and utilities. All things considered, her life was simpler now, even if more uncertain.

There was a sudden tap at the hotel room door. "Ms. Catherine," said a voice. "I have a message from Captain Natalie." Alarmed, Catherine jumped up and hurried to the door. Opening it, she saw an android steward with a white sheet of folded paper. "An Ubercab has been arranged. Please come down when you are ready," the android said handing over the paper.

"Okay," Catherine said confused. "Thank you."

"You're welcome, Ms. Catherine," the android said and, turning on his wheels, left. Catherine did not know what to think. *What is this?* she wondered and backed into the room to shut the door. Leaning on it, she read the note.

CATHERINE,

PLEASE PACK YOUR THINGS AND TAKE THE CAB TO THE AVIATION CENTER. I WILL SETTLE WITH THE HOTEL LATER.

I MISS YOU,

NAT

Catherine read the note three times, her eyes lingering on the different phrases. "Pack your things," "Aviation Center," and "I will settle later" all gave her a sense of unease. *Where are we going? Untas?* she wondered and then had a horrifying thought. *What if Nat is not going with me?* They never talked about what was ahead for them or even what they were going to do the next day. This morning, when Catherine was telling Nat about her situation, she could tell Nat was sympathetic and wanted to help. She had just assumed it was about helping find her father. *Not about sending me away to my aunt's.* Closing her eyes, Catherine felt sadness creep over her. Foolishly she imagined a future with Nat, but when in reality they only had a few days before Nat had to go back to the Space Rangers. Only now it sounded like they would not even have a few days. Feeling tears start to burn her eyes, she knew it was because she was just eighteen. Nat was worldly and experienced. *Why would she want to be saddled with someone like me?* The thought left a bitter taste in her mouth. Catherine knew she had more to offer than Nat apparently believed. *Well, I'll show her.* Pushing away from the door, Catherine went to pack. She was not going to go down without a fight.

WHEN CATHERINE'S UBERCAB arrived at the Aviation Center, she was surprised when it did not stop at the usual passenger terminal for public transports. Instead, it took her around the furthest end of the buildings to a particular area. It took her a minute, but then she realized it was a private launch pad for noncommercial spacecraft. There were rows of beautiful ships of all sizes and variations. Puzzled as to what was happening, Catherine looked until she saw Nat standing near an Avalon Mercury 3370 luxury spaceship. When Nat saw the cab stopping, Catherine watched her grin and walk toward them. Nat opened the door and held out a hand. "I thought you would never get here," Nat said as Catherine stepped out onto the tarmac. Nat motioned to the Avalon. "Well, what do you think?" Catherine could not believe it.

"You bought that?" she asked with surprise. Nat laughed.

"I wish," she answered. "No, I basically rented it. A gentleman is hoping to sell it to me, so he was willing to let me take it out for a long test drive. To Untas actually." Nat shrugged. "With a sizable deposit, of course." Seeing Nat's excitement and realizing there was no ticket waiting for her to take a public transport alone, Catherine laughed too.

"Oh, Nat," she said with relief turning to excitement. Never in her wildest dreams had she thought she would ride in the luxury of such a starship. "You are wonderful. I can't believe you did this." Nat slipped her arm around Catherine's shoulders and started to walk her to the ramp to enter the ship.

"I like you to feel special. Did I do okay?" she asked. Catherine nodded as she put her arm around Nat's waist and rested her head on the woman's shoulder.

"You have no idea," she answered.

THE AVALON MERCURY was gorgeous. Even though it was not a large-sized luxury cruiser, it was loaded with efficient amenities. As the two women embarked, they were met at the top of the gangway by an FR CisorMate 680 robot, "custom built to cater to any passenger whim," if Catherine remembered the comm link ads correctly.

"Welcome aboard, Captain Reynolds," the robot said in a clipped Earthstyle British accent. "My name is Frederick. I am at your service." Nat smiled and gave him a nod.

"Good afternoon, Frederick," Nat answered. "And this young lady is Catherine Porter." The robot bowed, his polished metal exterior gleaming.

"Catherine," he said. "A beautiful name for a beautiful face." Catherine giggled. It all seemed so surreal. "Please, walk this way, and I will show you the many features of the Avalon Mercury 3370. Unless of course, you would like to go straight to the lounge and relax. Have a cocktail perhaps? I make a wicked shaken martini." Catherine looked up at Nat to see what she wanted only to find the same expression on her face. They both laughed.

"Martini?" Nat said. Catherine had no idea what a martini tasted like, but it sounded like fun. She nodded. Nat turned back to Frederick. "Two martinis it is," she said, and they followed the robot to the lounge. It was beyond plush, with a black leather couch, a glass and chrome coffee table, all topped off with a giant screen comm link. Catherine had never seen anything like it outside of pictures.

"Is this suitable?" Fredrick asked when they arrived. Nat laughed.

"I think it will work," she answered. "How long until we take off?"

"I can check, Captain Reynolds. But I did overhear there were some delays. A mix up with a public transport schedule," Frederick said. Catherine could almost hear the disdain in his digital voice. "But please, make yourself comfortable. I will have the drinks shortly."

"Thank you, Frederick," Catherine heard Nat say as she slipped onto the closest couch and ran her hands over the leather. It was soft as silk. First the incredible hotel room and now this. She was almost ready to pinch herself to make sure it was not a dream. She felt Nat sit down near her and when Catherine turned, she smiled. "You look happy," Nat said. "I was a little worried."

"Worried?" Catherine asked, sliding closer to Nat and putting a hand on her arm. "Why? This is perfect." Nat took her hand and held it.

"I didn't want to assume too much. But getting to Untas sounded important, and this seemed like a fun way to go there," Nat said. "And it is a lot more comfortable than a public transport."

"And more private," Catherine said, trying to be bold. She had a lot to thank Nat for and wanted to show it somehow. She ran her other hand up Nat's arm and relished the muscles she felt there. Catherine licked her lips and glanced up to check Nat's face. The woman was staring at her with intense blue-gray eyes.

"Careful, Catherine," she murmured. "I've been thinking about you all day. Missing you." Nat leaned in closer until her face was less than an inch from Catherine's. "Wanting you." A bolt of desire ran through Catherine's body. *Why does hearing her say that turn me on so much?* she thought feeling warm in all the right places. A memory of Nat's hands on her in the shower popped into her head, and she sucked in a ragged breath.

"I missed you too," she said. Nat smiled a little and ran her lips over Catherine's cheek and down along her neck.

"Is that all?" Nat asked. Catherine leaned into Nat, feeling the woman's mouth on her skin like fire. She moaned but was nervous about answering. It was more than just foreplay. Saying what she was feeling out loud would be more like a confession. Clearly sensing the hesitation, Nat took Catherine by the chin and turned her mouth so she could kiss it. It was a tickle and left Catherine wishing for more. "Is that all?" Nat asked again. Catherine closed her eyes.

"No," she whispered. "I want you too."

CHAPTER 15
NAT

She wants me too, Nat thought. It was all she could ever ask, but as the reality of it settled in, the looming questions about their relationship made her pause. Pulling back a little, she looked into Catherine's eyes and saw such passion mixed with vulnerability it nearly broke her heart. *I can't let this keep going*, she thought. *I have to tell her the truth about our future.* Nat took a deep breath and tried to calm her racing heart and the burning desire inside her to simply push Catherine down on the couch and make love to her right there. They had to talk about things first. "Catherine," Nat started and saw a flicker of fear appear in Catherine's brown eyes. Seeing it, Nat almost lost her resolve. This was not what she wanted to do and kissing that look back out of Catherine's eyes would be so much easier. *But you can't do that.* It was time to stop living in a fantasy land. She took Catherine's hand in hers. "Catherine," she said again. "We need to—" Suddenly, there was a digital beep at the door of the lounge, and Nat glanced over to see Frederick was back with the martinis. Nat closed her eyes and let out a breath, both relieved and frustrated at the interruption.

"Cocktails have arrived," Frederick announced and he bustled across the space with a silver tray in his hand. Nat took a drink from him and handed it to Catherine. A quick look at Catherine's face let Nat know the girl was not letting her off the hook so easily. The woman was smart enough to know Nat was about to say something important. Suddenly, Nat did not want to have the conversation anymore. *Not today*, she thought. They should enjoy every last second together. *Besides, who says she wants to be with me after this trip anyway?* Nat almost laughed as she realized her line of thinking was arrogant as hell. *Maybe I'm the only one who's heart is about to be broken.*

Taking the second martini, Nat held it out to clink glasses with Catherine. "A toast," Nat said with a forced smile. "To new friendships." Catherine paused, and Nat could see the woman was thinking over the statement. Finally, she tapped her glass against Nat's.

"To a new everything," she said fixing Nat with a determined look and took a sip. As Nat watched her, it was suddenly so evident on Catherine's face she thought the drink tasted horrible, Nat chuckled with relief at the distraction. Sipping it herself, she had to admit the gin in it was a bit over the top.

"Not your favorite?" Nat asked. Catherine set the drink down.

"Maybe just a coke?" Catherine said. Nat nodded and put her cocktail beside Catherine's.

"You're not pleased, Captain?" Frederick asked sounding dismayed. "Perhaps something else? A margarita?" Before Nat could respond there was a chiming of a bell. It was the signal the Avalon Mercury was cleared for departure. "Oh good," Frederick continued. "Now we can depart. I apologize, but I must discontinue drink service while I pilot us out of the Prospo airspace."

"Of course," Nat said. "In fact, I'd like to come with you and co-pilot if you don't mind. I want to know how she handles."

"But of course," Frederick said. "You may both come if you like." Nat smiled and looked to Catherine who nodded.

"I would like that," she said, and although she was smiling, Nat could tell Catherine was still thinking about the aborted conversation. There would be no getting around having a heart-to-heart at some point, and Nat knew it. Clearing her throat nervously, she started to get up.

"Oh, Captain, one more thing," Frederick said suddenly. He took a piece of paper from a slot in his metal uniform. "I almost forgot. A message came for you." Nat knew what it had to be and paused. The communication was in response to her inquiry about Catherine's father. *Do I read this now with Catherine beside me?* she wondered as she took the note from Frederick. *She needs to know the truth, one way or the other.* Nat gave it a brief glance and frowned. The information was not horrible and, in fact, was more puzzling than anything.

"Thank you," Nat said looking up at Frederick again.

"What is it?" Catherine asked and Nat turned to her.

"I checked into your father's disappearance," Nat said. "And he took a transport to Helivian." Nat watched Catherine's face register surprise, then relief, and finally anger.

"Helivian? Why?" she asked. "A ticket like that would have cost all our credits and he had to know it." Catherine shook her head and Nat wished she could make sense of it all for her.

"Do you want me to reroute our flight to go to Helivian?" Nat asked. Catherine sighed and shook her head.

"No," she said. "Clearly he did not want me with him." Nat saw tears come to Catherine's eyes, but the woman brushed them away angrily. "Let's just go. It's time to take off." Nat nodded and hoped for now she could distract them both from all the turmoil in their lives with a little flying.

Although flying the luxury space cruiser was a treat and dinner, which consisted of steak and lobster with excellent red wine, was nearly perfect, Nat could not avoid the look of concern in Catherine's eyes. It was like the woman had read Nat's mind about their future and Nat knew the evening would not end until they had a talk about their upcoming separation. Twice over dinner, Catherine had tried to steer the conversation around to serious topics but Nat continued to keep things light by telling her stories of 1980's Earth culture. Even though Catherine showed some interest in learning about movies featuring DeLorean cars and time travel, Nat could see more anger starting to build in Catherine's eyes at the diversion. Now, as they were shown to their bedroom suite, there was no more hiding.

As soon as Frederick finished turning down the bed and left, Catherine whirled around on Nat, her eyes snapping. "What is going on?" she demanded. "Ever since I admitted how I felt on the couch, you won't even look at me! What was I? Some sort of conquest?" Nat's mouth fell open. *Conquest?* Nat thought. *Is that what she thinks?* Nothing could be further from the truth and Nat would prove it to her. She moved to Catherine in two quick steps and grabbed her by the hips to pull her close. Catherine resisted and put her hands on Nat's arms. "No," Catherine said. "You can't just kiss me and distract us from whatever you need to say. I want answers, Nat Reynolds." Nat paused and looked into the woman's furious and hurting eyes. The one thing Nat swore she would never do was happening. She only wanted Catherine to be happy and feel special. *And now I am making her miserable. Which will only get worse when I have to explain the reality of our lives.* Clearly seeing the hesitation, Catherine wrestled out of Nat's hold and went to stand on the other side of the bed. "You're dumping me, aren't you," she said. It was not a question. "It is because you think I'm too young?" The pain in Catherine's voice cut Nat like a knife.

"No," Nat said. "It's not like that. Please, come over here. We need to talk."

"About what exactly?" Catherine answered, not budging. "That you're dropping me off at Untas and then returning to the Space Ranger's without a look back?" Nat let out a long deep breath. There was not much she could say. Even though Catherine's words were full of anger, they were not untrue. She somehow had to make Catherine understand why it was the right choice.

"Catherine," Nat said softly. "You're the most amazing woman I've ever met. Every second with you makes me feel more alive. But, I'm not around and—" Catherine cut her off with a wave of her hand. Nat saw tears were streaming down the furious woman's face.

"Just stop," Catherine interrupted. "I'm sleeping in the lounge." She grabbed her bag and threw it open to pull out a few things before storming toward the door. Nat went to cut Catherine off, but before she touched her, Catherine had a finger in her face. "Do not touch me," she said. Nat froze and felt a pain like she never had before. Even the physical pain she endured in space battles could not compare.

"Please don't go," Nat asked. "I won't touch you. I promise. But please, stay." Catherine waivered and Nat could see the anger was turning to hurt resignation. In so many ways, that look was far worse to witness. Catherine shoulders sagged and she stepped back to the bed, dropping her things into her bag.

"I'll stay," she whispered.

JUST LET HIM GO, NAT," Shaun said. "You got two kills already. No need to show off." Nat laughed into the comm link. She knew her Space Ranger co-pilot was poking fun, but she could hear a tone of seriousness too. Shaun was always the more practical of the team. He balanced her out, but this time she was calling the shots.

"It's not showing off," she corrected. "I'm simply clearing the friendly skies of pirate scum. And this will be my last for today. Besides he's kind of pissing me off. He should have ran when he had the chance."

"True," Shaun agreed. "He is either very brave or very stupid." Nat smirked. From what she knew of space pirates in general, they were more likely very stupid. The fact a set of them

decided to invade planet Elivib airspace was a perfect example. *Everyone knew, even though it was sparsely inhabited, it was a well-patrolled area due to its extensive petroleum fields. Frankly, Nat could not figure out why the pirates would venture there at all.* But we made them pay for it, *she thought.* Two ships down and a third almost in her sights. *He's a tricky one though. This pirate ship was faster than the other two and clearly had a more experienced pilot. He had evaded sightlock twice already, but now Nat knew she had him. The craft was headed for a canyon, which Nat remembered had a lot of challenging, blind curves.* He will be forced to slow down and when he does, it will be goodbye to another piece of space filth.

"He's headed for the canyon," *Shaun said over the comm link. Nat knew he could see everything a little better than she could from the elevated position of his co-pilot seat behind her. After four years together, she trusted his eyes completely, but this time she was way ahead of him.*

"I'm already on it," *Nat said.* "He's toast now." *The comm link clicked like Shaun was about to respond, but there was a pause.*

"Nat, you sure about this?" *he finally asked.* "Kind of hard to see in there." *Nat grinned.* Shaun, always the cautious one, *she thought.*

"This will only take a second," *she answered and watched the small space pirate ship slip into the mouth of the canyon. Nat accelerated and followed him in. She had been in the canyon a dozen times before, but it was still challenging. Rocky outcroppings and dangerous overhangs threatened to wreck any passing craft. Not too many other Ranger pilots would fly there, but*

Nat loved it. It tested her skills to a new level. I'm a better pilot for it, *she thought.* And it is coming in handy now. *The brake lights on the pirate spaceship flashed ahead of her. With a smirk, Nat grabbed the control of her ship's laser cannon and turned on the locking device. It beeped as it looked for the target. Slowly it narrowed in and Nat waited for the welcome sound of the lock alarm.* Just a few more seconds. *The two ships raced around another curve and all of Nat's focus was on the pirate in front of her.*

"Nat!" Shaun yelled into the comm link. "Abort! Jesus, abort. It's a trap." Looking up, Nat saw he was right. A huge pirate starship, bigger than any she had ever seen, was hovering among the rocks. Hidden from view by the walls of the canyon, it was waiting for them. Nat instinctively jerked their ship up to try and clear the canyon, but she was too late. The pirate's spacecraft fired and the blast hit them. Suddenly, phosphorus fire was everywhere and she could hear Shaun screaming.

Nat screamed with him.

"Nat," she heard Catherine calling. "Nat, please wake up!" Shaking her head, Nat tried to orient herself. There was no fire and she was not in the hospital. Instead, she could feel warm hands brushing the tears from her face. She opened her eyes and saw Catherine's concerned face looking at her. "Nat. Baby," Catherine said softly. "You're safe. It's okay." Nat felt her heart surge with relief and something else. Feeling Catherine against her, with her hands holding her face, Nat realized she felt the last thing she wanted. She was falling in love. With a sob, Nat let the sadness of everything overwhelm her. As she stopped fighting it and started to cry, Catherine wrapped her arms around her and held her tight.

CHAPTER 16
CATHERINE

C atherine held Nat's head in her lap and stroked her hair
while the woman slept. Catherine had never felt such
tenderness toward any person. They had talked through
much of the night about Nat's dream and her horrible accident. Nat finally confessed the survivor's guilt she carried
over her Ranger co-pilot's death. Shaun was a close friend,
with a family and big dreams of moving up within the
Rangers. Nat blamed herself relentlessly for what happened
to him, even though she had been cleared of all responsibility
for the event. It was a space pirate trap, pure and simple. Nat
did not agree.

While Catherine listened, her heart hurting when she
saw the pain in Nat's eyes, much of the real Nat was revealed
layer by layer. The Space Rangers were her whole life, and
she felt she owed them for saving her in a way. Growing up
a lesbian in a small town and never fitting in because of her
tomboy look, it was only the dream of being a Ranger someday that kept her going. When she realized it was girls she
was attracted to, Nat decided leaving the planet and making
a career with the Space Rangers was her destiny. She never re-

gretted it, until her cockiness resulted in the death of someone who trusted her. "I will never forgive myself," Nat said
and, not knowing what else to say, Catherine had kept quiet and simply continued to hold her. Finally, Nat fell back
asleep.

What am I going to do with her? Catherine wondered
as she looked at Nat's face, which was finally relaxing as the
tears dried on her cheeks. Even while the woman spoke of the
accident, it was evident her devotion to the Space Rangers
was strong. Catherine was no fool and sensed it was this loyalty which was what had Nat so undecided about their relationship. The woman was torn, and Catherine hated putting
her through the torture. "I won't make you choose," Catherine whispered and realized she meant it. As much as it made
her hurt all over to think of a future without Nat, Catherine
resolved to never stand in her way. When they landed tomorrow, Catherine was determined to stay strong when the
goodbyes came, knowing she could weep as her heart broke
later. Tears slipped down her cheek as she thought of it, and
Nat, as if sensing Catherine's pain, opened her eyes.

"Hey," she said. Catherine gave her a weak smile.

"Hey back," she said and lowered down to kiss Nat's lips.
Although the touch set off a hint of passion within her,
Catherine pushed it away, wanting only to convey the tenderness she felt. In a way, it was a kiss goodbye already. Nat
pulled herself up to a sitting position and took Catherine's
face in her hands.

"Are you crying?" she asked. Catherine shook her head.

"No," she lied. Nat looked only half convinced but leaned
in to rest her forehead against Catherine's.

"Thank you," Nat whispered.

"For what?" Catherine asked softly.

"Holding me while I cried," she answered. "No one has ever done that. You, and only you." Catherine had to blink away more tears. She swallowed hard. There were no easy words to say and only a tap at the bedroom door saved her from having to confess the decision which was in her heart. Nat frowned and looked toward the sound. "Come in," Nat said. Frederick poked in his shiny, metal head.

"So sorry to wake you, Captain," he said. "But we've received a mayday call from a stalled ship." Suddenly Nat was all business.

"Are we the closest vessel?" she asked.

"Seems we are," he replied. Nat looked at Catherine.

"I'm sorry, but spacetime law requires us to respond and at least do a fly-by." Catherine nodded realizing this was the perfect example of how important duty was to Nat.

"Of course," Catherine said and could see Nat search her face, clearly sensing something was not quite right.

"Are we okay?" she asked. Catherine nodded and Nat hesitated as if knowing Catherine was not being honest.

"Really. Just go," Catherine said. Nat nodded.

"Okay. This won't take long. Then we can talk," Nat said. Catherine nodded again and watched as she climbed out of the bed.

CATHERINE COULD SIT in the spare seat at the edge of the cockpit and watch Nat pilot the ship all day. With the controls in her strong, capable hands, she exuded confidence. Catherine found it incredibly sexy and she wondered just how long it would take to respond to the distress call and how hard it would be to lure Nat back to the bedroom. The thought made her blush. She was feeling so bold now that their time was quickly growing shorter. If they only had a day and a night, Catherine wanted to relish every moment. Having Nat touch her so magically again would help lessen the sadness in her heart, at least for a little while. Glancing over, Nat caught Catherine thinking of just how she would talk Nat into doing things. Apparently, hints of passion were on her face, because Nat raised her eyebrows with surprise. Catherine giggled and put her hands to her hot cheeks. "What are you thinking?" Nat asked with a sly smile. Taking a deep breath, Catherine decided to be bold as hell. If she did not get Nat much longer, there was no time to play games.

"I'm thinking I hope we can take a shower soon," she said and bit her lip as she waited for Nat's response. A moment of doubt suddenly made her stomach ache. *What if I have this all wrong and she isn't interested anymore?* Catherine thought. She knew in a moment there was no need to worry. Hunger jumped straight to Nat's eyes and she grinned.

"I promise to make this quick," she said with a husky voice. "In fact, I have a visual on the stalled craft now." Catherine glanced out the window and saw an older spaceship. It was not as bad as her ED-90, but it was close. "No wonder they broke down," Nat said. "That NT line of ships is notorious for trouble." Catherine saw Nat press the comm link. "This is the Avalon Mercury to the NT-397. Do you copy?" There was no response. Nat turned to a different channel and tried again. Still, no answer and Nat pulled them closer. Frederick came to the door of the cockpit.

"Perhaps we can establish a visual?" he suggested. Nat nodded.

"I'm bringing us around now," she answered. As she did, Catherine saw a flicker of movement out the windshield. It was off to the left, and she leaned forward to look.

"Nat, what's that? Another ship responding?" she asked. Nat looked and then Catherine saw her face pale. "What? What's wrong?" Catherine asked, looking again. Whatever the ship was, it was moving at them fast. Immediately, Nat jerked on the controls and Catherine, with Frederick beside her, was almost knocked to the floor.

"Hang on," Nat said. "That is a space pirate ship coming and the distress call was sent to lure us in." Catherine felt panic climb up her spine. Everyone knew there was a slight risk of pirates along these routes, but it seemed so impossible to be happening now after Nat's dream.

Like it is fate, she thought. "Can you outrun them?" Catherine asked. Nat nodded.

"I think so. We got a good jump thanks to your quick eyes," she responded. "I just need to—" Her words cut off and Catherine turned to look out the windshield again. What she saw made her heart nearly stop. Two more small fighter pirate crafts were descending. The Avalon Mercury was caught between them and the larger one coming. "Frederick, what evasion maneuvers are built into this ship?" Nat asked quietly. Frederick looked frazzled, and Nat had to snap her fingers to get his attention. "Frederick!"

"I'm sorry, Captain, but the Avalon Mercury 3370 is not equipped with any defensive mechanism," he said. "It is built for luxury and speed, not battle." Catherine saw Nat grit her teeth.

"Catherine, I want you to hide," Nat said. "Depending on how many there are—" Catherine shook her head.

"No, I will not. We face this together," she said. Nat turned to her, clearly ready to argue when the comm link squawked.

"Hello there, Avalon Mercury. To whom do I have the pleasure of speaking with today?" said a man's voice. Nat turned to the comm link and prepared to press the button when Frederick held out a hand.

"Captain, wait!" he said. "Do not identify yourself as a Space Ranger to them." Nat looked at him and Catherine could see she was conflicted. Suddenly, Catherine knew their horrible situation just got worse.

"They kill Space Rangers, don't they?" she said almost choking on the words.

"Unless we kill them first," Nat answered boldly. "And I won't hide from these bastards." She pressed the comm link to respond. Before Nat could say a word, Catherine threw herself across the cockpit console and put her mouth to the comm link. There was no way she would let Nat sacrifice herself.

"This is Catherine Porter," she said trying to sound confident and perturbed instead of scared half to death. "Who is this? And what do you want?"

There was a pause and then a chuckle. "Well, now, aren't you a sassy one, Ms. Porter," replied the voice. "But since you asked, you can call me Rog. Now, I don't suppose you're the owner of that fine vessel?" Catherine's mind raced and she felt Nat's hand on her arm, trying to pull her back. She had no doubt the woman wanted Catherine to stop so she could throw herself on her sword to somehow save them. *Screw that*, Catherine thought and racked her brain for an idea. She knew little about space pirates other than they captured ships and held passengers for ransom. *Maybe that is all they want now?* Taking a deep breath, Catherine went for it. "No," she said. "Actually, my dad owns it. Senator Porter? Ring a bell?"

"What are you doing?" Catherine suddenly heard Nat whisper into her ear. "And who is Senator Porter?" Catherine waved her away.

"I know what I'm doing," she whispered back. *Or at least I hope so*, she thought. There really was a Senator Porter on Prospo. She was teased about it in high school, but she had no idea if he had a daughter or, if he did, how long it would take the pirates to figure out she was not the same girl. Finally, the comm link clicked again.

"Seems this is my lucky day then," Rog, the pirate said. "Who else you got on there with you?" Catherine turned to look at Nat before answering. She did not look happy about the turn of events, yet there was respect in her eyes as well. Seeing it, Catherine actually smiled a little, which seemed crazy under the circumstances, but maybe this was a chance to show Nat there was more to her than only a naïve eighteen-year-old.

"There is the ship's droid," she answered and held Nat's eyes. "And I have my bodyguard with me."

"I see," Rog said. "Is he going to be a problem? This body-guard?" Catherine raised an eyebrow at Nat and waited. After a moment, Nat shook her head. Catherine did not believe it for a second, knowing the warrior in Nat would try to have them escape the instant there was an opportunity, but hopefully, the ruse would buy them some time.

"She will not be a problem. So, what happens next?" Catherine snapped impatiently. There was another chuckle over the comm link.

"I can tell I'm going to like you, Catherine Porter," Rog said. "And what happens next is I will be sending over a couple folks in a shuttle. They'll say howdy and take over your ship, while you come visit me. How's that sound?" Catherine felt the panic in her start to flare up, but she took a deep breath and steadied her nerves. *In for a dime, in for a dollar*, she thought. It was another of her father's favorite sayings and Catherine knew this was no time to be timid now.

"Sounds repulsive, frankly," Catherine replied. "But I'll have Frederick our butler throw together a pitcher of margaritas. We can make it a party." This time a roar of laughter came over the link.

"Prepare to be boarded, Ms. Porter," Rog said. "And don't think about trying anything tricky. As charming as you are, I will not hesitate to blow your ship to pieces." The comm link clicked off and Catherine hoped she had not just made the mistake of her life.

CHAPTER 17
NAT

Nat had never been so impressed by someone's quick thinking and guts than she was with Catherine. The girl shocked the hell out of her when she jumped on the comm link and started spinning a tale of being a senator's daughter. *And she did it all to protect me*, Nat thought. She considered what would have happened if Catherine had not stopped her from telling the pirates she was a Space Ranger and the image was not a pretty picture. There were rumors within the corps about Rangers who were captured by pirates and torture was putting it mildly. The fact Nat was a female no doubt would have made it worse. Now she just had to find a way for them to escape before the truth came out. *And I will find a way. To save Catherine even if I can't save myself.* Nat knew she would do anything to keep the woman from harm.

"Well, that was quite creative, Ms. Porter," Frederick said. "Am I truly making a pitcher of margaritas?"

"I'd rather you find us the biggest knives in the galley, Frederick," Nat answered before Catherine could. Catherine shook her head and put her hands on Nat's arms to look in her face.

"No," she said. "Promise me no violence unless there is no choice. Maybe we can talk our way out of this." Nat paused as she considered the beautiful young woman's face and then sighed. It was not her nature to be passive and being taken captive went against her training, but the pleading look in Catherine's eyes made her nod in agreement.

"I will be patient," Nat said as she put her arms around Catherine. "But if it looks like anyone is going to hurt you, then all bets are off."

"I know," Catherine said and leaned in to kiss Nat on the lips. Nat expected it to be tender and soft, but instead, there was a possessiveness behind it. A passion and Nat pulled her closer, realizing there was a tiger inside Catherine Nat never expected. Nat pressed her mouth harder to Catherine's, suddenly hungry for her in the midst of all the uncertainty. With a gasp, Catherine pulled back. "I'll never let them hurt you, Nat," she said. "Never." Nat was about to explain Catherine needed to focus on saving herself when the sound of the pirate shuttle attaching to the airlock brought harsh reality back to the moment. "Okay," Catherine said. "Showtime everyone."

"Stay behind me," Nat insisted but Catherine shook her head.

"No, I want them to know we are not intimidated. I'm a spoiled senator's daughter, and you work for me. Remember that," she said. "Now, let's go meet them at the door." Again, Nat was a little shocked at the power behind Catherine's words. She meant business and Nat decided to let her run with it. *For now*, she thought. As they approached the exit door, there were more noises at the airlock and then a click. A light over the door turned green and then it slid open to reveal two pirates. One was a burly man with a severely pockmarked face. The other was a woman. Her black hair was cut almost razor short and her dark almond-shaped eyes were cold as ice. Of the two, she appeared to be by far the most dangerous. Nat looked them over from head to toe in an instant. Precisely like others she saw and battled in the past. An absurd mixture of modern armored space uniforms and leather pirate garb modeled after ancient pictures. *Those plasma guns they are carrying aren't ancient though.* The pair were armed to the teeth with knives and short swords as well. Already Nat was trying to figure out how she could disarm one of them and then remembered the threat over the comm link. Any trouble and the Avalon Mercury would be destroyed. Nat took a deep breath to try and relax. *Patience,* she told herself.

"Which one of you is Catherine Porter?" the male pirate asked. Nat saw Catherine toss her head.

"Which one of you is Rog?" she snapped back. The female pirate frowned.

"We will ask the questions," she said. "But I'll guess you are the senator's daughter."

"You guessed right," Catherine said not backing down. "But I'm going to make a leap here and say you are definitely not Rog." Nat saw a hint of color rise to the female pirate's cheeks. *Easy Catherine,* Nat thought. The other pirate barked out a laugh.

"No, she's not Rog and neither am I," he said. "But he's going to just love you, missy. Always enjoys the feisty ones." He waved a hand at his partner. "This here wench with the nasty attitude is Sal, and I'm Gruden."

"Shut up, Gruden," Sal growled. "They don't need to know any of this. Just cuff their hands so we can put them on the shuttle and get this circus over." She leveled a gun at Catherine and Nat clenched her fists, ready to react. No doubt sensing it, Catherine raised a hand to calm things.

"So, this means no margaritas then?" she asked with a sly smile. If Catherine was feeling any fear, Nat could not tell it. She hoped it was the same for the pirates. "Made with top-shelf tequila, I promise." Nat saw Gruden lick his lips and glance at Sal.

"Well, I don't know," he started but Sal shook her head and stepped up to point her gun at Catherine's face. Nat could not let it go and yanked Catherine behind her in an instant to stand face to face with the other woman. They were almost exactly the same height and weight.

"Point that gun someplace else," Nat snarled. Sal narrowed her eyes, not flinching.

"Or what?" Sal asked.

"Ye-haw, now this is fun!" Gruden said with glee. "A regular catfight." He looked at Catherine. "That's some bodyguard you got there. Sure she's not something else." He cackled. Much to Nat's displeasure, Catherine stepped out from behind her and put her hands on her hips.

"Let's just say she guards my whole body," she said. "Now how about we stop with all the bullshit and get down to business. I can't imagine Rog wants you to shoot me before we get a chance to say hello." Gruden clearly loved every minute of it, and Nat did not care for the gleam of lust growing in his eyes.

"Ease off, Sal," he said with a chuckle. "The pretty one's right. Rog would be pissed if you messed her up before he saw her." Regardless of Gruden's words, the tension in the air was still there. Nat continued to stare Sal down and finally the woman let her eye's skim Nat's face before ending with a smirk. "I would swear I smell the stink of a Space Ranger coming off of you but maybe not. The bodyguard, huh?" Sal said. "With benefits. How nice for you." Nat grit her teeth, but let the taunt go. She would not take the bait. Sal stepped aside and waved Gruden forward. "I still want them restrained." Gruden grunted and pulled out a couple pairs of handcuffs.

"You always were a kinky one, Sal," he said.

"Fuck off," Sal said with a glare at Gruden. "Just lock them up." Gruden laughed again but did as he was told. He started with Nat.

"Put your wrists out," he ordered. Nat hesitated. "Don't be stupid," Gruden snarled. "Sal will happily kill you and take your little pet. I can see it in her eyes." Nat knew he was telling the truth. The pirate was trouble on a lot of levels, but Nat knew she would die before she let her lay a hand on Catherine. *But now is not the time to make a move*, Nat thought and reluctantly put out her hands. Once he was done with her, the ugly pirate moved to put the cuffs on Catherine. As he approached, she obliged by putting out her wrists.

"Not sure I see the point of this," she said. "What are you expecting me to do? Use my kung-fu moves and save the day?" Gruden chuckled.

"I sure do like you, Catherine Porter," he said. "Too bad I'm so far down on the totem pole I won't even qualify for sloppy-seconds. Or thirds even." Nat saw Catherine's face pale a bit at the ugly threat and she wanted to kill the man right then and there. It was all she could do to keep from leaping at him. Out of the corner of her eye, she saw from Sal's expression she was not a big fan of Gruden's talk either and made a mental note to figure out a way to use the animosity there to her advantage. For now though, her only focus was on getting Gruden away from Catherine, especially when she watched him lick his lips as he ran his eyes over Catherine's body. "Damn, you are sweet though. I can see why both these women have hard-ons for ya," he said as he reached up and traced his dirty finger along Catherine's jawline. He licked his lips again and with a smirk, began to move his finger lower and along her neck. Nate knew where he was headed and started to lunge, but before she could jump, Sal moved like a flash of light, pulling her knife and putting it to the side of Gruden's neck. Nat blinked. She had never seen anyone so quick.

"Move that finger one more inch and I'll cut it off. Among other things," Sal threatened. Gruden was frozen. Nat saw him swallow hard, but then he grinned as he pulled his hand back.

"Well now," he said. "How would you explain all that to Rog?"

"I'd blame it on the droid," she replied without missing a beat. At this Gruden roared out a laugh and turned around.

"You're a piece of work, Sal," he said. "And I hope for your sake, Rog does give you this piece of ass. You've earned it." Nat watched as Sal shrugged and returned her weapon to its sheath at her waist.

"We'll just have to wait and see," she said with a glance at Nat. Their eyes met and Nat could read the hostility in the other woman's face. Nat returned the look with a glare of her own. Even with her hands shackled, Nat would happily step up and fight the pirate at any opportunity. *Especially where Catherine is concerned*, she thought. As if reading her mind, Sal smirked and then turned back to Gruden. "Help me lock them into the shuttle and then we can search the ship to make sure they aren't lying to us about other passengers," she said.

"Oh, I'm guessing it's just them. All romantic and shit," Gruden said and moved to grab Catherine by the arm, but she pulled away from him.

"I can walk on my own," Catherine snapped. "Besides, I think we've established the boundaries around you touching me." Gruden looked at her with surprise and then started laughing so hard he bent over and put his hands on his knees. Seeing the pirate vulnerable, Nat contemplated kicking him in the face. *If I can take him out, get his gun, maybe I can draw down on Sal*, she thought but then remembered just how fast the other woman had moved. *Lightning fast.* Nat knew she would only have one shot if she decided to act. *Do I dare put Catherine's life at risk on such long odds?* Nat knew she could not so she would wait until the moment was right. Then she would kill them, all of them, but especially the woman named Sal.

CHAPTER 18
CATHERINE

Catherine's entire body shook from the adrenaline still coursing through her. The confrontation with the pirates, particularly the leering Gruden, had shaken her badly. Once she and Nat were finally locked alone in the shuttle, Catherine lowered her head to Nat's lap and tried not to cry. Nat ran her bound hands up and down Catherine's back to comfort her. The woman's warm touch helped and Catherine let out a breath she had not realized she was holding. She was so thankful they were both all right. *At least for now,* she thought. There was no way to know what the future would hold as the shuttle lurched to life and disengaged from the Avalon Mercury. Catherine lifted her head. "How is it moving?" she asked.

"Remote control," Nat explained. "To keep anyone from trying to drive off with it." Catherine nodded.

"Someone like you," she asked Nat with a grim smile. "Nat, what are we going to do? I've never been so scared in my life." Taking Catherine's hands in her own, Nat gave a little laugh and shook her head in amazement.

"No one would know it, Catherine," she said. "You were amazing. So smart and incredibly brave. I've never seen anything like it. Where did that come from?" To be honest, Catherine was not sure how she pulled it off. Seeing Nat in trouble and knowing what would happen if the pirates knew the truth seemed to kick her survival instinct into overdrive. She had acted far braver than she felt.

"I have no idea," she answered. "I just knew I had to do something to stall for time. How long do you think we have?"

"I can't be sure," Nat replied. "It depends on how hard it is to corroborate your story. Please tell me there is a Senator Porter."

"There is, but I don't know if he has a daughter," she said. Catherine squeezed Nat's hands and racked her brain for an idea of how they could escape. It would not be easy, and she knew it. If Catherine had to guess, she had a feeling getting away from the pirate Sal would be the hardest. The woman looked ruthless and had moved so quick when protecting Catherine, it was frightening. *And she did protect me,* Catherine thought. There was no doubt about it in her mind, yet she was not sure what it meant. *Was Gruden right? Was it attraction?* The woman was masculine, but Catherine knew being tough did not always translate to being lesbian. Still, Gruden's lewd comments made her think Sal liked girls. Catherine closed her eyes and tried not to imagine what would happen if Sal made a real move on her. Nat would go crazy over it. As much as Catherine loved how safe Nat made her feel, it worried her too. *Would Nat die for me?* Somehow Catherine knew she would out of honor if not something more.

And what about me? Would I die for her? The thought gave her pause. It seemed impossible to care about anyone with so much passion so quickly and yet, Catherine did. Nat was all she wanted. *Yes, I will die for her if it comes to it. Besides caring for her, all of this is my fault and I won't have her suffer because of it.* Knowing she needed to tell Nat, she reached up and touched the woman's face. "Nat, I need you to listen to me," she said. "No matter what happens with that woman Sal, you have to let me handle it." Nat shook her head.

"You don't realize just how dangerous someone like her is," Nat started. Catherine put a finger to Nat's lips to stop her from going on.

"I need you to promise," Catherine said. "I'm not as naive as you think. I just proved that a little, didn't I?" Nat was quiet and Catherine could see so much tenderness and concern in Nat's eyes it touched her heart. "Promise me," Catherine said again. "And then kiss me and make me brave." Nat paused, her eyes studying Catherine's face, but finally, she leaned forward into Catherine. Their lips met and Catherine felt it all through her. There was no way to know when they would have a chance to embrace again and so Catherine relished every moment of their lips together. The heat behind it made Catherine's stomach tighten. Nat pulled back and looked hard into Catherine's eyes.

"I can't promise, but I will try," Nat said. "But you belong to me and I intend to make sure that bitch knows it." Touched by the force behind the words, Catherine never felt more wanted and she was about to tell Nat she loved belonging to her when the sound of the shuttle docking stopped her. Catherine scooted even closer to Nat and they turned to watch the exit. After a minute, it slid open and a different pirate, this one skinny as a rail and missing his front teeth, stuck his head through the doorway.

"You're going to cooperate, right?" he asked. "Not make me come in there and drag you out?" Catherine shook her head and stood up. Her knees threatened to shake and betray her, but she checked it and put back on her haughty exterior.

"I'd rather you did not. We are here to see Rog," Catherine said trying to sound as self-righteous as possible. The pirate raised his eyebrows, clearly not sure what to make of the girl's confident attitude.

"Well, that is the plan," he said. "The boss is really eager to meet you actually. Now I'm starting to see why. Let's go." The skinny pirate stepped back and Catherine walked out of the shuttle with Nat behind her. Another pirate, this one an alien of a planet Catherine did not recognize, waited for them in the hall. He had his plasma rifle at the ready and he was dressed in a variation of the same uniform as the others, but his alligator-like snout and beady yellow eyes set in scaly skin made him extra intimidating. Catherine tried not to flinch. "Lead on, Chuck," the skinny pirate said to the gator alien and the beast grunted and started to walk away down the corridor.

As they went through part of the ship in route to see Rog, Catherine took in as much as she could. Out of the corner of her eye, she could see Nat was doing the same. *And probably far better at it than I am,* she thought. A lot of what she saw was lost on her when it came to the electronics and machinery they passed. One thing she did know though was the ship was filthy. The paneled floor looked like it might have been a beige color once, but now it was dingy gray with a black stripe of scuff marks down the middle. The walls looked oily and when they went through a narrow hallway, Catherine was careful not to touch anything. Worst though was the smell. A stale hint of garbage rotting seemed to permeate the air wherever they walked. It made her wonder if the spaceship ever docked anywhere to let it be cleaned. *Do they just fly around in space all the time? Never landing?* she wondered and thought perhaps it was why they were so hard to catch.

Finally, the reached a set of double doors. These looked more polished than any of the others on the craft and when Chuck stopped at them, Catherine knew they must have arrived and now it was time to meet the one called Rog. The skinny pirate who had trailed behind them stepped up to the door's intercom and pushed the button. "It's us, boss," he said. "I've got that girl for you. Plus her bodyguard."

"Bring them in," Rog said. As she entered, Catherine did not know what to think. The man she assumed was Rog sat on a raised platform in a chair a few sizes too large for him. Although he was not standing, from the length of his legs, Catherine guess he was no more than three feet tall. His most prominent feature was his head, which was out of proportion to the rest of him, and he wore a black beard so long it ran down onto his chest. When he saw the group coming, he hopped out of the chair and came to stand at the edge of the platform. Catherine could see him appraising her. Apparently liking what he saw, he smiled and then looked at Nat. After only a moment, his smile faded. "Hold it," he said and looked at the skinny pirate. "You checked this one for weapons? She looks ready to slit my throat." Chuck and the skinny pirate looked at each other and then shrugged.

"I figured Sal or Gruden did it," the skinny pirate said. Rog frowned.

"Check again, just in case. She looks like trouble," he said. Catherine did not like the sound of his tone and knew she needed to get the focus off of Nat.

"What? You don't think I'm trouble then?" she asked. "And for the record, we don't have weapons." Rog looked at her, studied her face and body and then his smile came back. It was remarkably charismatic.

"You must be Ms. Porter, the senator's daughter," he said. "I'm Rog, the Pirate King." Catherine raised an eyebrow at his boast. There were always legends of a pirate king in the galaxy and it was even something parents told their children to get them to behave. *Or the pirate king will come and steal you away*, Catherine remembered. She never expected to be facing one. Before she could comment, she heard Nat mumble something under her breath. Apparently, Rog heard part of it too. "What did you just say?" he asked. Catherine felt a chill of unease. Nat had promised not to attack the woman Sal, but Catherine had not thought about what Nat might do when faced with the leader of the space pirates.

"Nat—" Catherine started but Nat raised her chin.

"I said you have got to be kidding me," she said. Catherine saw Chuck react and start to raise the butt of his rifle to strike Nat. Catherine threw herself in front of her.

"No," she said. "If you want me to cooperate with getting ransom from my father, then you will not hurt either of us." Chuck stopped and glanced up at Rog. Catherine followed his look. Rog's face was thoughtful and he stroked his beard. After a moment, he waved Chuck back.

"So," Rog started. "Nat is it?" Nat did not respond, the defiance in her face so evident it scared Catherine. After a pause, Rog frowned. "Is it because I'm a dwarf?" he asked. "You think I'm too small to be a pirate king?" Still Nat held her tongue. Rog nodded. "Probably smart you didn't answer that actually." He turned back to Catherine. "Are you going to keep you watchdog under control or do I need to take care of this?" Catherine looked at Nat's face and saw the deep hatred the woman felt toward the pirates. *Can I keep her safe?* she wondered. Their eyes held for a moment and Catherine saw a hint of sadness creep into Nat's look. Seeing it hurt Catherine's heart. All of Nat's life was about being the best Space Ranger she could be and trying to rid the world of pirates, and now Catherine was asking her to set all that history aside and cooperate with her sworn enemy. *But they will kill her otherwise.* There was no way she would let that happen. Finally, Catherine looked back at Rog and nodded.

"She will behave," she said. "I give you my promise."

CHAPTER 19
NAT

Nat took a deep breath and let it out slowly. She knew she needed to relax or the guy Rog would never believe Catherine's promise. *I need to play along with this. For both our sakes*, she thought. *And wait for the right time to strike.* In her heart, Nat knew she would not rest until she killed the pirate king, but for now, she gave the man a nod of agreement. As he continued to study her and stroke his long beard, she knew his decision could go either way. There was a long pause where everyone in the room waited silently and then the dwarf smiled to break the tension. "Okay, Catherine. I'll take your word," he said. "But don't think I won't have my eye on your bodyguard. I'm on the last leg of a longass journey, and I won't let anyone screw it up." Nat saw Catherine smile at the pirate in return.

"Well, you could always just let us go," she said.

Rog chuckled. "Don't you wish," he said. "But honestly, your luck is lousy. I mean, if you and your lovely little spaceship had not come along right when it did, I would not have bothered." Nat frowned. *What is he talking about?* she wondered. Catherine apparently was curious too.

"How so?" she asked. Before Rog could answer, the door to the room opened and in walked Sal, one of the pirates who boarded their ship.

"Sal!" Rog said and Nat did not miss how happy the pirate king was to see her. *A favorite*, she thought. Especially interesting because Sal's expression did not appear to be as excited to see him. "Did you secure their ship with the others?"

"Of course," she answered and Nat watched as her eyes skimmed over first her and then Catherine. "I searched it first, to make sure everything these two were telling us was true." At this news, Nat stiffened. It would not take much to figure out the spaceship did not belong to any senator. Sal met Nat's eyes and glared.

"And?" Rog prompted.

There was a pause and Nat prepared herself mentally for a fight. Her first move would be to attack Chuck and take his rifle. It would be difficult with her hands still bound in front of her, but there was no better option. Nat shifted her weight to be ready. Finally, Sal glanced at Catherine and smiled a little before turning back to Rog. She shrugged. "Out for a romantic cruise," Sal answered. "On daddy's luxury ship. Just like the girl said." Nat saw Catherine let out a breath of relief and unclenched her own hands. *Safe for now*, she thought and was relieved to learn Sal was less of a threat than she thought. Obviously, the woman was lazy or stupid if she could not find proof the Avalon Mercury was registered to a doctor, not a politician.

"Perfect," Rog said. "I'd have been pissed to learn there would be no payoff from this. When the time comes, I plan to make that senator pay a shitload of ransom for his pretty little girl." Chuck and the skinny pirate beside him laughed. Rog grinned and then went back to his original subject. "So, Sal," he said. "We were just discussing how unlucky Catherine and her watchdog are." Sal nodded.

"True," she said again fixing a stare at Nat. "If they were not so law-abiding and skipped checking on the disabled ship, they would still be free. Whose idea was it to respond?" Before Nat could answer, Catherine tossed her head and took a defiant stance.

"Mine," she answered. "Can you imagine the media frenzy if it got out a senator's daughter ignored a mayday?" Sal shifted her look to Catherine and narrowed her eyes.

"She has a good point," Rog added.

"I suppose," Sal said. "Still, like you said, bad timing. In a day we will be out of this airspace altogether and home." Nat froze at those words and worked to keep her face relaxed. *Is she implying this ship is about to land at the pirate's base?* she thought. The knowledge made her mind race. Suddenly, escaping from the pirate ship was not necessarily her primary objective. As much as Catherine's safety mattered to her, the idea the ship was headed to the pirate's hidden camp changed everything. The Space Ranger Corps, Nat included, had searched for years to find the pirate's base. With so many uncharted planets and moons in the multiple galaxies, trying to locate their stronghold had proven impossible so far. There was also the rumor the space pirates had acquired advanced cloaking sciences, which not only allowed their large galleon spacecraft to roam undetected so easily but was thought to be helping keep their home location secret. Nat's last ten years had been spent as a Ranger searching for the exact location of the pirate king's hideaway. It was on just such a recon mission when she chased the pirate craft into the canyon and was ambushed. Nat realized she could avenge her co-pilot's death by leading the Space Rangers to the camp. If Nat could go there and somehow send out a signal, it would be a game changer in the war against the space pirates.

"Wait a minute," Catherine said interrupting Nat's racing thoughts and sounding a bit alarmed. "Where are you going? I thought you were putting us up for ransom." Rog shook his head.

"Relax. All in due time," he said. "You'll have to be my guests for a little while. Then I'll decide what to do with you." Nat saw Catherine pale as the reality of how bad their situation was becoming set in. Catherine was smart enough to realize the chances of stealing a transport off of the pirate's ship were much better than trying to escape from a planet. Catherine shook her head and tried to regain her arrogant demeanor, but she was clearly upset.

"I will not agree to that," she said with a waiver in her voice. Rog chuckled.

"What? You don't want to see where I live?" he said. "We've been out raiding the galaxies for over four years, and at last I get to go home with my holds full of plunder. Forgive me for inconveniencing you in the process." Rog shrugged. "Besides, you might find you like it and decide to stay. There are a lot of benefits to being a pirate. Just ask Sal." The pirate king looked at the woman. "She joined our little party about a month after we started out. Best thing you ever did, right?" Nat saw Sal clench her jaw, but she nodded without comment. Rog laughed at her look and waved it off. "Don't mind her, she's a little bitchy about it. When we first captured her, she was a slave on the ship. Took her a good year to make her way over to the dark side." Nat heard Chuck and the skinny pirate chuckle at the comment. She checked Sal's face for her response and could tell the woman saw her watching. After a pause, Sal snorted a laugh and went along with the banter.

"Best decision I ever made," she said and turned to look at Nat for a moment before letting her eyes drift over to Catherine. "Especially considering the fun I get to have with some of our captives." Nat saw Sal give Catherine a wink and was happy to see Catherine shake her head with a hint of disgust. "Oh, come on now," Sal said and Nat watched her walk closer to Catherine. She stopped within inches of the woman and leaned in almost as if she was going to kiss her.

"Would it really be so bad?" Sal murmured and then glanced at Nat as if daring her to react. Nat hated the sight of the pirate being so close to Catherine, but she held herself in check. She knew the taunting was only meant to give Sal a reason to hurt or even kill Nat. Instead of making a move, Nat grit her teeth and glared at the other woman. No doubt seeing the animosity between Nat and Sal, Rog laughed hard and clapped his hands.

"Oh, this is absolutely perfect," he said with a grin. "A little love triangle. Here on my pirate ship of all places."

"Maybe we can have us a girl fight," the skinny pirate called out and Rog's smile grew bigger.

"Maybe," he said. "It would be a good one too, I imagine. This supposed bodyguard looks like she could kick some ass." Nat saw Sal frown and turn back to give Rog a dirty look. Rog held up a hand. "No offense to you, Sal. We all know you're the supreme badass on this ship." Rog nodded to Nat and Catherine. "I mean that too. Sal here has more individual kills than any of my men. A regular Space Ranger murdering machine." Nat felt her fury rise at the information and her whole body quivered as the hate built up inside her. She saw Catherine shift as if sending a signal for Nat to stay calm. Their hands were still bound and everyone else in the room was armed. Puffing out a frustrated breath, Nat twisted her neck side to side to work out the anger. Rog noticed and lifted his chin. "You got a problem with that?" he asked her. Nat knew now was the time to lie or they would kill her and no doubt give Catherine to Sal. She decided to follow Catherine's lead and run with it.

"Hell no," she said. "I'm no fan of Rangers. I was just thinking how much fun it would be to fight your friend so I could kick her ugly pirate ass." Nat loved seeing Sal narrow her eyes at the threat. *Bring it on*, Nat thought and set her feet.

"Oh my God," Catherine interrupted. "What is with all this? I am not a piece of meat!" Rog pounded the arms of his chair with amusement.

"This is classic!" he said laughing. "But she's right. How rude of us." He bowed his head to Catherine. "You are most definitely not a piece of meat. You are in fact quite lovely, hence the problem. What do I do with you?" Nat felt a sense of unease at the offhanded way Rog spoke about what to do with Catherine.

"I would suggest you think twice about what you do to a senator's daughter," Nat snarled. Rog raised an eyebrow at the comment.

"Or what?" Rog asked. "It's not like the senator can send anyone after me. The sorry bunch of clowns who call themselves the Space Rangers can't find my ships. They have never even seen my home." He hopped out of the chair and started to walk down the steps from the platform until he was in front of Nat. "I'm untouchable," he explained. "So, if I want to give your little girlfriend to a gang of my pirates, there is not anyone who will stop me." He paused and smirked at Nat as if daring her to say otherwise. Nat said nothing but instead poured all the hate in her being into the look she gave back to him. Rog stroked his beard for a second, but then looked over at Catherine. "You're sure you can keep this one on a leash?" he asked. "I do believe she wants to eat my liver." Out of the corner of her eye, Nat saw Catherine nod. After a minute, Rog shrugged. "All right then," he said and waved at Chuck. "Enough fun and games for today. I have a ship to run and it's time we got home. Chuck, walk these women to one of the cells." Sal stepped forward.

"I'll do it," she said. Rog raised an eyebrow.

"Can I trust you to keep your hands off until I figure out what I'm doing with them?" Rog asked. Sal glanced suggestively at Catherine but then nodded.

"I'll try," she said and pulled her plasma gun. She waived it at Nat in particular. "Let's go."

CHAPTER 20
CATHERINE

The walk down the long, dirty hallways to the cell block was uncomfortable. With Nat leading through each twist and turn, following Sal's barked instructions, Catherine was in the middle and the pirate was at her back with the gun. Catherine could feel Sal's dark-eyed stare boring into her and checking her out. The woman's interest was the last thing Catherine wanted. Not only did it make her nervous, but she knew it exasperated the already tense situation between Sal and Nat. Unfortunately, Catherine did not know what to do about it except for ignore Sal whenever she could.

When they arrived at a dark corridor filled with closed metal doors, Sal told them to stop and the woman walked past as she considered the different options. "Which rooms to put you in ..." she said under her breath and Catherine realized it was entirely possible she and Nat would be locked up separately. The idea of it horrified her. Knowing Nat was beside her and being able to see she was safe were the only two things keeping Catherine from losing her nerve altogether. *Do I try the senator's daughter bit again and insist we share a cell?* Catherine wondered. *Or will that make it even more un-*

likely? She bit her lip unable to decide as she waited. Finally, the pirate stopped at a door and turned back to Catherine and Nat. She looked thoughtful as if she truly could not
decide what to do with them. After a long pause, Sal took a
card out of her pocket and swiped it across a panel to open
the door. "You owe me a favor, Catherine Porter," Sal said
with a gleam in her eye. "Considering you look like you're
ready to puke, I'll be nice and keep you together. But don't
expect more special favors in the future. At least not if you
don't plan to return them." Sal smirked in Catherine's direction and she heard Nat suck in an angry breath beside her. Sal
laughed at it as she waved them toward the doorway. "I am
really enjoying pushing your buttons," she said to Nat as the
woman walked by. Nat glared at Sal as she passed.

"You're not bothering me a bit," Nat growled as she entered the room. Sal tilted her head with a grin and then as
Catherine started to pass by her, she reached out and combed
a stray hair away from Catherine's ear. It was a sensual touch
and Catherine flinched away from it.

"Please don't touch me," Catherine whispered. She heard
Sal chuckle.

"We'll see," she answered and took out an electronic key
to unlock Catherine's handcuffs. Once she was done, Catherine rubbed her wrists and Sal stepped over to Nat. They stood
face-to-face and Catherine saw they could not look more
alike while at the same time so different. Where Nat was
fair-haired and clean-cut, Sal was dark and sinister yet they
were both tall, confident women. *Who seem to want me*, she
thought and shifted uncomfortably while she waited to see
what was going to happen. Finally, Sal laughed. "Just a badass

bodyguard? Well, I suggest you be smart about this," Sal said. "I'm going to unlock you and if you take a swing at me, I'll kill you. You think you're big and strong, but I'm faster. I promise you." Catherine watched Nat consider her words. After a pause, she gave a curt nod and Sal slowly unlocked the cuffs. As soon as she was done, Sal carefully stepped back out of arm's reach and Catherine realized that for all the pirate's bravado, she respected Nat as being a dangerous adversary. Nat seemed to notice it too because now it was her turn to smirk as she rubbed her wrists. "Just a badass pirate?" Nat said in a mocking tone. "But at first a slave. That couldn't have been fun." Sal shrugged as if what Nat said did not matter and walked to stand near the exit door.

"Sometimes you do what you have to do to survive. You'll learn that soon enough," Sal said as she turned to go, but then she stopped and looked back over her shoulder. "And for the record, I don't believe for one second you two are who you say you are. There was nothing on that ship which said it belonged to a senator." Catherine's heart started pounding as she heard the words. *If she knows, what is she going to do with us?* she wondered. *And why didn't she tell Rog earlier?*

"It's a new ship," Nat lied. "Must not have the paperwork transferred over yet." Sal snorted a laugh.

"Of course," she said. Catherine could tell the woman did not believe it, but Sal started walking again and stepped into the hall. As she turned back to look in the room, she nodded. "Because what else could this be?" she said and then activated the control panel to slide closed the door.

The second they were alone, Catherine ran to Nat and threw her arms around her to hold her tight. "Thank you for not doing anything to get you hurt," she said. Nat wrapped her arms around Catherine and pulled her even closer.

"I did it to keep you safe," she said. "You are what matters to me." Nat kissed the top of her head and it was so comforting, Catherine closed her eyes and nearly wept. Never in her life did she feel so afraid yet so protected at the same time.

"You matter to me too," she said. "So much." They held each other for a quiet moment and then Catherine asked the question she was so afraid to ask. "Nat, what are we going to do? We have to get out of here before they make it to their hideout or help will never find us." Nat was quiet and Catherine knew she was thinking of their options, but there was a sense of hesitation too. Catherine opened her eyes and looked up at the woman. Nat gazed at her and a mix of feelings filled her blue-gray eyes. Catherine was confused. "What are you thinking?" she asked. Nat let out a deep breath and then took Catherine's shoulders to turn them both toward the narrow bunk on one wall of the room. As Nat took her hand and led her to sit down, Catherine tried not to think about the other people who were locked in the room before them and the despair they no doubt felt.

"Catherine, I need you to listen to me," Nat said taking both of Catherine's hands in hers. She looked into Catherine's eyes and held them. *Whatever she is about to say is very important to her*, Catherine thought still not sure what was going on. Finally, Nat cleared her throat. "I know this sounds crazy, but I don't want us to escape just yet." Catherine was shocked. *What Nat is saying is madness. Not escape?* "But," Catherine started and then shook her head in disbelief. The words sounded crazy. "When they find out we're lying, there is no telling what will happen." Nat took a deep breath and nodded.

"I know," she said. "We just have to hope our luck holds and they don't find out for awhile yet." Catherine let go of Nat's hands and rubbed her face to try and make sense of what Nat was saying.

"But why risk it?" Catherine asked. Nat stood up from the bunk and started to pace the small room.

"I'm not sure I can make you completely understand, but I have to go to the pirate's hidden camp," she said. "I need to know where it is so I can message the location to the Space Rangers." She stopped moving and gave Catherine a pleading look. "We've searched for their hideout for years. People have lost their lives trying to find it. And now we have a chance." Catherine watched as Nat quickly moved to kneel in front of her. "I have to do this and I need you to help me." Catherine did not know what to say. She could see the conviction in Nat's eyes and wanted nothing more than to help her, but she was afraid too. The pirates were dangerous and they scared her, no matter how much she pretended they did not. *Especially Sal*, she thought. She could still feel the woman's touch along her face and a shiver ran through her. Nat saw it and moved to sit on the bunk beside her. She put her arms around Catherine and pulled her in. Catherine rested her head on Nat's chest and sighed. Finding the pirate's home and then getting a word out to the Rangers was important and she knew it. *But at what cost?* The whole idea frightened her half to death.

"Nat, I'm so scared," she whispered.

"I know," Nat said. "I am too, but I promise I will keep you safe. No matter what I have to do." Catherine nodded her head against the fabric of Nat's shirt.

"I believe you, but I don't want you to be hurt either," she said. "And Sal wants to kill you already." Catherine felt Nat's body stiffen a little at the mention of the pirate.

"I'll especially protect you from her," Nat said with a growl. "I almost lost it when she touched you. No one but me should ever touch you like that." Even though Catherine was afraid and they were locked in the bowels of a pirate ship, hearing the possessiveness in Nat's voice made Catherine's heart happy.

"Thank you for saying that and for taking care of me," Catherine murmured.

Nat pulled back so she could look into Catherine's face. "I will always take care of you, Catherine," Nat said with such seriousness it nearly took Catherine's breath away and as the woman leaned into her, she felt Nat's hot, possessive lips against hers in a kiss she felt to her toes. Suddenly wanting to forget all about the horrible things going on around them, Catherine responded by wrapping her arms around Nat's neck and kissing her back with all the fierce passion inside her. She felt Nat's lips part and the touch of her tongue against her own. A thrill went through her. Slowly, Catherine pulled Nat down with her onto the blanket. Nat hesitated. "Are you sure?" she asked. Catherine nodded, not daring think about anything but the woman with her and the tenderness of the moment.

"I need to feel close to you," she said and ran her hands up Nat's strong arms. "I'm scared and I don't know what is going to happen to us so I want you to hold me and tell me everything is going to be okay." Nat did not hesitate and sank down to the mattress to envelop Catherine in her arms. Relishing the closeness, Catherine closed her eyes and prayed she could sleep. As a little girl, going off into her dreams at night was a perfect escape from her reality. Right now, in Nat's arms, she wanted to escape again. Even if only for a little while.

"Try and rest," Nat whispered. "I'll keep watch." Catherine sighed and forced herself to relax as much as possible. *Because tomorrow we will be at the pirate's hideout*, she thought. *And I need to be ready for anything.*

CHAPTER 21
NAT

"Rise and shine, ladies," a man's voice said through the intercom into the room. The sudden noise startled Nat from the half-slumber she was in and Catherine flinched in her arms. Nat gave her a squeeze of more reassurance than she felt.

"It's okay," she said to Catherine. "I think we've probably just arrived at their home base." Catherine nodded and Nat kissed her on the forehead before slipping her arms free and sitting up on the bunk. "What do you want?" Nat asked the voice.

"I'm going to open this door now, okay?" he answered. "And I don't want any ambushes or other bullshit. Get it?"

"We get it," Nat replied. Catherine sat up beside her and they both waited. As the door slid open, in sauntered Gruden, the pirate who boarded their ship before with Sal. Nat was not happy to see him as she remembered his lewdness toward Catherine. *Although now my wrists aren't in cuffs*, she thought and almost welcomed a reason to punch the ugly man in the face. For now though, he was all smiles. "Well don't you two look cozy," he said. "But no more time for cuddles. We've landed and Rog wants the ship cleared. Including the captives." Gruden pulled two pairs of cuffs from his pocket and tossed them to Nat to catch. "So, if you don't mind putting these on, we can get started." Being restrained again was the last thing Nat wanted, but leaving the ship and finally seeing the place the pirates called home was intriguing. *We have searched for so long.* The place she pictured was a festering pit of animals and based on the disgusting condition of the pirate's ship, she imagined she was not far off.

"Do we have to?" Catherine asked looking at the cuffs. "I don't plan to try anything." Gruden laughed.

"Yes," he said. "You have to. Especially your watchdog, although I don't imagine you will wear them for long. It seems Rog and Sal both think you're something special." Nat frowned. She did not like the sound of that.

"What the hell does that mean?" she asked. Gruden shrugged. "Rog just went on and on about how sassy the senator's daughter was and as for Sal, well ..." He grinned and it was full of suggestions. "I think you can guess how she was talking about your little girlfriend there." Nat felt Catherine shift uncomfortably beside her and Gruden laughed. "Aw, come on girly, you could do a lot worse. Think about it? You could have ended up with me instead." Nat stood up at that comment and started to take a step.

"Shut your mouth," she snarled and got ready to kick the ugly bastard's ass. Seeing her coming, Gruden pulled his plasma gun and leveled it at her.

"Don't even think about it. Nobody really wants you around too much," he said. Nat stopped but continued to glare at the man. She heard Catherine stand up and come up beside her to put a hand on Nat's arm.

"It's okay. Let's do what he says," she said with concern in her voice and Nat knew she was worried about what would happen after they got off the spaceship. Nat took a deep breath and taking the handcuffs, gently put them on Catherine first before slipping them over her own wrists. She looked at Gruden.

"Satisfied?" she asked. Gruden grinned.

"You bet," he said. "Nothing like watching a woman do what she's told." Nat shook her head and looked forward to when she would kill the ugly pirate who taunted them. *But for now, more patience*, she thought as Gruden waved them forward to exit the room.

"Go ahead, Catherine," Nat said. "I'll be right behind you." Catherine took a deep breath and then with a nod, walked out of the door with her head held high. Nat felt a surge of pride in how the young woman acted in light of all the things going on around them. *She's brave as hell*, Nat thought and it was just another reason she planned to do whatever it took to keep her safe.

"You're next, hotshot," Gruden said and, after throwing the man a dirty look, Nat walked out of the room to face whatever was next.

WHEN NAT WALKED IN a line with Catherine and the other captives down the gangway leading off of the pirate ship, she was shocked. Nothing looked like she had imagined. The landing pad the giant craft was settled on was right at the edge of a village where a few hundred people stood waiting and watching everyone disembark. They were not dressed in the rags Nat imagined, but instead in simple but clean clothes. The group was primarily human woman, but with a few female aliens mixed in, and the excitement of seeing their men returning safe after so long a voyage shown on their faces. Slowly, Nat realized this was not a den of vipers, but instead a relatively normal and civilized community like a person might find on many other planets. Taking it all in, Nat scanned the area and she realized she was correct in the guess the pirates were using cloaking towers to hide their settlement's location. The technology allowed Rog and his people to hide on a small planet almost literally under the noses of the Space Rangers. Although she was not exactly sure of their location, she would need to check a universal positioning device for that, she estimated they were no more than a day or two from Prospo. *This is crazy*, she thought. *And so damn frustrating.*

As the group reached the ground, a couple of the pirates guarding them waved everyone off to the side. Nat could feel the villagers' eyes on her and the others. "Why are they all staring at us?" Catherine whispered. Nat was not sure, but they were definitely being sized up.

"To see which of us they want to bid for," answered one of the other captives. "We're slaves now and they can do whatever they want with us." A murmur of unease went through the rest of the group.

"We should all make a run for it," whispered another captive. Nat thought the idea was a good one. It was not her style to be so passive and now might be the last chance she had to get Catherine to safety. She looked around. The village was surrounded by dense jungle with giant green trees, thick undergrowth, and drooping vines. Nat knew if she could get Catherine beyond the perimeter, hiding would probably be relatively easy. Slowly, Nat looked over her shoulder to see which of the others in her group looked like they wanted to try and escape. A teenage boy saw her look and nodded. Nat hesitated. *He's just a kid*, she thought. Seeing her doubt, the boy narrowed his eyes. "I can do it," he mouthed. Not wholly convinced but with no other choices, she nodded back to him and reached out to take Catherine's hand. The woman turned to her and Nat saw fear in her eyes, but also determination.

"When there is a distraction," Nat murmured. "We go." Catherine gave the slightest nod that she understood and Nat smiled to reassure her. *Finally, we are going to take some real action*, Nat thought. She had no idea what they would do once they got away and she still had every intention of returning to find a way to send a message to the Space Rangers. *But first, I need to make sure Catherine is safe.* Suddenly, a buzz of excitement went through the onlooking villagers. Nat followed their gazes and saw Rog, with Sal and what Nat guessed were other high-ranking members of his crew, exiting the pirate spaceship. A cheer went up and a few of the women rushed to the end of the gangway. As he walked down the ramp, Rog waved his hands at the crowd, clearly relishing the joyful return to his home. Nat knew this was the time to run for it and she took a step back while pulling Catherine with her. *It's now or never*, Nat thought and was about to go when she glanced one last time at the ramp and saw Sal was looking straight at her. Suspicion filled the pirate's eyes and as if knowing exactly what Nat was planning, Sal made a slicing motion across her throat. The message was clear. If Nat tried anything now, such as run for the perimeter, Sal would call for her to be killed.

"She sees us," Catherine murmured and held fast when Nat tried to pull her again. "We can't go." Frustrated, Nat started to argue when one of the captives, the boy who first suggested the idea, peeled off from the back and tried to run.

"Grab him," Sal yelled as she reached the end of the gangway and started walking toward the group. The guards jumped at the command and the boy who tried to run was quickly wrestled to the ground. While Nat, Catherine, and the others looked on, Sal went to stand over the struggling captive. He froze when her shadow fell across them. "Maybe I should have let you keep going," Sal said. "I doubt you'd last a week out there in the swamp." Slowly, Sal pulled her plasma gun from the belt on her holster. "But then that would set a bad example for the other slaves." The pirate raised her weapon and was going to shoot the teenager in the head. Nat knew she needed to do something or yet another victim would be executed by the pirates, but before she could act, Catherine stepped out from the group.

"Wait," Catherine said raising her bound hands to get Sal's attention. "Please don't kill him. He's just a kid." Sal turned to Catherine and Nat saw her face was filled with surprise.

"Why do you care?" Sal asked. "Do you even know this boy?" Catherine shook her head.

"I don't, but that doesn't mean I want to stand here and watch you kill him," she said. Sal hesitated.

"You're serious?" she said. Catherine nodded and after a pause, Sal laughed. "You're indeed one of a kind, Catherine Porter," she said as she holstered her weapon and then turned back to the boy on the ground. "Get him up," she barked and the guards lifted up the captive until he was standing in front of Sal. She tilted her head as she considered his face. "What's your name?" she asked.

"Colton," the teenager answered with defiance in his voice. Sal smirked.

"Well, Colton, I like your spunk, so maybe it's good I didn't kill you just now. But you owe your life to Ms. Porter. Do you understand that?" she asked. Nat saw Colton flick his eyes at Catherine before looking back at Sal. He nodded.

"I do," he replied. "I won't forget it." Sal smiled and turned back to the rest of them.

"Good," she said. "Now, as for the rest of you. Make a stupid decision and I'll kill you, no matter who begs for me to stop." Sal's gaze fell on Nat. "Are we clear?" Nat lifted her chin and glared at the woman. Sal smirked at the move and sauntered over to stand close to Catherine. Nat could feel the fury in her starting to rise. All she wanted to do was yell at Sal to get away from Catherine, but she also realized that was exactly what the pirate wanted. *So she can make an example of me*, Nat thought. Seeing Nat's restraint, Sal put a gentle hand on Catherine's shoulder and leaned in close to the girl. "You did a good thing," Sal said to her. "It makes me want you even more." Nat saw Catherine shrug off Sal's touch and the pirate chuckled. "You know what?" Sal said softly to Catherine.

"I think you need to be my guest at the welcome home banquet." A chill of unease ran through Nat at Sal's words.

"No thank you," Catherine said. Sal chuckled again.

"It wasn't a request," Sal said. "It was a fact." Sal waved to the guards. "Get a gun on this one. She's going to be trouble," she said pointing at Nat. "And then take her and the rest of them to the stock pens." Sal took Catherine by the arm. "You, my dear, will come with me."

CHAPTER 22
CAT

"Why are you doing this?" Catherine asked as she was led away from where Nat and the others were being rounded up to go in the other direction. Sal, who pulled gently but firmly on Catherine's arm, raised her eyebrows.

"Why do you think? I want to sit at dinner with a beautiful woman who has not been beaten down by circumstance yet," she said. "You're fresh and sincere. Something we don't get much in the pirate trade." Catherine was quiet. It was not the answer she was expecting, yet there was an honest ring to Sal's words. Still, she also knew Sal was aware her actions would infuriate Nat and that fact had to be part of her decision too.

"I don't know if I should believe you," Catherine said. Sal stopped and turned Catherine to look at her. The woman's dark eyes roamed her face. After a moment, Sal unlocked the handcuffs around Catherine's wrists and then turned to go. Not sure what to make of it, Catherine frowned. "Where are you going?" she asked. Sal glanced back over her shoulder but kept walking.

"The celebration feast," she said. "But I want you to go as my guest, not my prisoner." Catherine was stunned. *Not as her prisoner?* she thought. *But then as what?* The last thing Catherine wanted was any kind of connection to Sal, yet a part of her also knew there was some power in having the woman on her side. There was always the hope Catherine could get Sal to help Nat and her escape. After all, the woman had not revealed to anyone she knew Catherine was lying about being the senator's daughter. Catherine bit her lip with indecision and watched as Sal moved further away. A few other pirates and their women were nearby and had stopped to look at her. Although they did not appear hostile, Catherine noticed they did not seem particularly friendly. It dawned on her she had no place to really go if she did not follow Sal. There was no way she would survive long on her own in the jungle and if she went back to where Nat was, they would just put her in the stock pens with the other slaves. If that happened, she would be no help to Nat at all. Making up her mind, Catherine hurried after Sal.

"Sal, wait," she called and watched the woman slow her pace. As Catherine neared her, Sal turned and for the briefest of moments, Catherine would have sworn she saw a look of relief on the dangerous woman's features. Then it was gone and Sal smirked at her.

"Good choice," she said and retook Catherine's arm. Catherine shrugged it off.

"You don't have to pull me," she said. "I'm coming with you." Sal tilted her head.

"Maybe I just like to have my hands on you," she said with a sly smile. Words like that were not what Catherine wanted to hear. The last thing she ever needed was to make Sal think her decision to come along meant anything romantic.

"Keep saying that and I'm going back in with the other captives," Catherine snapped. Sal hesitated as if caught off guard by the fearless remark and then held up her hands in surrender.

"Okay," she said. "Fair enough. Don't run away. Let's just have some food and wine. Rog will be excited to see you too."

Catherine did not understand what she meant. Gruden had made a comment back on the ship about Rog's fascination with her too. "Why?" she asked. "There are dozens of captives. How am I so different?" Sal shook her head.

"You just are," she said. "Now, come on. The celebration is happening right in here." Sal guided them into a domed structure, not unlike the many which dotted the village, only larger and grander. Once inside, Catherine could hardly believe her eyes. Instead of being dark and dirty like the pirate ship, the open space was aglow with white light and shimmering crystals everywhere. An ornately carved wooden table was at the center and over twenty people were already sitting around it starting to eat and drink. Servants hovered and were quick to pour wine or refill a plate. Sal turned to Catherine and held out her hand. "May I?" she asked politely. For once, nothing was mocking in her tone and Catherine relented to place her hand in Sal's. Giving her a warm smile, which Catherine noted actually softened the hardness of her face, Sal guided her to a pair of empty seats just to the right of Rog. As they approached, the pirate king saw them.

"Sal!" he exclaimed and then clapped his hands when he saw Catherine. "And Catherine. Now, this is a pleasant surprise." He waved away a few people to make room for Sal to lead Catherine through to their chairs. "Sit. Drink," he said as they dropped into their seats. Once wine was poured for them, Rog leaned forward and glanced back and forth between Sal and Catherine. The gleam of pleasure in his appraising look made Catherine uncomfortable. *He is getting the wrong idea about this*, she thought but did not know what to do about it. Standing up to leave would no doubt be a mistake. She knew she would just have to run with it for now and so slipped back into her spoiled senator's daughter persona.

"Nice place," she said and picked up her wine to try it. After a sip, she smacked her lips and smiled. "Good wine too." Rog laughed and slapped Sal on the arm.

"You sure got lucky," he said. "Sassy and sexy. I can't wait to hear all the lovely details later." Catherine stiffened at the comment. *How many conquests did Sal have?* she wondered. *Enough to brag about, but then, where are they?* A sense of unease crept up her spine. *Does she toss them back as slaves when she's bored with them? Or worse?* Catherine took another sip of wine. The idea of a little extra liquid courage sounded terrific at the moment. Setting the glass back down, a middle-aged woman with dark-brown hair moved to refill it immediately. Catherine looked up to say thank you to the servant and then paused. The woman was staring at her as if she had seen a ghost. Their eyes met and Catherine sensed something familiar in the older woman's features. An eerie feeling settled over her and slowly Catherine touched her own cheeks to make sure nothing was wrong with her face. Noticing, Sal leaned toward her.

"What is it?" Sal asked over the sounds of Rog and other pirates talking loudly about the adventures of their long journey pillaging through space. At the same time, the servant woman dropped her eyes and moved away to pour wine for someone else. Catherine shook her head to clear the strange feeling inside her.

"It's nothing," she said and refocused on what Rog was trying to say to her.

"These are my wives," he said pointing to a group of four women gathered around him. Catherine nodded and smiled at them, trying to be polite. They did not seem happy to see her. Sal leaned in to whisper into Catherine's ear.

"They hate you," she said. "Because you're young and pretty and interesting. Rog likes you and frankly, if I had not claimed you, it would be his bed you slept in tonight." Catherine swallowed hard. The image of being forced to spend the night with Rog repulsed her and she was about to tell Sal so when the realization of her situation hit her. *Did she just say if she had not claimed me?* Catherine thought and turned in her chair to look at Sal.

"So, what are you saying?" she asked the woman and Sal shrugged.

"I think you know exactly what I'm saying," she said. "But I'll spell it out if you insist. You are my reward. My prize, if you will, for all my years of loyalty and hard work. Rog has given you to me." Catherine's mouth dropped open in shock. *I've been given to Sal*, she thought and was afraid to ask the next question but needed to know the answer.

"Then what bed will I be sleeping in tonight?" she asked. Sal raised an eyebrow.

"Now Catherine, you're smart enough to figure that out on your own," she said with a laugh. "Have more wine. You suddenly look like you need it." Catherine shook her head.

"I won't do it," she stated. "Send me back with the others." A hint of anger flushed Sal's cheeks and Catherine saw her considering what to do next. No doubt the woman was not used to people telling her no. Finally, Sal picked up her own wine and slugged back the contents. She licked her lips and then glared at Catherine.

"Yes, actually you will," Sal said. "Because if you don't, then Rog or some other member of the crew will claim you. Trust me, you do not want that." As she said it, the dark-haired servant woman from before returned to refill Sal's glass. Sal ignored the woman and leaned in to make sure Catherine heard her. "Face it, you're too sweet and pretty for your own good, Catherine Porter." Suddenly there was a crash and Sal leaped to her feet with her weapon drawn before Catherine had even registered what happened. Other pirates around the table had also stood and drawn guns or knives in alarm. Looking around, Catherine saw it was only the dark-haired servant. She had dropped the vase she was pouring the wine from and it had shattered on the floor. Rog, who was now standing in his chair, saw it and started to laugh.

"Sheath your weapons my mates, the only tragedy is the loss of some good wine," he roared. Slowly the others around the table started to laugh too and sat back down. Sal followed suit, but Catherine could not take her eyes off of the servant, who had now dropped to her knees to pick up the shards of glass.

"I'm so sorry," she repeated. "I'm so stupid and clumsy." Rog waved his hands to quiet her.

"Just clean it up and then bring us another," he said and sat down to start up the banter around the table once again. The servant did as she was told and once the mess was picked up, she stood up to go fetch more wine. Before she left, she looked back in Catherine's direction. Their eyes met again and for a second, Catherine thought she saw tears on the woman's cheeks. It made no sense. There was no way she knew the woman. *So why does it feel like I do?* she thought. After the servant turned away and left to get another vase, Catherine realized Sal was watching her as well.

"How do you know her?" Sal asked. Catherine shook her head.

"I don't," she said. Sal did not look convinced.

"Then why were you staring at each other?" she asked. Catherine frowned and wondered the same thing.

"I swear to you, I've never seen here before," Catherine answered. Sal tilted her head and gave Catherine an appraising look.

"Okay," she said. "But I'll tell you one thing. That woman may be older, but otherwise, the two of you look alike." Catherine paused as she thought about what Sal had said. After a moment, she nodded. Sal was absolutely right.

CHAPTER 23
NAT

N at's body physically shook she was so upset and angry.
Watching Sal lead Catherine away to who knew what
fate tore a hole inside her and all she could think about was
how to get away to go after Catherine. With every step she
took, Nat knew she was moving further and further from
wherever Sal was taking her prisoner. Although the village
was not large, there were dozens of buildings. Finding
Catherine would be nearly impossible if the woman were
locked in one of them before Nat could get to her. She needed to hurry. Looking around, Nat counted only two armed
guards escorting the group to what she saw was a big fenced
in stock pen not far ahead. It was empty but for some rags for
blankets on the ground. *This is where they hold captives until
we are auctioned off to be slaves*, Nat thought with disgust as
she appraised the layout. The walls were high, topped with
electric wire, and looked substantially built, which made Nat
all the more anxious about escaping now instead of trying later. Starting to feel desperate, Nat glanced around to consider
options. She saw Colton watching her. Of all the captives in
the pack, the teenager seemed to be the only one other than

Nat not willing to walk along like sheep to the slaughter. Slowly, Nat slipped through the group to walk beside the boy. After checking to make sure the guards were not in earshot, Colton leaned toward Nat. "Are you with the girl who saved me?" he asked.

"Yes," she whispered. "And I need to get away so I can go save her." Colton nodded ever so slightly to avoid attracting the guards.

"I'll help you. I owe her my life," he said as he glanced around to make sure they were still not being watched. "Do you have a plan?" Nat wished she had a plan, but knowing she had help, even if it was just a kid, gave her more options. The one thing she knew for sure was they were getting closer to the stock pen. An idea came to her. It was neither the best nor the most original, but sometimes brute force was the only alternative.

"Slow down and get to the back of the pack with me," she whispered. "Until we are near the guard behind us." Colton did not question her decision and started to ease in the direction she told him. "Easy," Nat said. "Don't attract attention to what we are doing. I need us last through the gate and when we do, trip and fall." Colton gave her a subtle nod. As everyone walked, the two of them continued to shorten their steps until they were in position. Nat watched as each prisoner was waved through the gate in the fence. When it was Colton's turn, he did exactly as Nat hoped and made a show of stumbling before falling to his knees. The guard swore and reached for Colton to get him up. As soon as the pirate was distracted and bending forward, Nat shot out a front kick with all her strength and fury. Her foot connected with the guard's face and Nat heard a satisfying crunch as the man's nose was crushed. He staggered and fell. "Run!" Nat yelled and Colton leaped to his feet in a flash. Sprinting toward the jungle, Nat moved to follow him, but then saw the second guard turn to level his plasma gun at her.

"You bitch," he growled. "Sal said to watch you, but I think shooting you would be easier." Nat's eyes widened as she expected the gun to fire, but at the last moment, Colton leaped onto the man's back. The blow knocked the guard's weapon upward. When he pulled the trigger, Nat ducked and the blast went high. *Missed me by a hair*, she thought as she turned to sprint toward the jungle at the perimeter of the village. Glancing back, she saw Colton was doing his best to wrestle the guard, but the man was bigger and stronger and was pushing Colton back toward the gate. In a minute, Colton would be in the stock pen with the others. Nat thought of turning back to go help the kid but knew if she did, the guard would most likely try to shoot her again. *And this time, I doubt he'll miss.* Vowing to go back for Colton once she figured out a better plan, Nat ran for the jungle and reaching the edge of the dense foliage, plunged through the broad-leafed bushes into the thick undergrowth. Vines and branches grabbed her as she battled to get clear of any pursuit by the guards.

After five minutes of struggling to get deeper into the jungle, Nat found a clear spot behind a thick tree and stopped to listen for the sound of shouts announcing her escape. If she could determine which direction the search was coming from she could sneak off in the other. Breathing deeply to settle her racing heart, she waited and was confused when she heard nothing. *Why aren't they coming after me?* she wondered. *Are they thinking a woman alone in the jungle is not worth pursuing?* Slowly, Nat looked around as it occurred to her there may be creatures who lived among the plants which were dangerous enough to deter the pirates from coming in after her. As if reading her thoughts, there was a rasping noise coming from the tree branches above and Nat looked up to see a snake winding its way toward her. Nat's eyes widened. Although she was not certain the species of this particular reptile and therefore could not be sure it was poisonous, the sheer length and breadth of its body was more than Nat wanted to wrestle with, especially considering she was weaponless and her hands were still bound. Backing away slowly, Nat watched as the creature advanced. It clearly had Nat in its sights as prey and even though Nat had no idea where she was going, she took off into the bushes around her to escape. As she fled, she had visions of the beast wrapping its body around her legs to trip her and the picture made her sprint deeper into the dark jungle.

Finally, she broke out into a clearing and was surprised to see a small cabin built from logs and vines. The structure was old and leaned precariously to one side, but Nat did not hesitate to duck in and hide. With no windows, the space was dark and Nat could only hope it was unoccupied by man or beast. Crouching down, Nat peeked out through a crack in the door and waited to see if the snake would appear. After only a moment, she saw movement at the edge of the clearing and slowly the dangerous creature which hunted her slithered out of the trees. As she watched, Nat guessed the beast was ten feet long at least and now that it was out in the daylight instead of the gloom of the jungle, its stripes of red, yellow, and black showed out against the dirt. Slowly, the snake lifted its head and used the senses in its flickering tongue to search for her. Nat held her breath and prayed the thing would not come to the cabin. She knew snakes did not see well and hoped it was not aware of the shelter only fifteen feet from it. The last thing Nat wanted was to have to shut and lock the door and be trapped with it outside. Every moment which passed meant Catherine had to survive on her own. Finally, after agonizing seconds passed, the reptile lowered its head and began to move away into the jungle again. Nat breathed out with relief. It was time to get back to the village and find Catherine. As quietly as she could, Nat slipped out of the cabin and went back into the jungle in the opposite direction of the snake.

Backtracking through the gloom of the jungle, Nat worried she was turned around. There was no sign of the pirate's camp. Frustrated, she continued to push through the thick leaves and brush until she literally stumbled into a wide concrete platform. Looking up, Nat realized she was at the foot of one of the cloaking towers which triangulated the village. Saying a little thank you to the universe for her good luck, Nat studied the setup. A transformer box was at the base, but it was bolted shut. She had no doubt if she could get it open, there would be electronics she could break to kill the towers stealth broadcast. *I need to find some way to get in there*, she thought and added it to her growing list of objectives. But first, she had to locate Catherine. *Where would Sal have taken her?* There were so many shelters to consider, including Sal's own quarters. The image of it made Nat grit her teeth with fury. Sal clearly wanted Catherine and Nat had no doubt if the woman could get Catherine alone, she would try to take advantage of her. *But Catherine will fight her*, Nat thought and she hoped Catherine could fend for herself well enough until Nat got to her. The question really was how aggressive Sal would be with Catherine. Even Nat had recognized the pirate had a soft spot when it came to the girl, but Nat could not decide if it was enough for Sal to be patient. Nat shook her head with frustration. *She's still a dirty pirate.* They were not known for being patient or respectful but instead were ruthless. *I've got to find her and fast.*

Moving at a crouch until she was closer to the village, Nat worked hard to stay hidden while scanning the landscape. Pirates, their mates, and servants all milled around the different buildings, but one shelter in particular seemed busy. It was larger than the other domed structures and Nat slipped as close as she could without revealing herself. She could hear music and laughter coming from inside. *A celebration of the pirate's return?* she wondered. It made sense. *But would Catherine be in there?* Nat nodded as she considered the question. Sal was arrogant enough to make Catherine go with her to just such an event. Using the girl as a trophy was definitely right in Sal's wheelhouse, especially considering how taken Rog the pirate king was with Catherine. *She's in there showing her off.* Nat wondered how Catherine was reacting to it and hoped for her sake she was playing along. *At least for now when other people were around.* Nat knew a time would come soon enough when Catherine would be alone with the woman and then would have to reveal who she really was to Sal. Thinking of the scene and the idea of Sal's unwelcome hands on Catherine made Nat's heart clench with fury. She had to find a way to stop it.

CHAPTER 24
CATHERINE

S al led her by the hand out the back of the banquet hall and through a door to the outside. Catherine knew Sal was angry at her, but whenever she tried to slow down and ask questions, Sal did not allow it. "We're almost there," she snapped when Catherine asked where they were going. Now that they were out in the open, Catherine saw they were near the giant pirate space galleon. Other smaller ships were settled around it, including the Avalon Mercury. Sal was headed straight for it.

"Wait," Catherine said and dug in her feet to stop walking. "What are we doing?" Sal turned back and grabbed Catherine's arm.

"Stop with all the damn questions," she said with a snarl and started to pull again. Catherine resisted and Sal whirled on her, frustration clear on her face. "Listen," she said. "We need to talk and this is the most private place I can think of, so let's go." Catherine still held back. The last thing she wanted was to be alone someplace with Sal where no one could find them and yet, the pirate's words confused her. *We need to talk?* Catherine thought. *What would Sal need to say?* It was one thing to have Sal continue to make sexual innuendos and threats, but somehow this felt different. Sal pulled at her arm again.

"Don't make me pick you up and carry you," she said. "Because I will." Catherine could tell she meant it and so started walking with her again. It did not take long to get to the Avalon Mercury's gangway and Sal led her inside. Frederick the android met them at the door. He was confused and upset.

"What is happening? Why are you here?" he asked. Sal waved him aside as she escorted Catherine past him.

"Shut up," Sal said. "Just bring me a bottle of the most expensive alcohol you have on this ship." Frederick paused as he considered the situation.

"Two glasses, ma'am?" he finally asked, clearly recognizing who was in charge now. Sal glanced at Catherine and then nodded.

"Definitely two," she said and pulled Catherine forward to the lounge. Once inside, Catherine yanked her arm away. Enough was enough. Being in the room where she had only the day before had such a tender but passionate moment with Nat gave her strength. She was sick of Sal being a bully, and pirate or no pirate, Catherine was done being a victim. *If I have to fight her, I will*, she thought and turned on the woman.

"I don't know why you brought me here," Catherine snapped. "But if you think it will seduce me, forget it. I want someone else." Sal narrowed her eyes and her look was cold as ice. They stared at each other for a long moment.

"Why did you ask me to save the boy?" Sal asked. The question caught Catherine entirely off guard.

"He was just a kid," she stammered in response. "I couldn't just stand by and let you kill him." Sal frowned.

"So you're saying you did it out of the goodness of your heart?" she asked.

Catherine nodded. "Yes," she said and then had a thought. Sal was not always a pirate and, in fact, had once been a slave. There was a life for her before that as well. Wanting to appeal to it, Catherine softened her tone. "Surely there was a time when you encountered people who did things simply because it was right. I don't believe you have always been so hardened." Sal's head jerked up at the words and her face flushed.

"You know nothing about me," Sal said. "So keep your speculations to yourself." Catherine instinctively wanted to apologize for upsetting her but did not. She had touched a nerve and knew she had to keep going.

"Why?" she asked and then decided to take a big risk. "Because I know deep down you're not the evil pirate you pretend to be?" In a flash, Sal was on her and had Catherine's long hair wrapped in her hand. Jerking her head back so they were face to face, Sal glared into her eyes.

"Trust me, I am evil," Sal whispered. "Don't pretend otherwise." Suddenly, Sal was kissing her, her lips hot and angry on Catherine's mouth. Catherine tried to jerk away, but Sal's hand was too strong in her hair. Growing furious, Catherine twisted her face to the side and pushed against Sal's shoulders with all her strength.

"Stop!" she said. "I know you're not really like this." For a second, Catherine was not sure if she was right as Sal continued to hold her close. Her lips brushed Catherine's cheek and then her neck.

"You know I could just order that droid to fly us away," she murmured. "Take us far from here. Just you and me." Catherine heard such wistfulness in Sal's tone, she stopped fighting her and held still.

"No," Catherine said. "I won't leave Nat." Sal froze for a moment and Catherine could almost feel the hurt run through the other woman's body. Then she thrust Catherine from her so hard, it sent her sprawling onto the couch. Sal strode to the door to the lounge.

"Droid! Where the hell is that bottle?" she yelled. To Catherine's relief, Frederick appeared in an instant.

"Sorry, so sorry," he said and held out a tray with a bottle and two glasses on it. Sal grabbed them and then motioned for him to go.

"Get out," she said and once Frederick hurriedly departed, Sal opened the bottle and splashed the amber liquid into a glass. When it was over half full, she picked it up and shot the whole contents before pouring herself another as well as one for Catherine.

"Damn you to hell, Catherine Porter," she whispered and then looked up to meet Catherine's eyes. As if just realizing she was still in the room, Sal laughed a little. "Why did you have to come along? Or even worse, why did your Space Ranger girlfriend let you get captured by pirates?" Catherine froze at the words. Sal knew the truth and it made her heart stop to think of what Sal might have done to Nat. Seeing her look, Sal smirked. "Oh yeah, I knew it from the first minute I laid eyes on her. Trust me, I know the look."

"What have you done with her?" Catherine asked. "Where is she?" Sal shot the second glass of liquid before answering.

"In with the others," she said. "For safekeeping. Probably fetch a good price at the slave auction tonight." Catherine felt sick to her stomach.

"So you know I'm not a senator's daughter then?" she asked. Sal shrugged.

"Didn't take much detective work. Especially since the guy doesn't have a daughter and this spaceship is registered to some doctor," she said. "You're lucky Gruden is such an idiot he didn't figure it out." Catherine closed her eyes. A feeling of helplessness washed over her. Sal knew the truth and now had all the power. A word to Rog about the lies Catherine and Nat had been telling and there was no doubt he would kill them. *I have to find a way to make her keep our secret*, Catherine thought and shuddered at the realization there was probably only one way to make it happen.

"What do you want?" Catherine asked. At first, there was no response, but then she felt Sal drop onto the couch beside her. She winced, not knowing what may be coming next.

"Relax, Catherine," Sal said. "It's not going to be like that." Catherine slowly opened her eyes and saw the pirate was looking at her. "And as for what I want, well, the list is so long, I don't even know where to begin." Sal sighed and took another drink. "So, where did you meet your Space Ranger anyway? Some grand rescue?" Not sure what to make of the change in Sal, Catherine slowly nodded her head.

"I was flying to Untas and I crashed. She saved me," she answered. Sal snorted a laugh.

"Of course she did," Sal said. "Which is why you are now so madly in love with her. The hero always gets the girl." She took another drink. "And we all know what happens to the villain." Catherine was suddenly not sure what to do. Sal was obviously slowly getting drunk and rambling, which meant she might have a chance to escape. *If only I can get her weapons away from her*, Catherine thought. *Then I could try and get to the cockpit and send a distress call out.* She shifted in her seat as she considered the best strategy to reach for Sal's knife and glanced to see what Sal was doing. Catherine froze when she realized the pirate was staring at her.

"What is in that pretty head of yours?" Sal asked. "Thinking of making a break for it?" Catherine blushed. It was exactly what she was thinking. Sal sighed sounding disappointed. "Catherine, where would you go? Even if you disarmed me, would you run straight back to your Space Ranger and try to get her out of the stock pen?" Catherine lifted her chin.

"That is exactly what I would do," she answered. "I'll do whatever it takes to save her." Sal shook her head and set down the drink.

"And then you'd both be caught and locked up until the auction. I can't protect you if you go that route," she said. "Is she really worth it?" Catherine considered what Sal was asking her. She thought of everything the woman said and knew it was true. Catherine was madly in love with her Space Ranger and even if it meant risking everything to be back with her, then she would do it.

"Take me back to her," Catherine said. Sal shook her head and drank the last of the liquid in her glass before setting it down. She looked at Catherine and her eyes were filled with sadness. *And regret?* Catherine thought trying to read the mixture of emotions in the woman's eyes.

"Things are not like you think," Sal said as she stood up. "I hope you will remember that." Catherine nodded although she was not sure what the pirate was telling her. Wanting to understand, Catherine stood up too and started to ask when there was a tap at the door. Sal whirled around at the sound.

"What?" she asked and Frederick slid open the door. He looked nervous.

"Excuse my interruption," he stammered. "But are you Sal?" Catherine saw Sal frown. "The reason I ask is they appear to be looking for you," Frederick continued in a rush. "It's coming over the comm link." Sal puffed out a frustrated breath.

"Oh for crying out loud," Sal said as she pushed past Frederick and went to the cockpit. Catherine rushed to the door to stand beside Frederick.

"What's happening?" Catherine asked him. Frederick shrugged his metal shoulders.

"This is Sal. What the hell is the problem?" Catherine heard Sal bark into the comm link.

"Where the hell are you?" Catherine heard Gruden fire back. "You need to quit banging your new girlfriend and get back to business. The chick's bodyguard has escaped." Catherine felt her heart leap. *Nat's free,* she thought with excitement and relief. Suddenly, Sal slammed her fist into the console so hard it made Catherine jump.

"That meddling bitch," she growled to herself. "I knew she was going to screw everything up." She pressed the comm link again to talk to Gruden. "I'm on my way. And if you catch her before I get there, wait for me," she said and stormed out of the cockpit only to stop in front of Catherine. "Stay on the ship. I mean it," Sal said. "And don't try sending any long-range messages. Rog has it blocked somehow. Understand me?" Catherine nodded and grabbed Sal's sleeve.

"If they catch her, please don't let them kill her," Catherine begged and Sal paused. Their eyes met and again Catherine saw a flicker of regret.

"No promises," Sal said and turned to stride off of the spaceship.

CHAPTER 25
NAT

Nat stayed hidden among the dense foliage at the edge of the jungle which surrounded the village and watched the door of the large domed structure where she hoped Catherine was inside. People came and went, but none were Catherine or even the pirate Sal. Shifting uncomfortably to relieve the pressure on the cuffs which still bound her wrists, she contemplated trying to sneak closer to the building and see if there was a way to peek inside. It would mean leaving cover, but the day was slipping away. *If only I knew for sure where Catherine was*, she thought and tried not to think about the possibility Catherine was actually alone somewhere with Sal instead of inside at the celebration. Whenever her mind drifted there, she felt rage start to build up in her and she knew letting her anger takeover would be a mistake. *I need to keep a clear head if I'm going to be any help to her and hiding here is not doing any good either*. Making up her mind to act rather than wait any longer, Nat stood up into a crouch and after waiting to make sure the coast was clear, she sprinted for the building. As she made her way through the dangerous open ground between the jungle and the wall of the shelter, she suddenly heard shouting. Looking around to see where it was coming from, Nat realized she was discovered. A pirate who Nat guessed was actually searching the perimeter for her started running in her direction. He had his plasma gun drawn and was yelling for her to stop.

Not hesitating, Nat took off in the other direction and hoped she could circle the building and get back to the jungle before the pirate had a good shot. She was almost in the clear when a second pirate appeared and blocked her path. Veering away, Nat was forced to run into the village, but her gait was slowed by the fact her wrists were locked together. Scanning as she went, she looked for a place to hide and raced toward some of the smaller domes. As she sprinted as best she could for cover, a shot rang out and she ducked as a plasma blast went over her head. It was a near miss and Nat realized if she did not find a way out of the village and back to the jungle soon, she was going to die. *And then what will happen to Catherine?* she worried. The thought gave her motivation to run faster. If she could just get past the next row of buildings, she was sure she could get away. Another shot fired and this time she zigzagged. The blast missed, but only by a hair. *Go, go, go!* She rounded the last of the structures with relief and saw the edge of the thick, green bushes not far in front of her. She knew she was going to make it and then a figure stepped out into her path. It was the last person Nat wanted to see and she slid to a stop. The new pirate was Sal and she had her gun pointed right at Nat's chest.

"You are a real pain in my ass," Sal growled and Nat saw her pull the trigger. She was too close to miss and as the energy of the blast hit her, Nat fell. *Catherine!* her mind screamed as pain racked her body. *I'm so sorry.* Nat hit the ground with a thud and could not move. Everything hurt, both through her body and in her heart. She waited to die and then realized Sal's gun had to have only been on stun. Things had not blacked out and she was still breathing shallowly. Thinking the pirate had made a mistake, Nat stayed still and did not open her eyes, hoping against hope the woman thought she was dead. Nat felt Sal step over to her and then she was whispering in her ear. "Whatever happens, don't move," she said. Confused as hell, but doing what she was told, Nat stayed frozen. She heard the sound of pounding feet and guessed it was the two other pirates who were chasing her. They stopped when they saw Nat dead with Sal over her.

"Well there you go," one of the pirates said. "Should have known you'd get the job done, Sal."

"Considering she almost got away, somebody had to do it," Sal snapped back. "You realize how pissed Rog would have been?" The two pirates shuffled their feet and did not comment. "Go get a damn cart so we can take this bitch to the pit," Sal instructed.

"You sure you don't want us to just drag her?" the other pirate asked. Nat heard Sal snort a laugh.

"What? Through the middle of the village where everyone is celebrating? And look like idiots because we let a stupid captive get away?" she answered. "Just go get the cart and we can sneak her around."

"You're the boss," the first pirate said and Nat heard them jog off. After a moment, Sal was kneeling down beside her. With a click, Nat felt the cuffs on her wrists release.

"Get up, Ranger," Sal hissed. "We don't have much time." Nat rolled over and looked at Sal. She had no idea why her enemy was helping her, especially if she knew Nat was a Space Ranger, but all she wanted was to make sure Catherine was safe.

"Where is she?" Nat asked. Sal smirked.

"I almost killed you and the first thing you ask about is Catherine?" she said and shook her head. "Well, your fair maiden is on the Avalon Mercury waiting for you. I suggest you follow the edge of the jungle back around to where all of the captured ships are sitting and get the hell off this planet." Sal put her plasma gun back in her holster and then tilted her head at Nat. "I'm assuming you can fly well enough to get away before they scramble some fighters to come after you?" Nat nodded.

"Damn straight," she answered and tried to get up. Her muscles still twitched from the stun blast and Sal actually held out a hand to pull her to her feet. It was so out of character along with the other things she had done, Nat had to know what had changed.

"Why are you doing this?" Nat asked as she shook out her arms and legs to get them working again. Sal looked Nat hard in the eye and Nat could tell she was considering how to answer. Finally, she chuckled wryly.

"One riot, one Ranger, all planets, all danger," she said. Nat's mouth dropped open with surprise. It was the time-honored Space Ranger motto and emblazoned on every Ranger's patch. *Is she saying what I think she is? No, it can't be true,* Nat thought almost in shock. Sal, the pirate, was actually one of them. Sal was a Space Ranger.

"But," Nat said and then closed her mouth as her mind started putting pieces together. Sal had spent four years with the pirates on their space galleon raiding the galaxies. Four years waiting for them to finally dock back at their hidden base. "You've been deep undercover all this time?" Nat whispered. Sal let out a long breath and nodded.

"And now you're about to screw it all up," Sal said. "So, if you don't mind, get the hell off my planet."

Nat shook her head. "I won't leave a fellow Ranger behind," she said. "Come with us."

Sal laughed. "I'm hardly still a Ranger after all I've done and you know it," she said. "I've had to kill in order to make Rog believe in me." Nat saw a look of sadness sweep over the woman's face and then Sal shook it away. "Including fellow Rangers. And if things were different, I would have killed you too if it meant keeping my cover." Nat stiffened at the information. It was hard to hear but stopping the horror of the pirates and the rape and pillage of the galaxies was a priority objective, regardless of the costs. *I would have done the same if it was me*, Nat thought. She knew it in her heart.

"Like you said before, Sal," Nat said. "You do what you must to survive. There's still honor in you regardless what you've done." Sal chuckled.

"Dear God, you and Catherine are definitely made for each other," she said. "Both good through and through." Sal turned to leave. "Go be with her and stop wasting my time." Although Nat's heart beat faster as she thought of Catherine, she clenched her jaw at the dismissal. No doubt seeing her mixed expression, Sal waved her off. "Besides, I can't leave now. I'm not finished," she said. "Until I can take out those cloaking towers, none of my sacrifices are worth it. I sure as hell won't quit now."

"I'll help you," Nat insisted and Sal gave her a long look.

"No," she said. "Go get Catherine to safety. But I do want one thing from you."

"Anything," Nat said, still having trouble getting her head around what Sal was telling her. The woman looked off into the distance with a wistful expression on her face.

"Don't tell Catherine," she said.

Nat frowned. "Why?" she asked.

Sal ran a hand over her face. "Let's just say it's because I don't want to put her at risk with the knowledge. You're a trained Ranger, I know you can hold up under questioning, but I worry about her if you get caught."

"I won't let her get captured," Nat said. Sal raised an eyebrow.

"Really? Because you're not doing so well so far," she said and then shook her head. "Doesn't matter. I need to keep my secret a little longer and if she is associated with a Space Ranger, they will kill her." Nat nodded.

"What is your plan?" Nat asked. Sal shrugged.

"Wait until they start the auctioning of the captives tonight. Slaves are always popular and everyone will be distracted," she said. "I am hoping to have time to disable the cloaking towers and then get out a call to the cavalry. We'll see how it goes." Nat nodded thoughtfully and held out a hand to Sal. Sal stared at it and then slowly took it to shake.

"Godspeed, Ranger," Nat said softly. Sal yanked back her hand as if the words burned her. Her face was twisted with anger, but Nat was not sure if it was at Nat or herself.

"Get the fuck out of here," Sal growled and walked away. Nat watched her go and was filled with indecision. She needed to protect Catherine and take her to safety. *But I can't leave a Ranger behind, no matter what she has done*, she thought.

After a moment, Nat heard the sound of the other pirates returning with the cart and knowing she was out of time, she ran for the jungle to circle around to the Avalon Mercury. For now, she would make sure Catherine was okay and get her someplace away from danger, but they would not be leaving the planet in the spacecraft yet. There was more work to be done and, in her heart, whether Sal wanted it or not, Nat knew it was her duty to help.

CHAPTER 26
CATHERINE

C atherine paced the lounge in the Avalon Mercury and could not decide what to do. Somewhere out there, Nat was on the run and she did not know how to help her. If she left the spaceship, she had no idea where to even find Nat, but also worried Nat would never think to look for her on the ship. Biting her lip, Catherine was sure of at least one thing, and it was she could not just wait around for Sal to return. Something was going on with the pirate, but Catherine could not put her finger on it. One minute, Sal was all cocky and mean, and the next, she was almost friendly and sweet. *And a little sad*, Catherine thought remembering some of the things she said about heroes getting the girl. It was clear Sal knew she was not the hero in anyone's story. *Not like Nat is in mine,* she thought. *If only I can find a way back to her.* The idea she might never see Nat again tore at her heart. She was so worried about what would happen if she was caught. *Will Sal kill her?* Catherine was not sure. It was clear Sal wanted her and Catherine thought of the passionate kiss Sal forced on her earlier. She remembered how the wanting had rolled off of the woman like a wave of heat. *Yet she stopped when I told her too.* Catherine was grateful for that if nothing else, but it did not translate to not fighting Sal if it meant saving Nat. *So that is what I will do.* When Sal returned, Catherine had to be ready to disarm her and force Sal to tell where Nat was taken. *And if Nat is dead?* Catherine pushed the image of Nat hurt or worse out of her mind. Surely fate would not be so cruel.

Moving with purpose now, Catherine stepped out of the lounge and looked around for Frederick. He was waiting against the wall for his next command and lit up when he saw her. "How can I be of service?" he asked.

"We need to knock the pirate out when she returns," Catherine said. "I need to take her weapons and find out where Captain Nat is being held." Frederick nodded.

"I will find a knife in the kitchen," he said and started to walk away. Catherine grabbed his arm.

"No, wait," she said. "Not a knife. I don't want to kill her." Frederick looked puzzled.

"Why not?" he asked. "She's a pirate and you may never have a better chance." Catherine paused. He was right. For a reason she could not quite understand, Catherine did not want to kill Sal. Knocking the woman unconscious was one thing, but dead was another. Something inside her believed there was good in Sal, even though she had no doubt the woman had done unmentionable things. Her mind returned to the kiss and how easy it would have been for Sal to force herself on Catherine. *But she didn't. Still, am I being a fool?* she wondered. *Was she just delaying something she intends to do anyway?* Catherine shook her head and did not believe it. Somehow, she knew Sal would never really hurt her.

"I just won't," Catherine finally answered. "So not a knife, but maybe a frying pan? Something hard with a handle." Frederick raised a finger with excitement.

"Brilliant," he said and bustled off to get it. He was back in less than a minute with a skillet heavy enough Catherine knew it would do the trick. Now all she had to do was stand by the door and let Sal open it to step in.

Not knowing when the pirate would be back, Catherine moved into position. She did not have to wait long as the pounding of footsteps running up the gangway sounded almost immediately. Catherine took a deep breath. This was her one chance to gain the upper hand and she knew it. Cocking the skillet back, she listened for the lock to be engaged from the outside. There was a click and a whoosh and then the woman was stepping in. Catherine swung with all her might, but Sal was quick enough to duck and only take the glancing blow on the shoulder. Then she was turning and, in an instant, Catherine realized it was not Sal, but instead it was her Nat. Catherine dropped the skillet and threw her arms around the woman. "Nat, oh my God, I'm so sorry," she gushed. "I thought you were Sal." Nat pulled her into a tight hug and held her for a moment.

"Catherine, thank God, you are safe," she said. "Forget about hitting me. I am just so thankful to find you."

"But how did you—" Catherine started wanting to know everything Nat had done to find her, but Nat pulled back to look into her face.

"I'll explain everything later, I promise, but right now we need to go," Nat said and took her hand to lead her toward the exit. "I don't know how long we have until they think to

look here." Catherine followed without hesitation. She trusted Nat completely and would go with her anywhere as long
as it kept them together. With Nat scanning in every direction, they hurried back down the gangway and onto the
packed dirt of the landing field. "We need to get into the jungle on the other side of the village." Catherine nodded and
ran with Nat toward the thick foliage. They had only gone a
few hundred yards, and Catherine recognized they were near
the large domed banquet hall where Rog was holding court.
Suddenly, Gruden the pirate stepped out of the shadows. He
was zipping his fly after pissing into the weeds and looked as
surprised to see them as they were him. Nat jumped for him,
but he was able to get his plasma gun free of its holster just in
time to stop her momentum.

"Hold it, bitch," he said. "What the hell? I heard you were
out running around, but Sal said she killed you and screwed
your girlfriend." Catherine's eyes widened at his words. *What
is he talking about?* she wondered. She saw his eyes narrow.
"But apparently, she lied," he muttered with a frown. "Why
would she do that?" He raised his weapon higher and put it
into Nat's face. "What is going on here?" he asked. Catherine saw Nat's eyes were fixed on the pirate's weapon and she
knew her hero was trying to figure out how to take it from
him without getting either of them shot. Gruden was the one
thing keeping them from making an escape.

"It's complicated," Nat answered. "Too complex for
someone as stupid as you to understand." Gruden flushed at
the insult but did not take the bait.

"Nice try," he said. "But I won't let you make a move on
me. I'm going to shoot you in the gut and then you know

what? I'm going to bang your hottie pet right here against the wall while you slowly die watching." Catherine felt the cold realization he was telling the truth tighten her stomach. She could hardly breathe and did not know what to do. Gruden grinned and she knew this was it.

"Wait!" Catherine said. "Please. You can do whatever you want with me, but don't shoot her." Gruden laughed.

"I'm going to do whatever I want anyway, and frankly, I'm sick of this one," he snarled and moved to fire. Before he could, a figure stepped out of the shadows of the building behind him and smashed a large wine vase down on his head. The glass shattered and Gruden slumped to the ground. Catherine was shocked at the turn of events and blinked with surprise when the dark-haired servant she felt a connection with earlier came forward.

She looked right at Catherine. "Are you okay?" the woman asked and Catherine nodded while the stranger walked to her. They stared into each other's eyes and Catherine could see the similarities were uncanny. The woman was older and had lines on her face from a life which was no doubt difficult as a servant to the pirates, but the shape of her features was so familiar. Mostly though, it was the eyes which captivated Catherine. *Who is this person? And why do I feel such a connection?* she asked herself. "Is your name really Catherine Porter?" the stranger asked. "Did you grow up on Prospo?" Catherine caught her breath at the question. Suddenly for reasons she didn't quite understand, her heart was beating faster.

"Yes," Catherine answered and glanced at Nat who was watching them both with a puzzled look on her face.

"Do you know her?" Nat asked the stranger. The woman suddenly looked embarrassed and lowered her eyes. Stepping back, she shook her head.

"I'm sorry," she said. "You need to go. He will wake up eventually and others will be hunting for you."

"But wait," Catherine started as she needed to know more about the woman who looked so much like her. "Who are you?" The dark-haired stranger started to back away.

"No one," she replied. "Now go. Hurry." Nat retook Catherine's hand.

"She's right, we have to go," Nat said and started to lead her away into the jungle. Catherine looked back at the re-treating figure of the woman.

"Will you be alright?" Catherine called to her. The woman waved.

"Yes, I always find a way to survive," Catherine heard her say and then Nat was pulling her into the thick bushes of the jungle. Once they were under the canopy, it was much darker and Catherine had to focus on her steps to keep from being tripped. The image of the woman's wave haunted her, but she forced herself to think only of helping them escape. Nat moved with determination as she pushed massive green leaves and thick vines out of their path.

"Where are we going?" Catherine asked.

"I know of a cabin where we can hide for a couple hours until dusk," Nat answered without breaking stride. "It's a wreck, but it has a door we can shut and it doesn't appear anyone ever goes there." Nat slowed and looked back. "It's at least a mile. Can you make it?" Catherine nodded.

"I will," she said forcing a particularly clingy vine aside. "Keep going." Nat obliged and continued on at a fast pace. Before long, Catherine was winded and prayed they were close. She was amazed Nat even knew of a building way out in the jungle. "How did you find this place?" she gasped. Nat did not answer immediately, but then glanced back.

"I was chased by a giant snake," she answered. Catherine almost tripped. *A giant snake?* she thought and immediately scanned the ground. It was hard to see under the trees and with all the plants. "We're almost there," Nat said to reassure her and Catherine found the energy to run even faster. Thankfully, the extra push was just enough and they broke out into a small clearing. At the center was a sagging shelter. It was not much to look at, but if it meant they could hide while Nat explained what was happening, Catherine was grateful to see it. Retaking her hand, Nat led Catherine into the building.

CHAPTER 27
NAT

T he space was even darker than under the trees and Nat wished they had a light, especially when she had to close the door. "Don't move," Nat said and began to search the space to determine what was inside the room. After a moment, her hands fell on a shelf and found what felt like a candle stub and matches. She lit one and started the candle burning. She heard Catherine sigh with relief. Using the minimal light, Nat surveyed her surroundings. It was clear the cabin had not been occupied for a long time, but overall the space was better than she expected. A small table with a single chair. Some collapsing shelves, which were sagging with the roof. Even a narrow bed. She was most thankful to see there were no snakes or other creatures. After setting down the candle, Nat stepped up to Catherine and took her in her arms. Catherine leaned into her and Nat felt tears of relief sting her eyes. "I was so worried about you," Nat murmured into her hair. Catherine let out a sob.

"I thought they were going to kill you," Catherine said. "I don't know what I would have done." Nat stroked her hair and kissed the top of her head.

"It's okay," she said. "We're safe in here for now." Catherine looked up at her, and in the flickering light, Nat had never seen anyone more beautiful. Light glistened off of the tears in her eyes and instinctively, Nat kissed them away. Catherine raised her face and then Nat's lips were on her mouth. At first, the kiss was tender, but it quickly turned hotter and Nat felt Catherine's need to be comforted pour out of her. Catherine's lips parted and Nat knew she was welcoming her in. Feeling a rush of desire, Nat kissed her harder, using her tongue to make Catherine gasp. Now the woman was clinging to her and as crazy as she knew it was, Nat picked her up and carried her three steps to the small bed along the wall. As she set her down, Nat's head spun with thoughts of all which had happened and still was to come. *Live in the moment*, she thought and reminded herself she might die tonight when she went back to help Sal. She and Catherine may never see each other again. The thought of it made her desperate and she pressed her lips to Catherine's again. The kiss was deep and so filled with all of the emotion Nat was feeling, it made her ache.

As if sensing the specialness of the moment, Catherine took Nat's face in her hands. "I want you," she whispered. "No one else ever. Just you." The confession touched Nat so deeply she almost could not breathe. Catherine was everything she ever hoped to find. She loved her and lowered her head so their faces were close.

"I love you, Catherine Porter," she said. At the words, Catherine slipped her arms around Nat's neck and pulled her down.

"Then make love to me," she said. "And make me forget everything for a little while." Nat did not hesitate and moved her hands up under the fabric of Catherine's shirt until she found the woman's full breasts. As her palms ran over the taut fabric covering Catherine's erect nipples, the woman shivered. "How can you make me feel so alive?" Catherine whispered and reached to push her lacy bra up so her naked skin was exposed. With a rush of passion, Nat lowered her head and took one of the hard nipples into her mouth and pulled on it hungrily. Catherine shook with excitement and ran her hands into Nat's short hair to pull her down harder. It was almost too much as Nat felt a throb of ecstasy tear through her.

She could feel the tightness building between her legs and lifted herself to move on top of Catherine. With legs entwined, Nat pressed down until her clit rubbed through the fabric against Catherine's hip. Sensing her need, Catherine pulled up Nat's shirt and ran her fingertips across the lean muscles of her back. With a growl, Nat pushed again and the pressure of Catherine under her was exquisite. Catherine moaned with the feel of the friction too and lifted her hips to meet Nat's next thrust. Nat shook with the sensation of their bodies moving as one.

"Catherine," she moaned. "Is this okay? Am I hurting you?" Catherine shook her head.

"You're not hurting me," she whispered. "Please don't stop." The words lit Nat on fire and she moved her hips faster, now using her arms to lift up and put more pressure on the focal point between them. She could look down into Catherine's face now and saw the woman's half-closed eyes filled with desire. Again, Catherine lifted up to meet Nat's down-stroke and moaned when the muscles in Nat's thigh rubbed her. She immediately lifted up again to match Nat's rhythm and the two of them moved in unison as the intensity continued to build. The pleasure was so extreme, Nat could hardly breathe. Faster and faster until Nat felt the tightness inside her start to explode.

"Oh my God," she whispered. "Catherine, oh my God, you are making me come." Catherine let out a cry of pure pleasure and pulled Nat against her so hard and with such wanting, Nat started to come a second time while Catherine bucked and shivered with an orgasm of her own.

"Nat," Catherine whimpered as the waves rolled through her. "How do you make me feel like this without even taking my clothes off?" Nat chuckled a little at her words. As selfish as it was, Nat loved knowing she was the only one who had ever made Catherine come. Slowly, she lowered herself to lay beside the woman's still quivering body and enveloped her in her arms.

"It's so intense with you," Nat confessed. "You make me crazy." Catherine smiled.

"I want to always do that to you," she said and rolled into Nat so they were face to face. Their eyes met and Nat could see a sense of seriousness come into Catherine's brown eyes. "Did you mean it?" she asked. Nat was not sure what she was saying.

"Mean what?" she asked gently. Catherine looked down as if almost shy.

"That you loved me," she said. Nat's heart skipped a beat at the question. The words had been spoken in the heat of the moment and now she took a second to consider them. *Do I love her?* she thought wanting to be completely honest. She had never loved anyone before and yet, she knew what was in her heart. Nat took Catherine's hands in hers and squeezed them.

"I love you," she said. "I don't know what our future holds, but I will love you until I die." She heard Catherine let out the breath she was holding and sigh with happiness.

She looked up and Nat could see the relief and the love she felt reflected in her eyes.

"I love you too," Catherine said. "I never imagined I could feel this way about anyone, but you've opened my eyes to so much. I know this is crazy and we could be captured again at any minute, but in some ways, I have never been happier. You make me feel alive." Nat knew exactly what she meant and kissed her on the lips.

"It's not crazy," Nat said. "I feel it too." Catherine was quiet and Nat could see she was thinking hard about something. Unsure of what was going on, Nat was patient. Finally, Catherine frowned.

"Nat, do you know what else is crazy?" she said.

"What else is crazy?" Nat asked. Catherine sat up in the bed and Nat raised herself to an elbow. She watched the woman run through the facts in her mind again and then she shook her head.

"No, it can't be possible," Catherine said and looked almost sad. Nat touched her arm.

"What is it?" she asked gently. Catherine covered Nat's hand with her own and sighed.

"For a second, I was thinking the woman who helped us, the one who hit Gruden over the head with the wine vase," she said. "I was thinking she might somehow be my mother." Nat blinked. The confession was not what she was expecting and she immediately replayed the scene over in her mind. It was true the servant who saved them looked like Catherine. *A lot actually*, Nat thought now that she was considering it. *And she was especially inquisitive about who Catherine was, but how could it be possible?* "I told you it was crazy," Catherine said. "It's just that both times I've seen her, I felt incredibly connected with her. Like we somehow knew each other." Nat raised an eyebrow at the new information.

"You met her once before?" she asked. Catherine nodded.

"When Sal took me to the celebration banquet," she answered. "The woman was serving us wine and I swear, when she heard my name was Catherine Porter, she dropped the vase in her hands she was so surprised." Catherine turned to Nat. "Do you think it is possible? I thought my mother was killed in an accident off planet. When a transport she was on exploded, but what if that was not what happened?" Nat paused. The whole thing sounded crazy, but not impossible.

"When did it happen?" Nat asked and she could see a glimmer of hope starting to come into Catherine's eyes.

"Fourteen years ago. She was part of a humanitarian coalition going to a planet which had just suffered a horrible series of earthquakes," she said. "My dad always said the spaceship blew up, but he never gave much more detail. He hated to talk about it." Catherine lowered her eyes. "He loved her very much, even though he never felt he was good enough for her. When she died, he never got over it." Nat squeezed Catherine's hand. *I could understand that feeling*, she thought now that she had met Catherine. If she died, Nat would never forgive herself.

"Did you ever know why the transport exploded?" Nat asked trying to put the pieces together. *What if it was space pirates after all?* she wondered. As if reading her mind, Catherine's eyes widened.

"Nat, what if it was space pirates?" she said excitedly. "No one ever seemed to know what happened or at least I was never told the details. It really could be her!" Nat took a deep breath as she realized Catherine's hopes were starting to soar. There was no way to know if what she was deducing was correct and if she was wrong, Nat knew Catherine would be crushed. Nat rubbed a hand over her face. Things were quickly becoming extremely complicated. "Nat," Catherine said. "I have to go back and find her again to ask who she really is. I need to know." Nat nodded. There really was not another option, because if it were true, it would change Catherine's life forever. Even though Nat was not close with her mother and they had their differences about Nat's sexual preferences, growing up without her would have left a gaping hole in her life. *If I lost her at four years old and now had a chance to find her again, nothing would stop me*, Nat thought.

"Alright," Nat said and sat up swinging her legs to the floor. "Once it is dark, I am going back. I need to see if I can disable the cloaking towers, but I want you to wait here. I'll find the woman and get some answers." Catherine shook her head.

"Absolutely not. There is no way I am staying behind," Catherine insisted. Nat took Catherine by the shoulders and looked hard into her face.

"Catherine, it is too dangerous," she said. Catherine put her hands over Nat's and Nat could see by the set of her mouth, there was no way the woman was going to do what she asked.

"I'll wait with you until dark, but then I go back. You take out the towers and I'll find my mother. Then can we please get off this planet?" Catherine asked. Nat took a deep breath and let it out slowly. Having Catherine put herself back into danger was the last thing she wanted, but she could also see how determined the woman she loved was about finding her mother. Finally, Nat nodded. They would get it done. Together.

CHAPTER 28
CATHERINE

As dusk fell, Catherine stood next to Nat amongst the thick leaves and vines at the edge of the village. They were holding hands and Catherine felt the lingering tingle of the lovemaking they shared in the cabin. *Please don't let anything happen to her*, Catherine thought. *I love her.* "Are you sure you won't go back and wait for me?" Nat asked as she turned to face Catherine. "I need you to be safe." Catherine shook her head and put her arms around Nat's neck to pull her into a kiss. They lingered for a moment and then Catherine stepped away.

"I have to do this," she said. "And I will be careful, but you better not let anything happen to you either, Nat Reynolds. I need you." A tender look came into Nat's face and she pulled Catherine close again for one more kiss.

"See you at the Avalon Mercury. Thirty minutes, and no longer," Nat said. "I love you." Catherine smiled and watched as the woman slipped away into the darkness to do what needed to be done. With no time to waste, Catherine circled the other direction to go toward the banquet hall where she hoped the woman she believed was her mother was still working. There was no easy way to get there without stepping out into the open and after carefully looking each way, she started across the dirt. Suddenly off to her left she heard shouting and froze. *Have I been seen? Has Nat?* she wondered as fear leaped into her throat. It was not coming from the direction she knew Nat was headed, and she took some relief from that, nor did she see anyone running toward her. *So what was it?* Worried now some other trouble was happening, Catherine snuck to the side of a smaller dome structure and peeked out. In the center of the settlement she saw all of the captives in a line surrounded by villagers who were raucously yelling out bids. Catherine realized it was the auction and as horrified as she was at the idea of anyone being sold as a slave, she was thankful to know the pirates were distracted. *Now is the time to do this.*

Going back to the path which led to the other side of the clearing, Catherine suddenly found herself face to face with two pirates she did not recognize. They looked surprised to see her, but then the older of the two narrowed his eyes. "Who the hell are you?" he asked. Catherine gulped down her fear and gave them a smile.

"Catherine," she said. "Sal's new woman." The two men looked at each other clearly uncertain if she was telling the truth. "What? You haven't heard? I'm surprised actually, considering the pirate king himself made the announcement over a toast of wine." The younger pirate scratched his beard.

"Huh," he said. "I wasn't invited. Only the senior guys got to go, but I might have heard Sal got a new bitch. Just no way to tell if it's you." Catherine swallowed her fear when she realized they were not buying her story and made a show of bristling at the insult. She was about to keep trying to sell her case when she felt someone step upside her.

"Did you really just refer to my woman as a bitch?" Catherine heard Sal ask. She saw the two men pale and the younger pirate started to back up.

"Sal. Hey, it was a joke, okay?" he said. "This girl, she's smoking hot as—" Sal closed the distance between them and was instantly in the pirate's face.

"I strongly suggest you shut the hell up," she snarled. The older pirate grabbed his friend by the collar and yanked him along hard as he started to move away.

"You're an idiot," the older pirate said to his friend. "Don't talk. Just come on, I want to go to the auction. He's sorry about his mouth, Sal." Catherine watched the two men hurry away and she sighed with relief. At least until Sal whirled around on her and Catherine saw the fury in her eyes.

"What are you doing?" she snapped. "I don't understand why you are still here." She furrowed her brow. "Where's your Ranger?" Catherine kept her mouth closed. Although Sal had just saved her and something was going on with the pirate Catherine was not sure about, she also did not trust her. If Sal knew what Nat was up to, Catherine was confident she would kill her. Sal rubbed a hand down her face in frustration. "Years in the making and this is what it comes down to," she muttered. It made no sense to Catherine.

"What are you talking about?" she asked. Sal waved her off.

"Forget it," she moved to take Catherine's arm. "Come on. You need to hide. Things are about to get crazy around here." Catherine stepped away from her.

"I'm not going to go hide. I need to find someone first," she said. Sal frowned.

"Who?" she asked. "Is your Space Ranger missing again?"

"No," Catherine replied. "It is the woman who served us wine at the banquet. I think..." She paused, not sure how to even explain. *Is this really even possible? Could my mother be alive and here?* she wondered. "I think she is my mother," she finished. Sal looked at her with disbelief.

"What?" she asked. "Why would you even think that?" Catherine felt a rush of emotion over all of it.

"It's complicated," she answered with tears welling up in her eyes. "But I have to see her and find out." Sal's face softened a little when she saw how Catherine felt and she let out a sigh.

"Okay, come on," Sal said as she turned to lead them to the large dome at the edge of the village. "But we need to hurry. I have shit to get done. Especially if Nat is out there running around like a loose cannon." Catherine quickly followed and wanted to ask Sal what she meant regarding Nat but was afraid to give up any information. Still, it seemed Sal was frustrated with Nat differently than before. As if they were no longer enemies. *Something has changed,* Catherine thought and planned to get to the bottom of it, but first, she had to see the dark-haired servant. Sal took them to the back of the banquet hall and paused to look around before going to the door there.

"I am hoping Rog and the rest of the crew have gone to watch the auction," Sal said. "Otherwise this is going to require a very complicated explanation." Sal opened the door and stepped in. There were two women just inside in what looked to Catherine like a pantry. When they saw Sal, both stepped back alarmed. Neither of them was the woman Catherine hoped was her mother. "Where's the wine server?" Sal snapped at them. "The dark-haired older woman." The two servants dropped their eyes.

"She's in the great room cleaning up," one of the women answered.

"Have the other pirates left?" Sal asked. Both women nodded and without bothering to thank them, Sal marched past while Catherine hurried after her. *This is it*, she thought with her heart racing. *Somehow, through some crazy twist of fate, I may have found my mother*. They burst into the room with the large table. No one was inside except for the woman they were looking for and when she saw them, she froze. Sal stopped and turned to Catherine. "Is this her?" she asked. Catherine did not answer but instead started walking toward the woman standing at the far end of the table with a dish in her hand. They stared at each other and slowly the stranger set the plate down and stepped in Catherine's direction.

"You know me, don't you?" Catherine asked as they came to stand to face each other. She could read fear and confusion but also hope in the woman's eyes. Slowly, she nodded.

"I can't believe it, but I think I do," she whispered. Tears welled up in the woman's eyes and one ran down her cheek. Catherine felt pain in her chest when she saw it. *All these years lost*, she thought and felt her own tears coming.

"When I was four, my mother was killed when a transport exploded," Catherine said. "All souls were lost, or so I was told. So how can you be who I think you are?" The woman glanced cautiously at Sal and then looked back at Catherine. Resolve crossed her face.

"We were boarded by pirates and kidnapped. They took us and then blew up the ship," she explained. "They brought us here and made us slaves. I've been here, waiting and hoping somehow, someday, help would come." She stepped forward and reached out to Catherine. "My prayers were answered, but not like I wanted. I never wished for you to become a pirate's property." Catherine took her mother's outstretched hands and held on tight. "I'm your mother, Catherine," the woman finished softly.

"I knew," Catherine said. "Somehow I knew." The two of them embraced, the tears flowing freely now. For a minute, they just stood and held each other. Then Catherine heard Sal clear her throat from behind them.

"Unbelievable," Sal said. Catherine could tell the pirate was trying to be gruff, but there was a hitch in her voice too. "I hate to interrupt this moment for you, but we really need to get the hell out of here before the auction is over." Catherine pulled back and wiped her face while her mother did the same. The mannerism was so similar Catherine choked out a laugh. *My mother*, she thought with wonder and grabbed her hand before turning to Sal.

"We need to get to the spaceship," Catherine said. "And wait there." Sal nodded and started toward the exit of the building. Catherine's mother resisted.

"What's happening?" she asked. "Where are we going?" Catherine looked back and smiled at the woman she had not seen for so long.

"We are going to go home," she said. There was a pause and Catherine could see the woman who was her mother could not believe it. "Just trust me," Catherine added. A determined look came into her mother's eyes and she nodded.

"I do," she said and together they ran after Sal. The pirate was already at the back door and looking out to check for anyone walking nearby. When the coast was clear, she led them quickly to where the spaceships were parked. The Avalon Mercury's gangway was still down and the three women hurried toward it. Sal slowed at the base as Catherine and her mother started up. Seeing the pirate pause, Catherine stopped.

"You've got to come with us," she said. Sal shook her head.

"I can't," she said. "I have things to finish here." She waved Catherine away. "Now go. Hide and wait for your Ranger. I know that is the plan." Catherine walked back down the gangway to stand in front of Sal. She looked into the woman's eyes and saw a mix of feelings reflected there but mostly she saw regret. Catherine impulsively reached out and touched Sal's face.

"Thank you," Catherine said. Sal froze at the touch and Catherine saw the woman search her face before taking the hand in her own and gently kissing Catherine's palm.

"No, thank you, Catherine Porter," she said and turned to go without another word. Before she was even out of the landing zone, an explosion sounded on the far side of the settlement. It reverberated through the air and Catherine's heart nearly stopped. *Nat!* she thought. Sal apparently came to the same conclusion.

"I'm so going to kick her ass," Sal said as she broke into a run. "She started without me."

CHAPTER 29
NAT

The force of the concussion when the cloaking tower's transformer blew was more than Nat expected and it knocked her onto her ass. *Not to mention making my ears ring like hell*, she thought as she shook her head to clear the cobwebs. Shooting the box with a full blast from the plasma gun she took from Gruden seemed like a good idea. She just had not considered the back blast and realized she was lucky to be alive. The other unfortunate side effect was the loud noise it made when it exploded. Any second now she expected pirates to descend upon her position and she knew it was time to exit stage right. Unfortunately, when she went to stand up, her left leg buckled precariously. *I must have twisted the knee when I was thrown backward. Not good.* Forcing herself up, she hobbled to the edge of the concrete base of the now sparking tower and ducked down to assess the damage. Looking at her pant leg, she saw there was more damage than just a sprain. A piece of shrapnel was lodged there. The wound throbbed as she pressed the spot with her fingers to decide if she could pull it free and the pain made her head spin. It did not take her long to figure out she was now in a particularly bad spot and as if she willed them into appearing, Nat heard the sounds of pirates approaching on the run.

Nat checked her plasma gun and got ready to battle. *I am a warrior*, she reminded herself and using the element of surprise to her advantage, waited until the voices were close before she rolled out from cover, aimed at her attackers, and fired. The closest two were easy shots and Nat dropped them with satisfaction. Her third shot went wide and the pirate was able to retreat back behind the edge of a domed building to return fire of his own. Keeping her head down, Nat moved back out of sight. More blasts hit the concrete near her and, even worse, she heard more shouts of other enemies coming. Looking around, Nat knew her only chance was to try and get to the jungle to hide among the trees, but the minute she went to rise, her knee shot pain through her. Putting weight on it was a problem. *I guess it's time to belly crawl*, she thought, but first Nat knew she had to drive them back or they would overrun her position before she made it.

As more blasts started to pound against the concrete base, Nat took a deep breath and made ready to roll out from cover again to return fire. Three quick shots, then she would roll back and start crawling. Waiting for a lull in the barrage, Nat began to move when another gun sounded. It was from further to the right and Nat worried for a second one of the pirates was flanking her to get a better angle. Knowing she had to focus on the new threat first, Nat forced her throbbing leg under her and shifted only to see a sight she would have never imagined. Sal was here and with a plasma gun in each hand, she was blasting the crap out of the pirates who had Nat pinned down. Inspired, Nat rolled out from behind the concrete as well and opened up on her attackers. More of them fell and after a minute, Nat could see they were either dead or had fled.

"Way to go, superhero," Sal said with a shake of her head as she jogged up to Nat. "You had to go and blow up the damn thing." Nat pulled herself into a sitting position.

"It seemed like a good idea at the time," she said as Sal knelt beside her and looked at the knee. Without asking, she reached down and yanked the piece of metal sticking out of Nat's flesh and then tossed it away. Nat was so surprised, she did not have time to scream, but the aftershock of the pain had her rolling over to puke in the dirt.

"You bitch," she said when she was done spitting out the last of the bile. "When this is done, I'm going to kick your ass."

"Fine, but right now I need you to get up and run. I think you did the trick taking down the stealth field over this settlement, but it does no good if we can't radio out for back-up," Sal said as she slipped an arm under Nat's shoulders to help lift her. "You ready?" Nat nodded and between the two of them, got her up. Limping, but thankful the shrapnel was out of her leg, Nat was able to keep up with Sal as she led across the clearing.

"Where are we going?" Nat asked.

"Back to your ship," she answered. "You can call from it at the same time as getting the hell out of here." Nat liked the sound of her plan until she realized Sal had not said "we."

"You're going with us," she insisted, but Sal did not bother to answer. "I'm serious, Ranger," Nat said. "I am ordering you to escape with us." Before Sal could respond one way or the other, Colton, the captive who helped Nat escape, came running at them. Nat realized the slave auction must have fallen apart when the transformer blew and shooting started. The boy was armed with a plasma gun and training it right at Sal. "Colton!" Nat yelled as she and Sal stopped in their tracks. "Hold your fire." Colton held up but his whole body shook.

"They killed my parents," he cried. "And she was going to kill me. So now it is my turn." With no choice, Nat thrust herself between Colton's gun and Sal to block him. The boy's face turned furious.

"Get out of the way," he said. Nat shook her head.

"I won't until you hand me that weapon," she told him. "This woman is a Space Ranger who has been undercover as a pirate. She is not your enemy and would not have shot you." Nat was not so sure the last sentence was true, but she forced it out of her mind for the moment. Colton waivered.

"We're wasting some valuable time here," Sal said. "Either shoot me or don't but make it quick."

"You're not helping, Sal," Nat said, but she could see indecision on the teenage boy's face. Nat held out her hand. "Give me the gun and come with us. I'm about to fly us all out of here and the Space Rangers will be on their way to rescue everyone else." Slowly, Colton lowered his weapon, but before he could hand it over, plasma blasts landed in the dirt near them.

"We got company," Sal said and turned to return fire. Nat grabbed Colton by the arm and with Sal laying down cover for them, the three managed to get to the holding area where all the spacecraft were waiting. As they approached, Nat watched the gangway descend. *Please let that be Cather-*

ine who was watching for us, she thought. In answer, she saw the woman come out the open door and run toward them.

"Get inside," Nat yelled. Catherine ignored her and was immediately at her side to help Nat hobble up the ramp.

"Oh my God, you're bleeding," she said and Nat looked down to see blood had soaked her pant leg clear to her ankle.

"A scratch," Nat reassured her even though it hurt like hell and she worried for a brief moment if the damage to the knee would be permanent.

"We're all going to have more than a scratch if you don't hurry up," Sal snapped as she continued to hold off the on-coming pirates with her well-placed shots. Even in the heat of the moment, Nat was impressed at her accuracy as she backed up the ramp behind them. Finally, they made it through the door and Frederick was waiting. He hit the button to close the door the moment they were through, but Nat could hear more plasma blasts pounding into the hull of the ship. *Not good*, she worried, knowing any one of those impacts could disable the luxury cruiser starcraft if the pirate got lucky. The hull of the Avalon Mercury was not made to hold up under such an attack. Nat looked at Sal and could see she knew it too.

With a look of resignation, Sal slapped the door's controls to reopen the door.

"What are you doing?" Catherine asked with alarm. "You can't go back out there."

"Watch me," Sal said and turned to meet Nat's eye. "Take care of her, Captain Reynolds." Nat hated what was about to happen and stepped forward to go with her when her knee buckled. Sal caught her. "Go make the radio call," she said. "I'll hold them off."

"No!" Catherine exclaimed. "I won't let you. They will kill you." Nat saw Sal give Catherine a wink.

"We all know what happens to the villain," she said and turned to go. Nat grabbed her arm.

"Wait, they will need to know who's calling it in and the code word to make sure it is not a trap," Nat said. Sal nodded.

"Codename is Athena," she said. "And tell them Salishan Bransen says hello." Nat froze. *Did she just say she was Salishan Bransen?* she thought with wonder.

"Hold it, you're a Space Ranger legend," Nat said. "They said you were dead." Sal gave her a wry smile.

"Not just yet," she said and ran down the gangway with guns blazing. Watching her go, Nat felt a chill run through her. The woman who held every record at the academy and was the most decorated sniper in the corps had given up her option to choose any career she wanted to go undercover and stop the evil of the space pirates. *And now she is out there saving our butts*, Nat thought and turned away from the door.

"Help me get to the cockpit," she said to Catherine and Colton. The two of them grabbed her under the arms and half carried Nat until she was able to sit in the pilot's chair. While firing up the spaceship's engines, Nat engaged the comm link. *I sure hope this works*, she thought. If taking out one of the cloaking towers did not wreck the grid and bring them offline, then they all were sunk. She pressed the button. "This is Space Ranger Captain Natalie Reynolds, call sign Catwoman, calling with a Level Red 10-85," she turned to the positioning system and watched the screen as the computer came online. At first, the screen was blank and Nat felt her heart sinking. The system would not be able to determine their location if the cloaking towers were still functioning. Behind her, she could sense Catherine was holding her breath. *Come on, come on.* Finally, a 3D map started to appear and the Avalon Mercury 3370's indicator began to blink in the middle of it. As she noted the coordinates, the comm link squelched and Nat's friend Dee, the Space Ranger dispatcher, replied to Nat's original distress call. "Catwoman, this is Base, what is your position? We are scrambling fighters now." Nat had never been so happy to hear a friendly voice and she rattled off their coordinates. She turned to Colton. "Tell Sal to get her butt in her. We're leaving," she ordered and Colton disappeared out of the cockpit. He was back in less than a minute.

"She won't come!" he said and Nat leaned forward to see Sal was hunkered down behind a fighter wing, shooting at any pirate who tried to advance on the Avalon Mercury. Angrily, Nat rapped on the ship's windshield as hard as she could and Sal looked over. When she saw Nat waving her to come on, Nat watched Sal grin and then, in perfect Space Ranger fashion, she snapped off a salute. Suddenly, a barrage of plasma blasts coming from the other direction rocked the ship. A red warning indicator light started to flash on the control panel. *Not good*, Nat thought. It was time to go and she knew it. When she glanced back to look at Sal, the woman was gone.

"Damn her," Nat muttered feeling a twist of sadness and regret in her stomach. The decision to leave was almost too much, but when another red light popped on to show the spaceship was sustaining too much damage, Nat started to engage the engines for a fast departure. "Everybody buckle in and hang on," she said and pulled back for liftoff.

CHAPTER 30
CATHERINE

"Nat, no!" Catherine cried. "We can't leave her." Catherine saw Nat grit her teeth in frustration at their predicament.

"If we don't go now, it will be all over for us too," she said. "You have to buckle in. We're going up." Not sure what to do or how they could still save Sal, Catherine hesitated. Nat turned to her and Catherine saw determination but also a hint of tears in the woman's eyes. "Catherine, please. We can't wait. I'm sorry." Realizing the situation was hurting Nat as much as it was herself, Catherine sank down into the jump seat and put on the harness. "Colton!" Nat yelled. "Is everyone ready back there?"

"Yes," he yelled back and Catherine could hear the nervousness in his voice as plasma blasts continued to echo outside the ship.

"Then we're going," Nat said and Catherine closed her eyes as she felt the Avalon Mercury start to lift in a hurry. *I'm so sorry, Sal,* Catherine thought as tears slipped down her cheeks. Even though she knew the woman was a pirate and had admitted to doing terrible things, she was also a

Space Ranger like Nat. *And I know in her heart, she was never the villain.* The spaceship shuddered as Nat turned it hard up and to the left to clear the larger ships on the ground around it. As she maneuvered, Catherine heard her click on the comm link. "Catwoman to Base," she said. "I am getting the hell out of here. Codename is Athena. I repeat. Codename is Athena." There was a long pause on the comm link.

"Base copies," Dee said over the dispatch. "Jesus, Nat, how did you get mixed up in this?"

"I hope to tell you over drinks real soon," Nat answered and Catherine felt the spaceship starting to accelerate and opened her eyes to see they were finally clear of the shelters and tall trees of the jungle. *We're going to make it*, she thought with a mixture of relief touched by regret. Sal was still down there. They could not save her.

"I'll be happy to buy, Catwoman," Base said. "Now go!" Catherine saw Nat nod and pull back on the throttle.

"Here we go everybody," she yelled. "Hang on." Catherine grabbed the edge of the seat as the craft began to shoot toward space. It was moving so fast it physically pushed her back. As she watched, the green of the trees grew smaller and she let out the breath she had not realized she was holding. *It's going to be okay,* she thought and then the first alarm sounded.

"What's that? What's happening?" she asked and saw Nat working the controls. The entire spaceship yanked hard to the right and then dipped back down toward the planet.

"Shit," Catherine heard Nat growl. "That was the sound of someone trying to get a sitelock on us. It means we've got company." Nat's hands flew over the console as she went into evasion maneuvers. Their craft began to twist and turn. A crash of something tipping over followed by a cry of alarm came from the back. Again, the sitelock warning sounded and again Nat twisted the ship to avoid the attack. Catherine saw the strain on Nat's face and knew they were in trouble. "Catherine, look through the windshield to the right and see if you can get a visual. I need to know how many are out there." Catherine unhooked from the seat and moved to look out. Her heart nearly stopped when she saw two pirate fighters right on their tail.

"Two," she said. "Nat, they are right on top of us." It seemed impossible they could miss.

"Get snapped back in," Nat said. "I've got an idea, but you will want to be hanging on." Catherine scrambled back to her seat and once Nat saw she was secured, she took the craft into a sharp nosedive. As Catherine watched out the front windshield, she could see the canopy of the jungle rapidly approaching. The sight was terrifying yet she trusted Nat with all her heart and if this was the way to stay alive, Catherine believed it.

"This is it everybody," Nat yelled. "Hold on, I'm going to hit the brakes." *What is she talking about?* Catherine thought and then she was slammed against the belts crisscrossing her body and holding her in the seat. Nat had engaged a full reverse thrust within seconds of plunging into the trees below. The two pirate fighters on their tail were caught by surprise and the first could not pull up in time. Catherine watched it shoot past them and into the treetops. The crash was beautiful to see as first the left wing and then the right was torn off by the thick branches, spinning the rest of the ship end over end until it hit a larger tree and exploded. Catherine wanted to cheer but then realized the second fighter, which also raced past them, was not going quite as fast. As the small but deadly craft wobbled while it fought to pull up and level above the trees, Catherine felt her hopes dash. She did not have to be a pilot to know now the Avalon Mercury was a sitting duck as it hovered in place.

Nat scrambled to recover and turn the ship to head them back out toward space, but Catherine could see the fighter out of the front. It was coming around in a long, lazy sweep to make a fatal pass. "Where is the cavalry?" Catherine heard Nat whisper and knew she was hoping against hope the Space Ranger fighters would arrive before it was too late. As the Avalon Mercury pitched while Nat tried to move out of the oncoming fighter's line of fire, Catherine saw an even more frightening sight. Coming in at lightning speed was another pirate fighter. As Nat noticed the second threat, Catherine saw a look of determination cross her face. "I have to ditch us," she said. "It's our only chance. Through the trees and maybe get to a clearing—" her words were cut off by the screeching of the sitelock alarm. Catherine could not believe what was happening. At any second, they were going to die and it seemed so unfair. *I only just found my mother*, she thought. *And Nat. I can't lose her now.* She watched as Nat did all she could to shake the fighter's lock, but the spaceship at her fingertips was just not made for it.

As she was about to tell Nat how much she cherished having had a chance to love her, the onrushing pirate fighter screamed past the windshield of the Avalon Mercury. It was so close both Nat and Catherine instinctively ducked and the sitelock alarm abruptly ceased. "What the hell?" Nat whispered clearly confused. "That guy just went through his buddy's sightline and ruined the shot." Seizing the chance, Catherine saw Nat yank on the throttle and turn to evade any further attempts. As she did, Catherine had a clear view of the two pirate fighters. They looked for a moment like they might collide and Catherine frowned trying to take it all in when suddenly the second fighter let loose its laser cannons and blasted the original pirate fighter out of the sky. Catherine's mouth dropped open with surprise.

"Did you see that?" she asked in total shock. Looking at Nat, she saw the woman was nodding and a grin was starting to spread over her face.

"I'll be a son of a bitch," Nat muttered but with respect and awe in her voice. She brought their spaceship around while the remaining pirate fighter came up alongside. Catherine unbuckled again and went to the windshield to look out. Through the glass, she could see the smirking face of Sal Bransen in the other cockpit.

"How many fucking times do I have to tell you to get off of my planet?" Sal said over the comm link. Catherine felt relief wash over her. Although her feelings toward Sal were different than with Nat, Catherine felt a specialness about the pirate. There was raw, untapped goodness in the woman, which she knew Sal would swear did not exist. *I should have known Sal wouldn't let them kill her*, she thought and with a smile realized she did not know much about the Space Ranger Corps, but one thing was for sure. The females in their ranks were badasses. Beside her, she heard Nat laugh with pure relief and excitement. She pressed the comm link.

"I never thought I'd say this," Nat replied. "But I am very happy to see you." Catherine heard Sal chuckle over the connection.

"Ditto, Ranger," she said. "Now let's get the hell out of here because I'm pretty sure more fighters will be coming."

Nat nodded. "Agreed," Nat said. "I honestly don't know how much juice this ship has to blast us out of the atmosphere, but I'll follow your lead." Without another word, Catherine watched Sal lift the nose of her smaller spaceship and start to climb. "Time to buckle in," Nat said to Catherine softly and when she looked into Nat's face, she saw the same relief she was feeling. They were leaving. Somehow, they survived. With tears in her eyes, Catherine leaned forward and kissed Nat. It was quick, but there was both passion and tenderness in it. *It's not over for us*, she thought and prayed it never would be. Pulling back, she smiled at her lover and then went to sit down. Buckling in, she felt Nat start to lift the ship. "Everybody still okay back there?" she yelled toward where Colston, Frederick, and her mother still sat.

"We are," Colston said. "But maybe you can tell us what is going on?" Catherine watched Nat grit her jaw with concentration.

"We are getting the hell out of here at last," she said and pulled on the throttle to blast them upward. Catherine felt the spaceship begin to tremble as it gained speed. There was no way to know how much damage from the plasma blasts the Avalon Mercury sustained. For the briefest of moments, Catherine worried it would be too much and they would not be able to get free of the planet's gravity, but then she forced the thought away. *We are going to make it*, she told herself. *All this did not happen so we fail now.*

"You got this, Nat," Catherine heard Sal say over the comm link. "Get your ass up here." Catherine grabbed hold of her seat as the whole spaceship started to rock and two more red lights started blinking on the control panel.

"Come on, come on," Nat growled and then they were through and Catherine could feel the release into weightlessness as the ship was enveloped in the blackness of space. A cheer came from the backroom and Catherine covered her face with her hands almost wanting to sob she was so happy.

"Oh shit," she heard Nat say under her breath and Catherine looked up. Out the windshield, she could see a line of Space Ranger ships coming straight at them and for a second did not understand why this was bad until she realized they were all aiming their cannons at Sal in her little pirate fighter. Nat jumped at the comm link.

"Everyone, hold your fire!" she ordered. "I repeat, hold your fire. This is Space Ranger Captain Nat Reynolds in the Avalon Mercury 3370 and that fighter is with us. Do not engage." Feeling the tension, Catherine watched Sal's ship start to dip lower. Nat slapped the comm link. "Bransen," she snapped. "You will hold your position." Then her voice softened. "Sal, if you try and run, they will shoot you down." None of the spaceships moved and as she watched out of the windshield, Catherine could almost feel Sal's hesitation. Quickly unbuckling, Catherine moved to the comm link.

"Please, Sal," she said. "You don't have to do this anymore." After a pause, Sal's ship slowly lifted back into line with the Avalon Mercury.

"How do I know I'm going to regret this?" Sal muttered over the line. "Okay, I'll behave." Catherine heard Sal sigh. "Space Ranger Squadron Leader, this is Ranger Salishan Bransen," Sal said. "I am willing to cooperate." There was a long pause before an answer came back.

"Copy, Ranger Bransen," the squadron leader finally replied. "Who called in the code word?"

"I did, squadron leader, but it was her successful mission," Nat answered giving Sal all the credit. "Code word Athena and this is the planet we have all been looking for. There are hostiles as well as captives and other civilians so proceed with caution."

"Understood, Captain," the squad leader said. "The Magellan Space Carrier is at our rear. I am sending you with an escort to that location." Catherine saw Nat exhale a long slow breath.

"Never sounded better," she said.

CHAPTER 31
NAT

Nat could feel the pain in her knee starting to come back as the medication wore off, but she was glad for it. Her month of rehab after the last accident in the canyon had taken her dangerously close to addiction. Mixed with the guilt and depression she had felt, it was a road to disaster and only thanks to the encouragement from the Space Rangers to get back in the saddle did she escape at all. Now more than ever, she wanted to avoid any risk and stay aware of everything around her, especially because sitting on the edge of the bed beside her was the beautiful Catherine. Her hand was clasped in Nat's and the smooth warmth of it was incredibly reassuring. "Is it hurting?" Catherine asked as she read Nat's face. Nat shrugged.

"Only a little, but I don't mind it. Having you here is the best medicine anyway," she said with a grin. The line was corny but ridiculously true. After all they had experienced over the last week, Nat felt more connected to the woman than anyone. *Ever*, she thought. Catherine smiled at the comment.

"I want to be here and I want to take care of you," Catherine said and leaned in to kiss Nat on the lips. The taste of her mouth made Nat feel a warm tingle run through her. She could hardly wait to get out of the hospital and spend time alone together. They needed a chance to talk about everything which had happened. *And where we are headed as couple*. Nat pushed the unwelcome thought aside.

Now that she had to stay in place to rehab for a while, there would be time to figure everything out. The doctor even warned Nat she would possibly never have full mobility again and may likely forever have a limp. The news concerned Nat. She knew the Space Rangers were strict about the capabilities of their pilots and if she was less than one hundred percent, there was no way to know if they would let her stay in the corps. Since the Rangers were all she knew, imagining a future without them was scary. *But then I could stay with Catherine*, she thought. *Assuming she wants me that long*. Again, Nat shoved the thoughts aside. It was time to live in the moment and Nat pulled Catherine even closer as she ran her hands up into the woman's long dark hair and held her as she took the kiss deeper. The slightest moan came from Catherine and Nat felt desire bloom within her. For a fleeting moment, she wondered who would notice if she pulled the woman onto the bed. As if reading her mind, Catherine pushed back gently to break the kiss.

"Nat," she breathed her voice heavy with passion. "We can't, but I hope they let you out soon." Nat chuckled and hoped it too.

Someone cleared her throat at the door and both Nat and Catherine jumped with surprise. Nat saw Catherine blush as she looked and saw Sal was standing in the doorway. She was watching them with a wry smile. "Should I come back?" she asked. Catherine laughed.

"No," she answered. "I need to go back downstairs to sit with Mom. She's very anxious." Sal raised an eyebrow.

"Is your father on his way back to Prospo?" she asked. "That was quick." Catherine glanced at Nat, who smiled and then nodded. She had pulled some strings to get Catherine's dad picked up and then raced back on a Space Ranger fighter. Catherine smiled in return.

"Nat took care of it," she said and then bent down to kiss Nat again. Suddenly feeling possessive with Sal looking on, Nat turned the gentle kiss into something with more heat before she let Catherine walk away. Catherine blushing again, this time from passion rather than embarrassment, giggled and turned to go. "I'll see you soon," she murmured. Nat winked.

"Tell your mom hello. I am hoping the reunion is perfect," Nat said. Catherine nodded, her face filled with both worry and hope.

"Me too. I so much want that," Catherine said and moved to leave. Sal stepped aside with a mini bow and Catherine smiled at the courtesy before she was gone down the hall.

"You need to quit flirting with my girl," Nat said with a joking tone, but there was also a hint of bite to it. Sal waved her off.

"That is one you don't need to worry about," Sal said. "She's so in love with you it is ridiculous. Trust me, I tested the waters." Nat felt a stab of anger at the offhand comment but swallowed it and gave the woman a nod.

"So she told me," Nat said. "Catherine seems to think you were quite honorable about the whole thing considering." Sal shrugged.

"I have my moments," she said and walked closer to the bed. "I guess the real question though is what you are going to do with her. Can't exactly take her along on your next mission. And you don't strike me as a 'one in every port' sort of gal."

Nat sighed. It was a good question and she did not honestly have an answer yet. Knowing Catherine had changed her through and through, but it did not overcome the challenges which would be ahead for them. If Nat stayed with the Space Rangers, and she could think of no other way to live her life, their relationship would be long distance. Nat had sworn after Olivia she would not put anyone through that again. Catherine deserved better and since she was only eighteen, she had so much to still experience it would not be fair to tie her down.

"You're taking an awfully long time to answer considering the amazing woman is madly in love with you," Sal said. "Don't tell me you think you can do better or I'll kick your ass right now, bad knee or not." Nat shook her head. Sal was right. Catherine was in love with her and was not ashamed to admit it, even though Nat was the one and only woman she had ever been with. *And I'm in love with her too*, Nat thought, which was the problem. She wanted to be with her as long as Catherine would have her.

"Damn," Nat said. "Why does life have to be so complicated?" Sal snorted a laugh.

"You're preaching to the choir," she said. Nat chuckled too. Sal had a great point. Compared to the ex-pirate's situation, Nat was on easy street.

"Do you know what they plan to do with you yet?" Nat asked. It took every favor Nat could pull to keep Sal out of jail, but she knew it was probably only temporary. Mission or no mission, Salishan Bransen had crossed lines the Space Rangers were having trouble forgiving. Sal ran a hand over the short black hair of her scalp and shook her head.

"Not exactly," she replied. "There will be a court hearing tomorrow and everything will be brought out into the open." Nat noted a hint of regret in Sal's eyes as she looked away out the room's window. "I don't imagine it will go well for me." Nat sighed with understanding. She did not think it would go well for Sal either but did not want to admit it after all the woman did to save her and Catherine.

"Maybe they will just discharge you and be done with it," Nat said.

Sal continued to stare out the window. "Maybe," she said. A thought occurred to Nat. *What if Sal is like me and there is no life beyond the Space Rangers?*

"If they do, what will you do?" Nat asked. Sal shrugged.

"I'll figure something out," she answered. "I have some funds." Sal looked back at her. The woman's eyes were cold as ice now and any regret was long gone. "Probably shouldn't mention it, but I do happen to know where all the pirate's off planet stashes are hidden. I figure it's my due." Nat frowned.

"You're right, don't tell me stuff like that," Nat said. "Although I'm sure you'll do the right thing tomorrow and confess those locations at the hearing as well." Nat and Sal's eyes met. It was suddenly crystal clear the woman had no inten-tion of sticking around for any hearing. Nat lifted her chin and for the moment, tried to stop thinking like a Ranger.

"Where will you go?" she asked. Sal shrugged.

"Here and there," she said. "The galaxy is a big place." Nat nodded and could tell Sal was about to go. There was, how-ever, one more question in Nat's heart, which she needed to ask Sal, but a part of her dared not do it. Memories of the race through the canyon a year ago, while she chased a talent-ed pirate pilot into a trap, still haunted Nat. Even after taking revenge by exposing their hidden base, Nat could not let go of the regret and responsibility she felt over Shaun, her co-pi-lot's, horrible death. *Could the other pilot have been Sal?* she wondered, not for the first time. Setting such a cunning trap seemed right in line with something the woman would do. *She could have just been doing it to appease Rog. Or did she do it just to kill?* Nat could not be sure and a part of her realized she needed to be. Nat swallowed.

"I need one more thing from you, Sal," Nat said. "Before you disappear into the wind." Sal tilted her head and nar-rowed her eyes. She paused a moment before answering.

"What?" she asked.

Nat took a deep breath. "About a year ago, on the planet Elivib, did you lure a Space Ranger fighter into the canyon there?" she asked. Sal raised an eyebrow.

"Why would you ask me that?" she said. Nat did not like the lack of a direct answer and she felt her heart start to beat faster.

"Did you?" Nat said. Sal looked hard into Nat's eyes, but her expression was unreadable. In that moment, Nat knew

Sal was the one and then Sal shook her head and looked away.

"I don't know what you're talking about," she said. "Now, if you're done with the interrogation, I have places to go and women to conquer."

"We're done," Nat said her voice hard. Without another word or a look back, Salishan Bransen walked out the door. Nat watched her go and knew they were even and there was nothing more to say. Leaning back on her pillow, Nat closed her eyes and tried to forgive herself for what happened in that canyon. Suddenly there was the sound of loud voices in the hall and Nat looked up to see her friends Vic and Dee come in.

"Holy crap," Vic said as she walked up to Nat's bedside. "Was that who I think it was? Fucking Salishan Bransen?" Nat grinned.

"You just missed her," she said. Vic's eyes widened and she was speechless. Dee snorted a laugh at her friend's starry-eyed look.

"Chill out, Vic," she said and then looked at Nat. "Although she's a bit of a legend at Base. Was she really an undercover space pirate like they are saying?" Nat nodded.

"Yes," she said. "A true badass and you know coming from me, that means something." Vic laughed.

"True that," Dee said. "It takes one to know one. How's the knee?" Nat was about to answer it was sore but getting better when Vic butt in.

"Nat, do you think she would give me her autograph if I asked her?" Vic said. Nat considered the question for a moment before answering and then shook her head.

"I wouldn't ask," Nat said. "She's not particularly friendly."

"Damn," Vic said looking disappointed. "Well, maybe next time."

"Maybe," Nat said, but somehow knew there would never be a next time.

CHAPTER 32
CATHERINE

C atherine held her mother's hand in the coffee shop just down the street from the hospital. Both of them were nervous and Catherine kept giving the hand a squeeze to reassure them. It was so surreal to be sitting there next to the woman Catherine believed most of her life was dead. *My mother is alive and beside me*, Catherine thought for the hundredth time and now her dad was on his way back to Prospo. Although she was still not clear on the details as to why he left her without word, she was excited to have him home again. It was incredibly sweet of Nat to arrange for him to be brought back in a fighter as it could travel so much faster than a transport. Catherine knew waiting even one minute longer than she had to would be torture to her nerves. She had decided not to tell her dad about her mother and how she had been rescued. She especially left out the part about her here waiting to see him. It would be shocking enough to hear it in person. Feeling impatient, even though the Space Ranger Base had been kind enough to contact her to say her dad would be arriving soon, Catherine had to do something. "Can I get you a snack? Are you hungry?" Catherine asked her mother. The woman smiled and patted Catherine's hand. It was clear she was overwhelmed with the reality of the situation as much as Catherine was at the moment.

"Honestly, my stomach is in such knots, I can't imagine putting anything in it right now," she answered. "But thank you." Catherine smiled back.

"You're welcome, and you're right. Eating something right now is about the last thing I want," she said. "But I'm going to check outside again. I don't want to miss him." Her mother nodded and Catherine slipped out onto the sidewalk. Her excuse to go outside was two-fold. Catching her dad first before he came into the building, felt like the right thing to do. She wanted to prepare him. *Not to mention ask him a bunch of questions too*, she thought. There were things she wanted answers to and foremost was how he could just up and leave her like he had with no credits and no options. As she was thinking of it all, she saw an Ubercab turn the corner and head her way. In her heart, she knew it was him and took a deep breath. The craft stopped and her dad stepped out of the backseat. When he saw her, she saw tears well up in his eyes and in the moment, Catherine did not care about the whys and the hows. She was simply happy to see him safe and here with her again.

"Catherine," her dad said as he held his arms out to her. "I don't know how you did it but thank you for helping me get back to Prospo." Catherine went to him and wrapped her arms around his waist.

"It wasn't really me," she said. "A friend did it. She someone who... well, she makes things happen."

"I hope I get a chance to thank her," her father said as he hugged her tight. For the first time in a long time, he did not smell of alcohol and it caught Catherine off guard. In fact, he seemed healthier overall. Stepping back, Catherine looked into his face and saw the constant five o'clock shadow with bloodshot eyes were gone too. Catching her look, her father gave her a timid smile.

"Dad, where have you been?" Catherine asked more confused than ever. Her father looked away.

"I went to a special rehab," he said and then turned back to her and there was resolve in his eyes. "I know I have a lot of explaining to do, but please believe me I did this for love." He stepped forward and took Catherine's hands in his to look in her eyes. "Catherine, I was killing myself and after you turned eighteen, I realized you would leave and I would lose you to the real world if I didn't change."

Catherine shook her head. Everything was so overwhelming. *He did this because he loves me,* she thought. *And now I have him back and he's actually sober.* "Why didn't you just tell me?" she finally asked. "I thought you were dead." She saw his face fall.

"God, I never wanted that to happen. It was supposed to be a week so I figured you would think I was on a bender and then I could surprise you when I returned." He ran a hand over his face and Catherine could see the remorse he felt. "But I was a tougher nut to crack than they thought. What was supposed to be a week was a month and I was not allowed to leave or contact the outside world," he said. "Including you." Catherine was thoughtful while she put all the pieces together. It seemed crazy yet made sense and slowly she realized everything was going to be okay after all. *And he doesn't even know about Mom yet,* she thought. *Or Nat.*

"Oh Dad," she finally said and hugged him again. "I'm so proud of you." She felt him let out a big sigh of relief.

"Thank you," he whispered into her hair. "I never meant to scare you." Catherine just hugged him tighter.

"Excuse me," a voice said from behind her and Catherine realized it was her mother. Excited now, Catherine stepped back and turned to see the woman. She looked nervous and Catherine went to take her hand before looking back at her dad. When she did, her father was frozen in place and staring at his wife. Slowly he lifted his hand to reach toward her. His eyes were filled with confusion, but also hope.

"Miriam?" he asked. "But how—" Catherine's mother stepped forward and took the man's outstretched hand.

"It's me," she said. Catherine stood with tears in her eyes mesmerized by the moment. Both of her parents, alive, and back here together again. She watched as her dad pulled Miriam into his arms and held her.

"I always knew," he said. "Somehow. Someway. I knew you were alive. I felt it in my heart."

CATHERINE RAN BACK to the hospital. All she wanted to do was tell Nat everything. Her parents, although shy and confused, were settled in at the coffee shop to talk for the first time in fourteen years. *It is all so perfect,* she thought, smiling as she went. As she came to the front doors of the building, Sal was walking out. They both froze when they saw each other. Sal recovered first and gave Catherine a sly smile. "I did not know if I would have a chance to say goodbye to you or not," she said. Catherine tilted her head.

"Where are you going?" she asked. Sal shrugged.

"It's a big galaxy. I'm sure I'll find somewhere I'm welcome," she answered. The reply was meant to be a flip answer, but Catherine could see there was a bit of sadness behind the words. It made Catherine's heart clench. Although Catherine knew Nat was the only woman she would ever love, Sal would always be special. *After all, she saved us in the end*, she thought. Stepping closer, Catherine touched Sal's arm.

"I can never thank you enough," she said. "We all owe you our lives. If I can ever—" Sal put her hand on Catherine's and held it with a surprising fierceness.

"Do not say you need to repay me, Catherine," she said. "It is you who rescued me." In a flash, Sal closed the distance between them and she searched Catherine's face. Catherine caught her breath. The woman was so intense. "Do you love her?" she asked in a whisper. "Like a love which will never end?" All Catherine could do was nod. In her heart, there was no doubt. After a pause, Sal stepped back and laughed. It was not a happy sound.

"Well, she's lucky as hell then," Sal said. "And I could say something asinine like 'if she ever stops being good to you...' but you know what? That Ranger loves you so much it is ridiculous." Catherine's heart fluttered at her words and she smiled. It was a mutual feeling. Sal saw the look and shook her head as she held up a finger. "But," she started. "She's proud and stupidly loyal to the Space Rangers. If she starts some crap about duty and not being fair to you, tell her to shut the fuck up. Got it?" Catherine nodded and Sal walked to the curb to hail a cab. One stopped almost immediately and Sal turned back as she opened the door. It looked like she was about to say something else, but then paused to reconsider. Catherine stepped toward her.

"What?" Catherine asked. Sal smirked and shook her head.

"Nothing important," she said and slipped into the cab. Before Catherine could even get to the window, the vehicle was zipping away into traffic.

CHAPTER 33
NAT

"So, hey, we got you a get-well gift," Vic said holding out a wrapped box once she had stopped mooning over the idea of meeting Salishan Bransen. Nat took it with a grin.

"You did not need to do that," she said but was eager to open it. After all she had been through, something simple and fun sounded good. Vic shrugged and glanced at Dee.

"Figured you needed a new item for your collection," Dee said. Nat raised an eyebrow and pulled off the paper. When she opened the box, she saw a vintage t-shirt with a Catwoman logo on the front. "Not easy to find," she added. "I can't understand why you like that old Earth stuff personally." Nat gave her a big smile as she held the shirt up to look at it.

"I don't expect you too, Dee," she replied. "But from what I hear, it was the best of times and places." Dee snorted a laugh.

"If you say so," she said. "I prefer the here and now, thanks."

"Hey, speaking of the here and now, what are you planning to do next?" Vic asked. Nat wished she knew the answer.

There were so many parts to the decision, she was not sure which direction to go. *And how does Catherine fit into any of it?* she thought. Nat felt a stab of sadness in her heart at the possibility of losing her. Even through the most stressful and dangerous of situations, their passion toward to each other had endured, yet now Nat worried about what a normal life would do to them. *We've been living in a fantasy of sorts so far.* The question now was would Catherine still want Nat for the routine day-to-day. "Hello?" Vic said waving a hand in front of Nat's face. "Prospo to Nat. Is the question so hard?"

Nat chuckled. "Sorry," she said. "I was thinking, and actually, yes, the question is hard." Nat saw Dee nod.

"This has to do with Catherine, doesn't it?" she asked, but Nat could tell she already knew the answer. "Let me guess, you fell in love with her already and now the idea of leaving her for months at a time while you go on missions concerns you." Nat nodded.

"Exactly," she said. "How can I ask her to tie herself down? It's not fair to either of us. Besides, she is downstairs right now having a reunion with her father and mother. I don't know how that will impact us either."

"Reunion?" Vic asked with a puzzled look on her face. "What kind of reunion?"

Nat shook her head. "That is a hell of a complicated story and even I don't know all of it," she said. "I am just hoping it is going okay for her. Being stuck up here in this bed is driving me nuts because if things do not have the happy ending she wants, I can't be there to console her."

"Which is what it comes down to," Dee interjected. "You wanting to be there. To take care of the woman." Nat considered Dee's words and knew they rang true. She did want that and slowly she nodded.

"Yes," she admitted. "It is what I want." Dee tilted her head.

"More than your career with the Space Rangers?" she asked. Before Nat could answer, Catherine spoke up from the door.

"Why are you making her choose?" Catherine asked and when Nat looked over, Catherine was glaring at Dee. "You don't think I can handle being a Ranger's girlfriend? That I won't be faithful?" Dee raised her hands, palms out in surrender.

"Whoa," she said. "I'm not saying that necessarily, but from what I've heard and seen, it's no easy street." Catherine came to stand beside Nat at the head of the bed and put her hand on her shoulder. The touch was loving but possessive, and Nat loved the feel of it.

"I think we've already proven we can survive more than the average couple," she said and bent down to kiss Nat on the lips. "I'll wait for you always," Catherine said softly to Nat as she pulled back. "Always."

"Well, there you go," Vic said playfully. "Happy, Dee?" Nat looked at her longtime friend and saw she was conflicted. It seemed she wanted to believe Catherine but was wary too. Trying to ease the tension, Nat changed the subject.

"How did it go with your dad and mom?" she asked and was relieved when Catherine's face lit up at the question.

"Better than I could have ever hoped for," she answered. "I have a lot to tell you, but for now they are talking in the coffee shop." Catherine shook her head. "Everything is so incredible and I have you to thank for all of it, Nat. All because you love me." Nat saw Dee tilt her head at Catherine's last statement and Nat decided it was time to let her friend know how deeply she felt for Catherine.

"I do love you, Catherine," she said. "And I know you won't make me choose, but I've decided the Space Rangers are not for me any longer. I want to start a new chapter in my life. And I want you in it." Nat saw Catherine shake her head as she took Nat's hands in hers.

"No," she said. "I won't make you give it up. I can handle it." Dee waved her hands interrupting the conversation.

"Okay, okay," she said. "I get it. You love her and she loves you."

"Aw, come on, Dee, don't be a bitch," Vic said.

"I'm not," Dee snapped at her friend. "In fact, I'm pretty sure they are going to be damn happy about what I'm going to say next." Nat frowned.

"What are you talking about?" she asked as Catherine looked at the woman too. Dee shook her head.

"I'm probably going to catch hell for this since it is not public knowledge yet," Dee said. "But even with your injury, the Space Rangers want to keep you. So, they are going to offer you a teaching position at the Academy on Untas." Nat's mouth dropped open.

"Are you kidding?" she asked. "Why didn't you tell me?" Dee shrugged.

"I wanted to know how serious you really were about Catherine before I muddied the waters with the option," she answered and then Nat watched her friend look Catherine hard in the eye. "But I can see she does love you enough, so there you go."

Nat looked at Catherine and saw tears starting to spill down her cheeks. "Would you do it?" the woman asked. "Would you settle for being an instructor?" Nat smiled and took Catherine's face in her hands.

"Nothing would make me happier," she said. "The real question is do you want me to? It will mean you're stuck with me hanging around." Catherine laughed out a sob of happiness.

"I do. I so do," she said. "I could not ask for anything more."

THE END

Enjoy this book?

You can make a big difference

Honest reviews of my books help bring them to the attention of other readers. If you've enjoyed this story, I would be very grateful if you could spend a couple minutes leaving a review (it can be as short as you like) on the book's Amazon or Goodreads page.

If you enjoyed KC Luck's *Rescue Her Heart*, read on for an exciting new preview of

DARKNESS FALLS

IF THE LIGHTS GO OUT forever, can love survive?

When four women from different walks of life are brought together by fate to witness the end of the world as they know it, each must find a way to survive against the odds as well as learn to rely on each other.

The end of the world is only the beginning.

DARKNESS FALLS - CHAPTER 1

The attic was dusty and dark but for the single bulb hanging on a cord in the middle of the large space. Thankful she brought a flashlight, Anna Patten snapped it on and looked around. Years of keepsakes were piled everywhere. Boxes and furniture, clothes on racks, and old sporting equipment. *This is what happens when a house stays in a family for three generations,* she thought and started to work her way to the back of the attic. It seemed like a good enough place to start as any. Shining the light in her hand to the left and the right, she stopped when it fell on a box with her name written in marker on the side. *Keepsakes from my childhood?*

After Anna moved away and the house was empty, but for her parents, her mom had converted Anna's bedroom into a quilting room. Anna had never been sure what happened to her softball trophies or shelf after shelf of books. *Now I know*, she thought and set the flashlight on a table where it shone at the box. Opening it, Anna smiled as memories immediately began to wash over her. Her senior yearbook from Astoria High School was right on top, and Anna picked it up to flip through some of the pages. As if by fate, it opened to a photo of Anna and two of her closest friends joking around after a home football game. They were all decked out in purple and gold spirit wear, and Anna was even wearing a letterman's jacket. It belonged to the team's all-state running back, Mitch Wallace. *Now that brings back memories.* Their relationship had been complicated even by normal high school standards. Mitch was gay but afraid to death of anyone finding out. In a small town in Oregon in the 1980s, being a star athlete did not pair well with having an alternative lifestyle. So Anna was his beard, so to speak, and she never minded. It kept all the other boys from trying to get in her pants. *And the ruse helped with other things too, Anna Patten, and you know it.*

Not wanting to think about all of those details right now, Anna flipped the page and scanned the other pictures. She realized she was in a lot of them. As senior class president and one of the top academic students, Anna remembered being extremely busy and it showed in how well she was represented in the annual. The hard work had paid off though, and she earned a full-ride scholarship to Stanford. *That opportunity to leave town and head out of state could not have come at a better time*, she thought. Her life in Astoria had become complicated and confusing. Thinking of it all now, Anna paused. A part of her wanted to flip to the autograph page at the back of the book, yet another part of her was uneasy. *Why is my heart beating faster while I consider this?* Feeling foolish for hesitating about something so silly, Anna defiantly turned to the last page of the yearbook. At first, she did not see the words she was looking for and then her eyes fell on them. In neat, clear script were five words and reading them now made Anna catch her breath.

WHENEVER YOU ARE READY,
LEXI

NOT MORE THAN FIVE miles away down a dirt country road, Lexi Scott walked with her two golden retrievers along the fence line of her twelve-acre property. Even though it was early, the sun was warm for an April morning. The tall grass was damp though and Lexi knew she would have to rub her two dogs down before she let them back in the old farmhouse she called home. As if wanting to let her know it was worth it, Rosy came bounding alongside her with a grin on her face. Her brother Clem was right behind her, and the two of them romped in a circle around Lexi. "What are you two crazies up to this morning?" Lexi asked them. Clem barked as if he could understand her and Lexi chuckled. "You don't say?" Picking up a stick from the grass, Lexi held it up for her two dogs to see and the animals immediately paused in their antics to focus on what their master was doing. "Sit," Lexi commanded, and both dogs obeyed instantly. "Now wait for it ... one, two, three!" Lexi threw the stick with all her might, and the dogs tore after it. The throw was a good one, and Lexi smiled. Even at forty-three, she knew her arm was still better than most.

When she was eighteen, the college recruiters had come knocking with softball scholarships, but she was not interested. To her, the game was a hobby, and so she settled for going to the local community college to take writing classes. In the end, the decision was the right one as her talent at creating imaginary worlds proved lucrative. Although she knew she would never be a Stephen King or a Nora Roberts, Lexi had a strong base of followers who always bought her books, and so she cranked out one or two a year in order to live very comfortably. It was with those funds she was able to buy the old Reynolds' place five years before and slowly fix it up. The project was a challenge from the start as Lexi knew little about remodeling, but it turned into a labor of love as she found joy and fulfillment in bringing the house and the land back to life. *Not to mention it was the distraction I needed at the time*, she thought with a heavy sigh. *I should never have gone to that damn high school reunion. It was dumb then, just like it is dumb thinking about it now.*

With a shake of her head to try and clear the unwelcome thoughts, Lexi started walking again and called to her dogs. Before the animals could get all the way back to her, Lexi's cell phone rang and, grateful for the distraction, she answered. "This is Lexi," she said.

"Good morning, big sister," Lexi heard her sibling Jackie Scott say. "Out walking the fence line I assume?" Lexi chuckled.

"You know it," she answered. "And let me guess. You're racing way too fast down the I-5 through the heart of Seattle because you're late for a meeting."

"Actually, I'm on the 405, but pretty much yes," Jackie said, and Lexi could tell she was smiling. "But I did not call to chit chat about directions. I want to know if you're still coming up the weekend after next for my birthday."

"Wouldn't dare miss it," Lexi said even though the last thing she wanted was to drive three hours into big city traffic, but this was a milestone birthday, and Lexi was pretty sure Jackie was not looking forward to it. *All the more reason to rub it in*, Lexi thought and grinned. "After all, you are turning the big four-oh," she said. There was a pause on the phone.

"You're loving this, aren't you?" Jackie said. Lexi laughed. "More than you can imagine," she answered.

TAYLOR BARNES WAITED in the guard's booth at the end of the parking ramp and checked her Apple watch for the time. She was happy to see Jackie Scott was due any minute and checked herself in the small mirror. Taylor knew she was being ridiculous carrying a crush on the classy but infinitely sexy CEO of Vibrant magazine, but the flirting was harmless, and the extra attention always made Jackie smile. As if on cue, the familiar red Audi R8 coupe came screeching around the corner and shot down the ramp. As it slowed for the gate, Taylor watched to see if the driver's side window would roll down. It was a cue Taylor had learned early on. If it went down, Jackie was in a good mood and would be willing to chat for a minute or not. Taylor was pleased to see the window dropping and stepped out of the booth. "Good morning, Ms. Scott," Taylor said as she leaned forward to look into the car and make a quick appraisal of Jackie's designer outfit. Taylor was indeed no expert, but if she had to guess the soft gray dress was expensive. *Considering how fantastic she looks in it, I'd say the money was well worth it*, Taylor thought.

"Good morning to you too, Taylor," Jackie said with a smile. "Are you working tomorrow?" Taylor lifted an eyebrow. Tomorrow was Saturday, and therefore she usually had it off although other than spending the day at the gym and the evening with a good book, she had no plans.

"Depends on who is asking," she replied. Jackie tilted her head. It was a flirtatious move and Taylor wondered if Jackie knew she was doing it. *Probably not*, Taylor thought. Although Taylor had only been working as a guard for three months, she had yet to see Jackie with anyone, but her guess was the woman was straight. *Unfortunately.*

"Well, I'm asking," Jackie said. "I have a late afternoon meeting so I'll need someone to let me into the garage." Taylor hesitated. As much as she found Jackie attractive, she was not someone's puppet either. Twenty years with the Army Military Police Corps taught her a lot of things, but a big one was to make decisions with your head and not your heart. *Or any other part of your body*, she thought. Still, Taylor knew she could get in a long workout in the morning and then come in to pick up a few extra hours. Although her retirement pay allowed her to live more than comfortably, there was never anything wrong with some extra pocket money.

"I can help you out," she finally answered. "What time?"

CHAPTER 2

Jackie walked out of the conference room and let out a sigh of contentment. The teleconference call with Los Angeles had gone well. *Very well, in fact*, she thought, and it looked like she was about to have another feather in her cap for signing a deal with an excellent up and coming design photographer. The man was going to be expensive, but worth it as he had proven already to be exceptionally gifted behind the lens. As she strode down the hall and walked into her office, her handsome young assistant, Daniel, rushed in behind her. He was carrying a handful of pink memos, all of which Jackie knew were from people eager to talk to her. "Ms. Scott," Daniel said as they entered the plush corner office. "I have a few notes for you as well as the confirmation for next Saturday."

Before bothering to answer, Jackie went behind her desk and dropped into her expensive leather captain's chair. Kicking off her shoes and wiggling her tired toes, she looked at Daniel. "So there's no problem then with the reservation?" she asked. "The Space Needle is ours for the whole evening after all?" Jackie had made big plans for her fortieth birthday, including spending significant cash to reserve the SkyCity at the Needle restaurant. The arrangements were made over a year ago, but then in the last week, the owners were trying to back out. Apparently, the same night as her birthday party, a spectacular northern lights show was expected. Jackie did not budge and even had Daniel threaten them with a lawsuit. Apparently, the restaurant had finally relented.

"Yes," Daniel answered. "The threat worked, but they were not happy. No doubt seats to watch the solar storm effects on our night sky would have come at a premium." Jackie rolled her eyes. She had been hearing about this 'once in a lifetime' natural phenomena for weeks and could not completely understand the excitement. *And I'm sure as hell not going to let it mess up my birthday party*, she thought.

"Well good," she said. "The whole thing was ridiculous anyway. Who cares that much about a few lights in the sky?" She saw Daniel raise an eyebrow. He was gorgeous and gay to the hilt, but all Jackie cared about was the fact he was efficient as hell. Plus, he was smart enough to keep his thoughts to himself, but Jackie was curious what his take was on the whole northern lights thing. "You disagree?" she asked. Daniel shrugged.

"There is something special to be said about Aurora Borealis," he said. "And on that Saturday, it will show its stuff to the 10th degree. At least that is what the weather folks on the internet are saying. And I quote 'a better light show than any fourth of July.'"

Jackie leaned back in her chair to consider Daniel's words. "Fine," she said and smiled. "Sounds absolutely perfect and will just make my birthday that much more memorable."

LEXI POURED THE KIBBLE into the two metal dog bowls as Rosy and Clem looked on. They were both in a down and stay position, but Lexi could feel the excitement running through them. Dinner was a highlight, or at least it was until it was gone in four bites and a squirrel ran through the yard. Stepping back, Lexi gave them a nod, and her pets attacked the food with such pleasure it made her chuckle. *If only I could get as excited about what to eat*, she thought and wandered from the pantry into her kitchen. Although she would never consider her life lonely, bothering to make dinner for one often seemed a waste of time. Often, like tonight, she would skip cooking a full meal and instead grab a few handfuls of the early season sweet peas from her garden, some locally grown lettuce, and a greenhouse tomato for a quick salad. It was one of the reasons her body stayed so lean. Add in the physically demanding work on the remodel and around the property, and Lexi was proud of the toned body it earned her. She might have more gray hairs and wrinkles than she did in high school, but her jean size was the same.

Turning on some music, Lexi puttered around the butcher block island throwing together her food and was sitting down to eat when her cell phone buzzed. A quick glance at the screen to see if whoever was calling was worth interrupting her dinner, Lexi raised her eyebrows when she saw it was Diana Malone. They were friends from way back, but certainly not close. Diana was a bit of a gossip, and Lexi stayed well clear of any small-town drama. Still, it was odd the woman was calling at six on a Friday night. Deciding to answer it, Lexi pressed the connect button. "This is Lexi," she said.

"Lexi!" Diana said sounding thrilled to have her answer. "How are you tonight?" Lexi tilted her head. *What is this all about? A fundraiser maybe?* she wondered. It was not unusual for the booster club to ask Lexi to donate an autographed copy of her latest novel for a school auction.

"I'm good," Lexi replied. "What can I do for you tonight? Need a signed book or something?"

"Oh, no, nothing like that," she said. "I was really just calling to catch up." *Hmmm*, Lexi thought now wondering what was going on. Diana never had in the thirty years she knew her called to just "catch up."

"Well, I'm fine. Thanks," Lexi said. "Everything okay?" This time Diana actually giggled and Lexi realized the woman might be a little tipsy. Lexi thought she had heard somewhere Diana liked her wine a little bit too much. Figuring it was time to get back to eating, Lexi was about to say goodbye when Diana blurted out a sentence which froze Lexi in place.

"Anna Patten is back in town," Diana said. "And she's divorced."

WITH A POPULATION OF around ten thousand, the city of Astoria was quaintly small and a beautiful jewel along the Columbia River and the Pacific Ocean. It also boasted some of the best restaurants for miles around although the selection was a little limited. After a week in town already, she had tapped out the best spots to have dinner and a glass of wine and so restlessly drove around town trying to decide what to do. Since her hotel room had no kitchen, it was eating out or nothing. Of course, the idea of sitting at a table for one yet again was depressing, to say the least as well. *Which is all your own fault*, she thought. It was true she had a number of friends still in town she could ask to eat with her, but Anna was not ready for an inquisition yet. Coming back here recently divorced to pack up her family's old home was mettle for gossip, and she knew it. Of course, people would be respectful considering Anna's mother was now in a special memory care facility down in Los Angeles. Add in the fact her father died of a heart attack when she was twenty and Anna knew she was a bit of a sad case. The idea she was a pity piece made her madder than if she was a scandal. *Maybe I should just go look up Lexi then*, she thought and immediately regretted it. Not only was it not nice, but the last thing she wanted was to stir up anything from the past. She was in town for one more week and then she would never be back. *Ever.*

Finally seeing a place she had not tried, Anna pulled into a parking place and wandered in. There were a few couples at the table, tourists, Anna guessed, but still plenty of room for her to take her pick of a spot. As she pulled off her jacket, a man came to the table with a menu in his hand. When he reached the table, he paused, and Anna looked up to see if something was wrong. As soon as she recognized him, Anna felt her stomach clench. It was a boy from high school. Jeff. *I guess he's officially a man now*, she thought and gave him a weak smile.

"Anna Patten," he said. Anna nodded.

"Hi, Jeff," she said and reached out for the menu. "Long time." He smirked at her and Anna immediately remembered why she never liked the guy. He was a bully back in the day, and she was guessing he still was from the look on his face.

"Yep, long time," he said. "You look good though." His eyes roved over her body, and Anna felt a little creeped out. *Maybe I'm not as hungry after all*, she thought, but before she could make a move to leave, Jeff was sitting in the chair opposite her. "I heard you were in town," he said. *Fabulous.*

Anna nodded. "For another week is all," she said. "So, hey, I just realized I left my wallet back at the hotel, so I'm afraid I have to go get it." She grabbed her jacket and started to stand up.

"Whoa, hey," Jeff said. "I can pay for your meal. Happy to do it." He gave her a wink, and Anna almost laughed. She was not a scared teenager anymore, and this loser son of a bitch was not going to intimidate her. After all, she was a highly respected nurse practitioner with her own clinic in Los Angeles. *Not some small-town waiter*, she thought and continued to stand up. He stood up with her.

"No thank you," Anna said. "I'll just go." She walked toward the exit, and Jeff matched her steps. At the door, he moved to open it and then held it shut while he looked at her face.

"Sorry you need to go," he said. "But I don't suppose you'd like to go out? Maybe next Saturday to watch the northern lights show? Could be romantic." Anna smiled sweetly at him and nodded. Seeing her willing reaction, Jeff opened the door so Anna could leave. She walked out and then turned back to talk to him about the date.

"Not on your life, asshole," she said and then strode to her car without a look back.

CHAPTER 3

As a light April rain fell, Lexi walked along the rows of local vendors at Astoria's Saturday farmers market. The booths were showing off early season fruits and vegetables. Unable to resist, Lexi bought a pint basket of strawberries and immediately popped one in her mouth. Savoring the burst of sweetness on her tongue, she smiled. Nothing could offer the promise of summer ahead more than the taste of a freshly picked strawberry. She was ready for the warmer weather to arrive. Living so near the coast, a significant number of wet weather storms passed through during the winter months. Still, it was all part of living in the Pacific Northwest, and Lexi had no desire to ever live anywhere else.

Feeling the rain starting to pick up, Lexi ducked under the awning of the vendor she was hoping would be there. Handmade artwork of cut and polished metal wall sculptures, which always took her breath away, adorned the numerous displays. Her plan was to buy one for her sister Jackie as a birthday present. Even though her sister had evolved into a powerful executive up in Seattle, Lexi knew Jackie always had an eye for talent and appreciated raw beauty. These pieces were precisely that, and so she browsed to find the perfect one. As she searched, she contemplated a particularly unique wall art cut to look like a windswept coastal scene. The polished metal finish shined like a subtle rainbow from copper to silver hues. *It's perfect*, Lexi thought and moved to talk to the vendor who was also the artist. He smiled when he recognized her. This was not her first purchase as a few choice sculptures adorned the walls of her farmhouse.

"Find something you like?" he asked. Lexi smiled.

"I like all of it," she answered. "You do amazing work." The author blushed a little.

"Thank you. Always nice to hear that. Now, which one caught your eye today?" he asked. Lexi turned to show him, and as she did, she nearly crashed headlong into the woman standing behind her.

"Oh, I'm so sorry," Lexi started. "I didn't realize someone was—" She froze. The woman behind her was Anna Patten. Lexi saw Anna's eyes widen when she realized it was Lexi. Neither of them seemed able to say a word until the artist cleared his throat.

"Um," he said. "Is everything okay?" Slowly, Lexi nodded but did not take her eyes off of Anna's face. She had gotten a glimpse of her at the high school reunion five years before, but she was with her husband and thus had seemed to want to avoid Lexi at all costs. Now though, Lexi could see the woman up close. She looked incredible. Like Lexi, there were more laugh lines, but her hair was still a rich dark brown. *Longer than in high school*, she thought. *But it suits her well.* Finally, realizing she was staring, Lexi forced a smile.

"Hey," she said. It was lame as hell, and she knew it, but thankfully it broke the ice and Anna laughed.

"Hey back," she said. No two words had ever made Lexi happier.

WHEN THE WOMAN TURNED around, and Anna realized it was Lexi, her heart rate immediately jumped up a notch. The woman looked good, great even. Her sandy blonde hair showed a few bits of white now, but it only added character. The eyes though, blue-gray, looked exactly the same and as she stared into them, a million memories flooded her mind. Before she could sort any of them out, Lexi had saved the moment and simply said, "Hey." It was such a flashback to the start of thousands of old conversations, Anna had laughed.

"Hey back," she said and smiled. "I was wondering if I might run into you." Lexi raised an eyebrow, and again Anna was struck with deja vu. *As if not a day has passed,* she thought. It was almost surreal.

"Was it going to be a good thing to run into me?" Lexi asked. *Bold as always*, Anna thought and nodded.

"Of course," she said with a tilt of her head and then realized she was dangerously close to the edge of flirting. Dialing her emotions back although her heart was still racing, Anna shrugged. "Why wouldn't it be?" Lexi snorted a laugh and looked on the verge of a sarcastic response, but then seemed to reconsider. Instead, she nodded.

"Well, it is good to see you. Take care of yourself," Lexi said and started to move to slip past Anna, but then paused. "So, how long are you in town?"

"Not very long. Only until next Saturday," Anna blurted before she could stop herself, but suddenly she wanted Lexi to know there was not a lot of time. *For what?* Anna wondered. *I'm acting like an idiot. Why would she care?* Still, Lexi smiled, so Anna plunged ahead. "So maybe we can do lunch before I go?" Her heart fell as she watched Lexi shake her head.

"I'm not really a 'do lunch' kind of person," she said. "But..." Her voice trailed off, and Anna wanted to know what she was not saying.

"But what?" she asked, but Lexi was quiet and instead of answering looked at the ground as if lost in thought. Anna could not decide what she wanted to have happen next, but somehow, she could feel whatever Lexi did next could change both their lives. *If she's not interested in being friends again, so be it*, Anna thought. *I deserve it.* As if reading Anna's mind, Lexi looked up and met her eye. There was a hint of hurt in the blue-gray and Anna had a sudden urge to pull Lexi to her. To hold her.

"You hurt me," Lexi said softly. "I'm not sure I am ready to forgive all of it." Anna felt a ball of guilt curl up in her stomach. She always knew leaving town without even saying goodbye to Lexi was a horrible thing, but it was twenty-five years ago and a part of Anna hoped time would heal the wound. She realized now she was foolish to even think for a moment Lexi would want to associate with her again. Flustered now, Anna started to back away.

"Of course," she said and turned to go. She had the sudden urge to literally take off running through the rain. Suddenly, Lexi touched her arm.

"Wait," the woman said. "Let's not do this. I'm sorry I said that." Anna did not meet her eye.

"It's fine," Anna said.

"No, it's not," Lexi said. "Let's start over. I want you to come see my place. The old Reynold's farmhouse." Anna heard her pause. "Come to dinner," Lexi finished.

TAYLOR WAS A BULLET as she screamed along the surface streets of downtown Seattle on her jet-black BMW K 1600 motorcycle. Thanks to seeing a fender bender where she had to provide her info in case either party wanted a witness, Taylor was now running late to meet Jackie at the office high-rise. Gritting her teeth with frustration, she gunned it to get through a yellow traffic light and leaned deep into the final corner before her destination. As she made the turn, she noted Jackie's car was just arriving. It stopped at the closed gate, and Taylor pulled up along the driver's side. Chuckling at the perplexed look on Jackie's face, Taylor unhooked the chinstrap of her black helmet and pulled it off. "Fancy meeting you here," she said, and Jackie's face changed to one of amusement.

"Well look at you, Taylor," she laughed. "I should have known." *Interesting. What does that mean?* Taylor thought and wondered if she would have a chance to find out. *Not likely and you know it, Casanova, so just cool your jets and open the gate.*

"Let me get that gate open for you," Taylor said and goosed the bike forward to the locked control panel. In a minute, the metal grid was rattling back out of the way. Once it was moved, Taylor watched Jackie drive into the garage with a wave out of the car window. There was no reason for Taylor to stick around. The gate would automatically open if a car approached from the inside to ensure no one was ever locked in. Still, it did not sit well to know Jackie would be alone in the empty garage. Even though it was a secure space, Taylor learned long ago nothing was as black and white as it looked. *I think I'll just do a little zip around the levels*, she thought and coasted the bike down the ramp.

Jackie had already parked and was getting out when she saw Taylor. "Everything okay?" she asked walking toward her. Taylor could not help but notice the way today's slightly more casual pantsuit hugged the woman's curves just right. Forcing herself to not lick her lips, Taylor shook her head.

"Nothing wrong," she said. "I just thought I'd cruise around to make sure everything is cool."

Jackie gave her a sly smile. "Taylor, are you protecting me?" she asked, and although the playful comment was undoubtedly an innocent one, Taylor felt a shiver of attraction run through her. *Oh, you have no idea*, she thought but instead shrugged.

"Just doing my job, ma'am," she answered with a mock salute. Jackie laughed as she started to walk away toward the elevators. When she got to the doors and pushed the button, Jackie surprised Taylor by looking back at her.

"Well for what it's worth, I feel a lot safer knowing you're here," she said just as the elevator doors opened and she walked inside. Before Taylor could respond, she saw the doors close, and Jackie was on her way upstairs.

ABOUT THE AUTHOR

Army veteran KC Luck is a freelance technical writer living in the Pacific Northwest with her beautiful wife, their two little dogs, and four rambunctious cats. Although she had contemplated writing fiction for decades, it was not until a bet with her wife that she finally sat down and did it. "Rescue Her Heart" is her debut romance novel and hopefully more action adventure stories with strong female leads in loving lesbian relationships will follow.

KC Luck's would be thrilled to hear from readers (kc.luck.author@gmail.com) or go to the KC Luck's Facebook page at facebook.com/kcluckauthor and click Like to follow her.

Made in the USA
San Bernardino, CA
27 March 2019